The Runts of the Litter

The Runts of the Litter

Garret Baker

A. & A. Farmar

© Garret Baker 1999, 2000

First published in 1999 by Pale Blue Books

Published in 2000 by
A. & A. Farmar
Beech House
78 Ranelagh Village
Dublin 6
Ireland

Tel: +353-1-4963625 Fax: + 353-1-4970107
Email: afarmar@iol.ie

ISBN 1-899047-65-4

Printed by GraphyCems
Navarra, Spain

Contents

1. Money

'I'm sick of the whole damn thing,' Ernest said.

He picked up the cue ball, threw it in the air with his right hand, and caught it with his left.

'It's the uncertainty of it,' Jon reflected.

'It's the not getting paid,' Ernest said as he hit the cue ball with force against the triangle of coloured balls.

'Technically,' Jon said, 'you're not supposed to do that. Technically, you're supposed to use the cue.'

'What we need,' Ernest said, 'is a get rich quick scheme.'

'We could win the lotto,' Jon suggested. 'That would be instantaneous.'

'A to B,' Ernest said. 'It's as simple as that.'

Jon hit the number seven ball into the right-hand corner pocket.

'I'm stripes,' he said. 'You're spots.'

With his next shot he played a neat snooker behind two of his own balls.

'What,' Ernest asked, 'are spots?'

'I thought you said you were familiar with the game.'

'I'm extremely familiar with the game,' Ernest countered.

He picked up one of the balls from the table.

'These are solids,' he said. 'I've never even heard of *spots*.'

'Technically,' Jon said, 'you're not supposed to do that.'

After the game they sat at a table and drank more of the bar's most expensive beer. They were going to have another game but somebody had put some money on the table.

'I hate that rule,' Ernest reflected as he sipped his beer. 'You should be allowed to play at least two.'

'He was bigger than us,' Jon pointed out.

'But there was only one of him,' Ernest said. 'What sort of a man plays pool on his own?'

'You should ask him,' Jon suggested. 'If you're curious. Go up to him and say "What sort of a man are you?"'

Ernest sniffed loudly and stared around the room.

'I don't like Paul any more,' he said. 'He's too wealthy. He's doing too well for himself.'

'Don't you worry?'

'Constantly.'

'About being bitter. Don't you worry you'll be overcome?'

'I already am overcome,' Ernest said. 'Look at me. I'm losing my hair.'

'From bitterness?'

'It's not even the bad hair. It's the best bits. I'm losing all my best hair.'

Jon nodded sympathetically.

'Look at this forehead,' Ernest said, his voice suddenly consumed with passion. 'It needs covering up. It demands it.'

'You shouldn't worry,' Jon counselled. 'Some people say it's psychological.'

'I won't worry then,' Ernest said sarcastically. 'I'll just stop.'

They finished their drinks. Jon went to the bar to get more.

'Something quicker,' Ernest instructed. 'Lager is too slow.'

He returned with a bottle of tequila and two glasses. They did not bother with the salt or lemon.

'Maybe that's what's wrong with today's society,' Jon said. 'Everybody wants to get rich quick. Nobody can be assured of a lifetime's work with one company in today's cutthroat ruthless world. Therefore all sense of loyalty is being eroded. Everyone is out for themselves. It's a fast food culture. People want to make enough money quick, to live out the rest of their lives in leisure. People are greedy.'

'I know all that,' Ernest said. 'That's why we're here. That's why we've got to jump on the boat, shag the bandwagon, raid the piggybank.'

'You're mixing your metaphors again,' Jon observed.

'A to B,' Ernest said. 'It's simple. Maybe we should get into sales. What do people want? What are they willing to pay money for?'

Jon thought a moment.

'Sex, drugs, cars, property, washing-up liquid, computers, television. I could go on.'

'Well then,' Ernest said.

'Well then what?'

'I don't know. I lost my train of thought.'

Ernest knocked back a shot. He clicked his tongue against the roof of his mouth and shut his eyes tightly. When he opened them again they were pierced by the bright light of the pub.

'I hate these places,' he said. 'Why have they got so many lights in here?'

Jon shrugged.

'And on top of all this,' he said, 'they're threatening me with cutting off my dole.'

'They can't do that,' Ernest countered.

'Well, they seemed to think they could. Apparently there's been legislation newly passed whereby if you don't accept the jobs they offer you in your given field over a certain period, they cut you off.'

'But they haven't offered you anything.'

'Yes,' Jon said. 'That's what I told them.'

'And?'

'And he said I was being unrealistic. He said it was unlikely I'd ever get any work as an actor.'

'He's seen your work then.'

'Ha,' Jon said. 'No. Otherwise he would have cut me off for not declaring. Anyway, even if he did see it he could not possibly have recognised me.'

'I recognised you.'

'I told you about it. Besides, half a day as an extra in a long shot on a TV crime reconstruction shoot does not qualify as work.'

'You got paid for it,' Ernest said gloomily. 'More than I have ever gotten in my own artistic field.'

'Well, he didn't recognise me. He just said this out of the blue.'

'The cheek of him,' Ernest said. 'The bare-faced cheek.'

'I know,' Jon said. 'I said to him, "I didn't realise you were a talent scout and not some mere civil servant working in an ineffectual government body." He wasn't very pleased. He said he would cut my dole. He said he could do it tomorrow if he wanted.'

'Bastard,' Ernest said. 'They're all conspiring against us. Which is exactly why we need a plan.'

'We need a flat,' Jon said.

'You are not thinking on the correct scale,' Ernest complained. 'I am talking long term. I am talking money. I'm talking buying our own publishing firm, our own studio. A casting couch full of buxom beauties.'

'It wouldn't bring happiness,' Jon said.

'Who cares?'

'Well, that's the point, isn't it?'

'Money,' Ernest said. 'Money.'

When they had run out of money they fell out onto the city streets. Ernest nearly got sick into his hat but at the last second decided against it.

'I nearly got sick into my hat,' Ernest explained as they both stared at the pile of sick on the footpath. 'I don't know why.'

Jon shivered.

'What are we going to do?' he asked.

'Ah, I'll think of something,' Ernest said. 'Maybe we should go to Land's End and jump off.'

'Land's End is in England,' Jon pointed out. 'We are not.'

'Well, it's an island isn't it?' Ernest countered. 'It's got to end somewhere: the land. We'll go there and jump off and then they'll be sorry.'

'Who'll be sorry?'

Ernest spun around on one foot. He clutched his belly with his hands.

'I'm getting fat,' he said. 'I'm getting old and fat and bald and I'm already out of money.'

'I don't think we should have spent the whole deposit,' Jon said.

'Money,' Ernest said. 'Money. Money. Money.'

'I have a rich uncle somewhere,' Jon said. 'Somewhere in America.'

'That's it!' Ernest said.

'What's it?'

'We'll go to America and murder your uncle,' he said, clutching at Jon's collar. 'Then we'll steal all his money and sell his children.'

'I don't think it would work.'

'No?'

'Unless you're in their will, you can no longer murder rich people for their money,' Jon said. 'It's all in the bank. They no longer keep it in safes or under floorboards.'

'Bastards,' Ernest yelled. 'Bastards!'

'Who are you calling a bastard shithead?' a young man with a sour face said as he approached Ernest.

Two other young men watched on with small smug grins from the side. Ernest began to shake with fear. The young man stared him belligerently in the eye.

'Not you,' Ernest said. 'Somebody else.'

'You fucker. You drunk fucking bastard. I'll kill you if you shout that at me again.'

'Of course,' Ernest said. 'I'm sorry.'

But the man was not satisfied. He spat on Ernest's shoe and for a long time stared him in the eye before finally, with a leering grin, walking off.

'Bastard!' Ernest yelled after him.

Ernest turned to Jon as the young man froze.

'Run!' he instructed helpfully before taking off as fast as his short legs would carry him.

Ernest and Jon ran through the darkened streets for as long as they could maintain their breath, before finally resting under the fuzzing lights of a 24-hour convenience store. For several seconds they occupied themselves with regaining the use of their lungs. Ernest sat down on the wet pavement.

'I feel like a kebab,' he declared finally.

'You look like a kebab.'

'Why is it,' Ernest said, 'that men feel they should beat me up as a matter of course at every available opportunity. I have nothing but love for them.'

'I think,' Jon said, 'if that is the case, you're sending mixed messages.'

'Let's steal a car,' Ernest said, standing up suddenly.

'Why?' Jon asked.

'Because we have no home. We could steal a mobile home and kill two birds.'

Jon looked around them.

'I don't see any mobile homes,' he said.

Ernest shook his head, trying to rid himself of blurred vision.

'I can't see,' he said finally. 'Where are we?'

Jon looked around again.

'I don't know,' he said finally. 'Town?'

'Maybe we're dead,' Ernest said hopefully. 'Maybe that guy caught up with us and killed us and we're in some new place that looks like town but is, in fact, some kind of heaven or hell or purgatory.'

'Good to see they have 24-hour shops in heaven,' Jon said.

'Ah, what difference does it make?' Ernest said gloomily. 'We have no money. You see? It was lies. All lies. All that stuff about how the poor would inherit the earth and here we are in heaven and we can't even afford a packet of Hula Hoops.'

'I never believed it for a minute,' Jon reflected.

'If this is heaven we might as well steal a car,' Ernest said. 'Nobody will mind. They'll forgive us.'

'It's Pearse Street,' Jon said.

'What?'

'I think it's Pearse Street,' Jon said. 'I'm not sure. I'm basing it on that sign over there which says it is.'

Ernest looked up at the faded street sign.

'Oh well,' he said. 'Let's steal a car anyway. But first we need more drink.'

'We can't drink and drive,' Jon said. 'It's too dangerous.'

'Well, then you come up with something,' Ernest said. 'I've already had two good suggestions.'

'We could call in on Paul,' Jon said. 'He has a car.'

'But does he have drink?'

'I don't know,' Jon said. 'But one out of two isn't bad.'

'So we're agreed,' Ernest said. 'We're going to kill Paul, steal his car and drive it off Land's End.'

'Why do we have to kill him?'

'Because he has a job, is making money, is six months younger than me and has good hair.'

'Fair enough,' Jon said.

'You'll have to do it,' Ernest said. 'I'm a pacifist.'

'I'm not killing him. He's a friend of mine.'

'You're selfish. That's what's wrong with today's youth. You won't do anything for your fellow man. All I ask is a small favour. I'll hold him down, you can cut his throat with a butcher knife.'

'This is no good,' Jon said. 'I'm starting to feel sober.'

'Okay,' Ernest said. 'This is a crisis. We're in crisis mode. If you're starting to feel sober that means pretty soon I'm going to start feeling sober. This is horrible. To think what I've been through. All the effort I put in. All for nothing.'

'I blame Copper,' Jon said.

'We should have murdered him,' Ernest said. 'We should have ripped out his miserable heart and made him look at it in his dying moments.'

'They have no morals,' Jon reflected. 'Landlords. I mean, we've never even been late with the rent. Well, never more than three weeks. I always thought we were good tenants.'

'We should have trashed the place,' Ernest said.

'Then we would not have gotten our deposit back,' Jon pointed out. 'And we would not have been able to get drunk.'

'What's the use?' Ernest said. 'If we can't stay drunk? What's the point? Where's the justice? What is the capital of Belarus?'

'I thought it was a city.'

'I don't know. I don't know. Drink, drink, drink.'

'Paul might have some,' Jon said. 'He may have a drinks cabinet.'

'A cabinet?' Ernest said, perking up suddenly. 'Let's go.'

'We can't,' Jon said. 'He lives in Bray. Bray is a long way away.'

'It can't be,' Ernest said, starting to walk. 'It's a small city. We'll be there in no time.'

'Bray is in Wicklow,' Jon called out. 'You're going the wrong way. Besides, we can't walk. It won't work. We need a mode of transport.'

'We'll steal a car,' Ernest said, walking over to a green Mini parked by the pavement. 'This one will do. It's not the colour I'd choose but what the hell.'

He tried the door of the Mini. It was locked. He turned to Jon.

'Fetch me a brick,' he said.

Jon shook his head.

'We're too drunk,' he said. 'We're too drunk and neither of us can drive.'

'I can drive,' Ernest protested. 'Well, all right, I can't, but how hard can it be? I've been in cars. I've seen people driving. I can't see it being beyond my capabilities.'

'We're too drunk,' Jon repeated.

Ernest was busy looking for a brick.

'We'll have to use your fist,' he declared finally. 'We've no other choice.'

Ernest grabbed Jon's fist and began readying it for its assault on the window of the Mini.

'How are we going to start it?' Jon asked.

Ernest let go of his hand.

'I don't know,' he said. 'I hadn't thought of that. Can't you hotwire?'

Jon shook his head.

'Well, at least I'm willing to try,' Ernest said. 'Oh God. I'm starting to feel sober. We don't have a flat. We have no money, no jobs, no girlfriends, not even an inflatable doll. What sort of life is this to lead?'

'I have an idea,' Jon said, walking off down the road.

'Where are you going?' Ernest said. 'I need your fist.'

'Grafton Street,' Jon said. 'We must go there to act out my plan.'

Ernest began walking but was not convinced.

'We're going to busk,' Jon explained as they walked. 'For the tourists.'

'It's too cold for tourists,' Ernest complained.

'They don't mind the cold. They wear jumpers. They expect it.'

They arrived at Grafton Street.

'Well, I mind the cold,' Ernest said. 'It's degrading. We have no instruments.'

'Oh yes,' Jon said. 'I forgot about instruments.'

'I hope you don't expect me to dance,' Ernest warned. 'Because I never dance unless seriously drunk.'

'You are seriously drunk.'

'But there's no music. I never dance unless I am seriously drunk and there's music playing. And never for money. I am a poet. I have standards to live by. Besides, the drink is wearing off.'

'Exactly,' Jon said. 'Exactly, the drink is wearing off. That's the situation I am trying to deal with. I am trying to get us the money we need to keep us drunk. To keep out the cold. To keep out the fact that we've not only lost our innocence and our belief in God but we've also lost our flat.'

'Well, get on with it then,' Ernest said. 'You're not going to make any money making speeches. I liked my idea better. If you had an ounce of decency in you right now we'd be crashing through the window of an off-licence with that Mini.'

'I need a guitar,' Jon said.

Ernest looked up and down the street. He spotted a small traveller boy a little way down, strumming a plastic guitar and singing an Irish ballad out of tune.

'There,' he said, pointing to the boy.

Jon and Ernest walked over to him.

'Give us the guitar,' Ernest said, towering over the small boy. 'Or we'll beat the living daylights out of you.'

'No,' Jon said. 'We won't do that.'

'Shut up,' Ernest said. 'Give me that guitar or I'll shake you upside down till your teeth fall out.'

The traveller boy stood up, held the guitar out and with one swift motion smashed it between Ernest's legs before running away. Ernest lay on the ground and moaned and groaned.

'I don't think you ought to have scared him like that,' Jon said as he picked up the guitar. 'After all, he was just a little boy.'

'What's wrong with me?' Ernest asked as he stared up at the black rooftops against the dark blue sky. 'Why do people want to hurt me all the time? I'm an agreeable sort of fellow. I don't actively pursue minorities. I voted Yes in the divorce referendum. I once sent an Amnesty postcard to the warden of an Alabama prison. Why has God got it in for me? Is it all the masturbation? It's a compulsive disorder. I need love. One way or the other. I don't hate anyone. Why do they all hate me?'

'I suppose,' Jon said. 'It's because you're different.'

'Yes,' Ernest agreed. 'That's it. It's because I'm different. Because I don't fit in.'

'Well, that, and the fact that you can be a bit of a disagreeable bastard.'

Ernest sat up. He was beginning to regain feeling in the more delicate areas.

'Why aren't you playing?' he asked Jon. 'We're wasting time. Any minute now I'm going to be sober.'

He grabbed the guitar from Jon's hand.

'How does this thing work?'

Jon took the guitar back.

'I think maybe I should play,' he said. 'Seeing as I know how.'

'Well, get on with it,' Ernest instructed.

'Evening, lads,' a policeman who appeared from nowhere said. Ernest nearly had a heart attack from the shock.

'You scared me half to death,' he complained.

'Shush,' Jon said. 'Good evening constable.'

'Eh, not constable actually,' the policeman said. 'No, that's England.'

'Do you want something?' Ernest asked.

'Shushh,' Jon said.

'Busking are we?' the policeman asked.

'I don't know,' Ernest said. 'What do you play?'

'Shushh.'

'Will you stop shushing me,' Ernest snapped.

'Well,' the policeman said. 'I hope you won't be playing too loud. Because, if you do, I'll have to ask you to move on.'

'Busking is legal in this country,' Ernest pointed out.

'That's true,' the policeman said. 'But loitering, noise pollution, and causing a public nuisance are not.'

'Fascist.'

'Shushh,' Jon said, before turning back to the policeman. 'We're very quiet.'

'Yeah,' Ernest said. 'We play easy listening.'

'Really,' the policeman said, nodding several times to show he understood entirely. 'Well, take care now. There's a few drunks about at this hour. A few unsavoury characters. They might try stealing your pot.'

'Pot?'

'Or perhaps assaulting you,' the policeman went on. 'Sometimes they just do that for no reason. Come right up to you and smack you in the mouth. Or stab you with a broken twisting bottle. Or threaten you with a needle infested with HIV blood.'

'Thank you,' Jon said. 'We'll be very diligent.'

'Don't be too loud though,' the policeman said and walked off.

'I don't feel well,' Ernest said. 'My head is pounding. I must have bumped it in the fall. If I ever catch that little bastard I'll kick him into the middle of next Thursday.'

'Make it a Friday,' Jon suggested. 'That way he'll have the weekend to recover.'

'Shut up and play,' Ernest instructed. 'I'll sing.'

'What do you want me to play?'

'Something that will earn us lots of money,' Ernest said, clasping his hands together. 'Something the public will appreciate. Something which will draw large amounts of ready cash.'

'I get the idea,' Jon said.

'Pop.'

'I beg your pardon?'

'It'll have to be pop,' Ernest said. 'That's what the kids want to hear. Something happening. Something crap and catchy.'

'I'm not writing the song,' Jon said. 'Just name something.'

'Play some Beatles,' Ernest said. 'Everybody loves the Beatles.'

'Right,' Jon said. 'Which song?'

'If you don't start playing soon,' Ernest warned, 'I'm going to smash that guitar over your head repeatedly.'

Jon nodded. He got himself into a comfortable seated position. He steadied himself. He shaped his left fingers onto the guitar in the chord of A and was about to strum it when, out of nowhere, a drunken man appeared and approached them.

'What the fuck are ye doing?' he asked.

'Not a lot,' Ernest replied.

The drunken man had a red raw face and smelled of stale wine and chips.

'D'youse . . . d'youse want to . . . to know something?' he said. 'I nearly fucking killed a man back there. What d'you think of that?'

'Very impressive,' Ernest said.

The drunken man nodded. He swayed for several seconds, as if battling a sudden gust of wind, and then stood still for a long time, opening and closing his eyes in slow motion.

'And I'll tell you another thing,' he said suddenly. 'I would have done it.'

Ernest and Jon nodded.

'I would have done it,' the drunken man said with a satisfied nod. 'But for that copper.'

'We met a copper,' Ernest said. 'Perhaps it was the same one.'

'I could have done it too,' the drunken man said. 'I had him in me clutches.'

The drunken man blinked and laughed a gurgled spitting wretched laugh. He took a grizzled half-smoked cigarette from his pocket and lit it.

'I'll tell youse something,' he said. 'I liked what youse were playing and if I was a rich man I'd give you some money but I'm not . . . Many years ago I died in a car crash and what you see is only the shell of what I was. D'you hear me?'

He waited for Ernest and Jon to nod before going on.

'I have a power,' he said. 'A power. A power over life and death. It has power over you. Not over me though. I have it, within me. Two roads diverged in a wood. D'you hear me? Two roads diverged in a wood and I took the one least travelled by. I took the one least travelled by.'

With that the drunken man wandered off down the street.

'Well,' Ernest said.

'Yes,' Jon agreed.

'You see the problem with that,' Ernest reflected, 'was that we were too sober and the ugliness and stupidity were too apparent.'

'Yes.'

'Which is why you should hurry up and play something and make money so that we can get drunk.'

'Aren't you afraid?'

'All the time.'

'Of ending up like him,' Jon continued. 'All twisted and mishmash of truth and half truth. Drunken conviction that you are the centre of the universe.'

'I am the centre of the universe,' Ernest said. 'Play, goddamn you, play.'

At that precise moment the drunken man reappeared and grabbed Ernest roughly by the collar.

'Here you,' he said violently. 'D'you see what I said about the woods?'

Ernest nodded. He could smell the death from the drunken man's teeth.

'What I said about the woods,' the drunken man repeated as his grip tightened, 'is a secret no man will share and live. It's mine. D'you hear me? If you repeat that secret I'll come and find you wherever you are and, one way or the other, you'll get your justice.'

The drunken man threw Ernest to the ground and stumbled off down the street.

'How sad,' Jon said.

'You see?' Ernest said, as he rubbed his back. 'Why did he choose me? Two men present, of roughly equal height and build, sitting outside a ladies' hairdressers on Grafton Street, just trying to earn some money to stay drunk, and who does he choose to perpetrate his threats and violent behaviour upon? Me. Dear, sweet, innocent me. I'm beginning to develop a complex.'

'How sad,' Jon reflected,' that a man could convince himself that he wrote another man's words of beauty.'

'You don't need to tell me,' Ernest said. 'You're just a mere actor. A mimic. I'm the poet. I'm the one with the manuscript. I'm the one who's poured his soul into verse. All you do is say other people's lines.'

'Personally, I prefer it that way,' Jon said. 'Writers don't seem too happy to me. The good ones in any case. The good ones all seem quite miserable. I am quite happy being just an actor.'

'Maybe I should read from my manuscript,' Ernest said. 'I've seen it before. Street poets. Maybe that would get us the money we need.'

Jon shook his head.

'No,' he said. 'It wouldn't work. They don't want original poems.'

'Why not?'

Jon shrugged.

'They want famous poems,' he said. 'Poems by people with names they recognise. Poems by people with grand Irish names like Flanagan and Shaughnessy and O'Hushín.'

'Well, I don't do other people's poems,' Ernest said. 'I don't even read other people's poems. I don't like anybody's but my own.'

'You don't even like poetry.'

'That's right,' Ernest said. 'It's terrible. Dreadful. It needs a revolution. The blueprint for which is in this manuscript.'

Ernest held his manuscript in the air as if it were an Olympic torch.

'If only the bastards would publish it,' he said, suddenly losing his enthusiasm. 'Right now I'd be rolling in cash. Swimming in it. I'd have an Olympic sized swimming pool full of cash.'

'That's not very wise,' Jon said. 'You ought to keep it in a bank.'

'My God,' Ernest said. 'You're right.'

He calmed down when he remembered he didn't have any actual money. There was silence for a long while as the two men immersed themselves in thought.

'Isn't something supposed to be happening?' Ernest said finally.

'Something *is* happening.'

'Something else.'

'I don't know.'

'Well find out.'

'How?'

'What how?'

'How, how?'

'Hee haw.'

'Jim jam.'

'Cat spam.'

Jon began strumming the guitar as they went on and for a while both men whiled away the time singing in nonsensical sentences.

'Stop,' Ernest said suddenly.

Jon stopped strumming.

'That was it. I've remembered. You were supposed to be busking.'

'What about you?' Jon asked.

'I'm going to collect the money,' Ernest said, taking off his hat. 'You need somebody to collect the money from the passersby. You don't think people are just going to come and give you money do you?'

'I had thought that was the general idea.'

'Well, you're wrong. You need someone to shout at them.'

'I don't think they're going to give us money if you shout at them,' Jon said.

'Who is this "they" you keep referring to?' Ernest said. 'I don't see anyone.'

'The people walking by.'

'Oh yes,' Ernest said, noticing them for the first time.

They were of a variety of ages, all shapes and sizes. Mostly, though, they were young, and in groups. A few young couples desperately clutching each other as if the wind might pick up at any moment and blow the other away. Older couples walking in separate respectful units, staring at the shop windows. Giggling teenage girls in short skirts and low-cut tops. Large groups of men with clenched fists and bloodied mouths.

Ernest shook his head and did not recognise in any of them anything of himself. He turned to Jon.

'Well, go on then,' he said.

Jon strummed the guitar.

'What's that?' Ernest said.

Jon stopped strumming.

'What?'

'Don't stop,' Ernest said.

'Well, I can't hear you.'

'What was it anyway?' Ernest asked. 'What were you playing?'

'It was called the "I've just realised this Fisher Price guitar doesn't actually play anything more than three notes" song.'

'Never heard of it,' Ernest said. 'Play something else.'

'Ernest?'

'Yes?'

'I've just realised this is a Fisher Price guitar and that it doesn't play anything more than three notes.'

'What?' Ernest said, picking up the guitar. 'Oh, yes. Damn.'

He shook his head in disbelief.

'Still,' he said, 'I suppose, ordinarily, real guitars aren't made out of luminous pink plastic.'

'Yes,' Jon said.

'What are we going to do?' Ernest asked.

'Tune this,' a deep-voiced man behind them said.

Ernest and Jon looked up. Standing above them was a tall burly-looking man with a beard dressed in a blonde wig and a light blue dressing gown. Behind him stood a small thin man with a moustache and a long dark dusty coat that seemed to weigh his slight frame down. Underneath the coat he was wearing a long black evening gown.

The bearded man in the wig was holding out an acoustic guitar to Ernest and Jon.

'Tune this,' he said, 'and I will give you a reward.'

Jon took the guitar in a daze as the two men sat down beside them with large sighs.

'I myself,' the man explained, 'am entirely and indefinitely tone deaf. I tend to find someone who will tune it, however. What I offer in return is my gratitude and a reward.'

The man spoke with a harsh Northern English accent.

'This is Gladys,' he said, motioning to his friend. 'I am Drake.'

'I am Horatio,' Ernest said. 'This is my friend Delilah.'

Drake bowed respectfully and winked at Jon/Delilah.

'Can you tune it?' Drake asked them. 'Do you have the ability?'

Jon nodded.

'I'll see what I can do,' he said.

'I am completely tone deaf,' Drake went on as he took a large joint from his pocket and lit it. 'I cannot distinguish one note from the other. But I can play. I can play all right. Once it is in tune.'

He handed the joint to Ernest who took a long deep grateful drag. Gladys declined the joint so Ernest took another long deep drag and nearly passed out.

'Strong,' Drake said. 'Good stuff.'

Ernest nodded in the general direction of the disembodied voice and contemplated eating his own hat.

'I am a coal miner from Newcastle Upon Tyne,' Drake said. 'Like my father and his father before him.'

Ernest nodded dreamily as Jon continued to tune.

'Gladys is a Dublin magician,' Drake went on. 'He used to do kids' parties but the parents grew too afraid.'

'Ah,' Ernest said.

'The dresses,' Gladys said, shaking his head sadly.

'We are disenfranchised,' Drake said. 'Doomed to walk the streets forevermore.'

'So are we,' Ernest said. 'Only just today. By our landlord from Galway.'

Drake nodded knowingly.

'With me it was Margaret Thatcher,' he said. 'I once successfully spat at her from fifty yards.'

Gladys laughed quietly at this.

'My father and his father and his father before him,' Drake said, his eyes lost in the past, 'all went down the pit when men were men and real men wore dresses. My father and his father and his father before him. We drank and smoked and lived in constant filth. We mined and carried and broke our backs by day and by night we wore women's clothes and danced with each other in the darkness.

'It was wonderful. We were all part of a prestigious club. My father and his father and his father before him.

'Part of it was the way they felt. The glamour, the silky smoothness. Nothing was smooth down the pit. All rough edges. We felt alive wearing women's clothes. And then Margaret Thatcher came along and destroyed it all. Her and those damned environmentalists. Bastards! Ignorant fools. Clean energy! Who wants clean energy? Not me. Not me.'

Jon was salivating as he watched the joint being passed between Drake and Ernest and back again. He put down the guitar.

'I'm taking a tuning break,' he said, taking the joint from Ernest. Drake snatched the joint away from him.

'No, no,' he said. 'No. No. No. When you've finished.'

Jon grumpily picked back up the guitar and once again began to tune.

'Clean energy!' Drake said contemptuously. 'There is no such thing as clean energy. There's energy you can see and energy that you can't. I'll take black choking smoke over the invisible stuff any day. At least you know where you are with smoke. That's why we're all dying. That's why we're all dying out here from unknown causes and unseen filth. Because we turned our back on coal. On what we could see. On what burned and let us know, not seeped and leaked and creeped unseen.'

'Well said!' Ernest yelled.

'There'll never be another life like it,' Drake went on. 'And now we're all doomed. They all thought they were saving themselves but they were condemning us. Condemning us to extinction from clean, green, invisible deaths.'

'It is tuned,' Jon said holding the guitar aloft.

Sweat poured down his face. Saliva dripped from each corner of his mouth. He reached, with trembling hands, towards the joint.

'Wait!' Drake ordered.

He reached over and gently picked up the guitar. He played the E-string. He nodded his head and murmured approval. He played the A-string. He nodded his head and murmured approval. He played the D-string. He nodded his head and murmured approval. He played the G-string.

'Not right,' he declared.

'Not right?' Jon said. 'I thought you said you were tone deaf.'

'I am,' Drake said. 'But I know when it is not right.'

'Well, in that case,' Jon said. 'Why don't you just fiddle with the knobs till you hear that it no longer sounds wrong, thereby tuning the guitar?'

'Do you want your hash or no?' Drake said.

Jon nodded resignedly and resumed tuning.

'My friend and I,' Ernest said, 'are trying to busk so that we can gain enough money to stay drunk for the foreseeable future.'

'You shouldn't drink,' Drake said. 'Drink is a terrible thing. It has ruined many a moral man. Hash, on the other hand, is a celestial plant sent by God to demonstrate a sense of spirituality.'

'Are you a Rastafarian?' Ernest asked.

'No,' he replied. 'I am a transvestite.'

Ernest nodded.

'I see,' he said. 'A transvestite.'

'No,' Drake said. 'A transcendentalist. Well, a transcendental-ist transvestite.'

'I see.'

'No,' Drake said. 'No, you don't. When you have lived as long as I have in deep dark holes and danced contentedly in high-heeled shoes with face as black as soot and had your world torn asunder, been wrenched from your home amongst the brave and the dirty, wrenched up into the harsh white light of despair, then, and only then, might you have half an inkling.'

'Half an inkling,' Gladys said, nodding sadly.

'Like Gladys here,' Drake said. 'A simple soul with nothing less than affection and love for all creatures who walk this earth and a penchant for wearing designer frocks. A man with no greater ambition than to make every child he comes upon light up with laughter.

'Now, I ask you, what greater indictment could there be of our society that a man like him, a man of extraordinary kindness, of poise and dignity, be forced out of the only job he loves – to entertain a child – simply because he does not follow the rules of convention.'

'I see,' Ernest said.

'No,' Drake said. 'No you don't. You don't know the man. How could you? This man has a gift. A gift for making the most unhappy child smile. For making a room full of children of any age, race, physical or mental ability or disability, cry with tears of laughter. He could do it, simply by walking into a room. Simply by looking at a child a certain way. Something that you or I can never know or truly understand. Something that we have all forgotten as we have grown older.

'He understands children and they understand him. Something happens between them. Something holy. Something magical.

'And how did they treat him? This gifted man, this singularly brilliant man. They hunted him down as if he were a rabid dog. All for unfounded lies and rumours. Fear and ignorance. They are the world's worst sins and the most prevalent.'

'I've got it,' Jon cried.

He passed the guitar to Drake as carefully as if it were a porcelain vase.

Drake played the E-string. He nodded his head and murmured approval. He played the A-string. He nodded his head and murmured approval. He played the D-string. He nodded his head and murmured approval. He played the G-string. He nodded his head and murmured approval. He played the B-string. He nodded his head and murmured approval. He played the high E-string. He nodded his head and murmured approval.

'I sense nothing wrong,' he pronounced.

Jon smiled with relief and reached for the joint.

'Wait!' Drake instructed. 'The true test is to play the song. Only when I play the song can I be sure.'

Drake held his fingers poised over the guitar. He steadied himself. Jon began to sweat.

'The devil!' Drake began singing as he strummed the guitar. 'The devil! The devil! The devil!'

For ten full minutes Drake played the same chord over and over again as he repeated the only lyric.

'The devil?' he sang. 'The devil! The devil! The devil!'

Finally, he put the guitar down as Gladys and Ernest clapped. 'Very good,' he told Jon. 'It is in tune.'

Jon giggled an almost mad giggle and reached for the joint.

'Sorry,' Ernest said as he exhaled the last drag. 'I'm afraid it's all gone.'

'It can't be!' Jon wailed.

'Don't worry,' Drake soothed. 'I am very grateful to you. You will not go without. I am a man of my word.'

Drake took out a crumpled coke can from a plastic bag and a small lump of hash wrapped in tinfoil from his dressing gown pocket. He stared at Jon with a small grin as he burned and crumbled the hash onto the top of the coke can.

'Are you ready?' he asked him when he'd finished.

'I am,' Jon said.

'Put your mouth to this hole at the side of the can,' Drake said, pointing. 'And when I tell you to breathe, breathe.'

Jon nodded. Drake lit the crumbled hash at the top of the can. The brown turned to bright red and then to smoke.

'Breathe,' Drake yelled.

Jon breathed. He took deep inhalations of the pure drug. He held it within his lungs till the smoke seeped throughout his body and clouded his brain into a murky thoughtlessness. When the fog lifted, some time later, Jon could see Ernest was already sucking on the can.

'Sent by God,' was all Jon could murmur.

Gladys laughed and patted him on the back. At some stage he must have got wine from somewhere because he was now elegantly sipping from a tall glass. Jon laughed at the fact that Gladys was drinking wine and Gladys patted him on the back again. The force of pressure made Jon fall forward. Gladys grabbed him just before his nose hit the ground. Jon began laughing and Gladys patted him on the back again, nearly knocking him over and then catching him. This procedure was repeated several times over the next few minutes, the laughing, the patting and the grabbing before injury.

Jon then picked up the guitar and began strumming and singing Drake's devil song. Ernest and Drake joined in. Gladys laughed gleefully. Jon stared down the street as they sang and spotted something that made him think he was hallucinating. A large group of angry men were heading towards them, clutching sticks and bats and spades and brushes. At the forefront of the group was the young traveller boy from whom Ernest had stolen the plastic guitar.

Jon giggled to himself and marvelled at the power of the drug they were smoking. Ernest turned to see what was so funny and nearly had a heart attack.

'Oh shit oh shit oh shit,' he said. 'We are all going to die horrible, bloody deaths.'

He tried to stand up but only succeeded in falling over, which made the other three men laugh.

'We've got to run,' Ernest tried to say but, in his state, it came out as loose-tongued babble.

'Yes,' Jon said giggling. 'I entirely agree.'

Ernest looked back down the street. The travellers were walking a terrible slow-motion march. Their mouths opened and closed in unison as they called the battle cry. Saliva dripped from their yellow protruding teeth. The little boy at the front was playing a tin drum and singing a song of violent revenge.

Ernest grabbed Jon by the collar.

'We've got to run,' he managed to get out finally in actual words.

The fog over Jon's mind began to clear. He stared at the group approaching them.

'Are we in danger?' he asked.

Drake turned around and stared at the group of travellers.

'No, no,' Drake said. 'The travellers are an honourable people. They live by moral codes more sophisticated than our own, passed down from generation to generation over thousands of years. These men are clearly looking for someone who has wronged them. Someone who has perhaps harmed or dishonoured a member of their family. We have nothing to fear from them.'

Ernest nodded silently. He tried to swallow but found he had no moisture. The young traveller boy at the head of the group spotted them. He stood perfectly still and pointed. The whole group of travellers stood perfectly still and stared at them. For some reason this image finally released Ernest and Jon from their stupefied paralysis. Both men jumped into the air and ran.

'You have nothing to fear,' Drake called out after them as they took off, 'but fear itself.'

Jon and Ernest ran unsteady Pinnocchio steps. The person in charge of steering in their brain kept veering them dramatically to the right so that as they ran they continually bumped into walls or buildings. They could hear but not see the chasing pack.

They ran down Grafton Street and turned right up Nassau till they came to Trinity College. Here they scrambled over the large gates into the green college playing fields and hid face down in the darkened grass.

'We know you're in there,' came a deep country voice from the darkness. 'We have these grounds surrounded and shortly will descend upon you. There is no chance of your escape or that you will breathe for much longer. I am speaking to the shorter one. The one with dark hair. If the other wishes he may come to us now and give up his friend, and we will let him go gladly. We have no bone to pick with him. He should come now or he'll be sorry later.'

'Jon?' Ernest whispered. 'Jon, where are you? You're not going to go are you? You don't believe him?'

'I'm thinking,' Jon said.

'Don't be a fool,' Ernest whispered. 'They'll kill us both.'

For a long time there was silence.

'Jon,' Ernest whispered desperately. 'Jon, don't do it.'

'I've made a decision,' Jon said. 'I've decided that, even if it would be in my best interest to go, I can't. I'm too much of a chicken.'

'Good. You won't regret it.'

'I might regret it,' Jon said.

They lay on the dew-drenched grass and listened for sounds of the approach of certain death. For a while they heard nothing. Then a faint rustling. A footstep, followed by another. Whispered voices.

'We should run,' Jon said. 'It's our only chance.'

Ernest considered this.

'You're right,' he decided. 'We should run immediately.'

'Agreed,' Jon said.

Both men lay very quietly and still.

'You go first,' Jon said finally.

'No,' Ernest replied.

They lay deathly still and only breathed when absolutely necessary. A pitchfork suddenly hit the earth approximately three inches from Ernest's face.

'Ahhhhh!' he shrieked.

Ernest stood up, plucked the pitchfork from the ground and ran screaming through the oncoming crowd of travellers. He felt the fork pierce something soft and let go of it, continuing to run and scream as bodies flew left, right and centre. Jon ran screaming behind him through the newly created gap.

They ran till they could no longer feel their legs and still kept going. They were sure that the travellers were right behind them and that, at any minute, they would be struck down by heavy, fatal blows.

The travellers stood in a respectful circle around the body of their dead leader, the pitchfork jutting out from his stomach.

'The king is dead,' one of the men said, choking back the tears.

'Whatever happens after this day,' the eldest traveller said, 'we shall not rest until those two men are dead with him.'

'Who will be king?' someone asked.

'I will,' a young man stepping out of the crowd, said. 'He was my brother. I want to avenge him.'

'We'll need a contest,' several people said. 'There is no right of succession.'

'A contest,' another man said approvingly. 'To decide amongst the best contenders. Tully can fight in it and avenge his brother as king if he is good enough.'

'No,' the eldest traveller intervened. 'This will not do. Nothing like this has happened before. There are outsiders involved.'

'Rules are rules,' the first man argued.

'No,' the eldest said. 'Whosoever finds and kills those two boys.

He will be the next king.'

A murmur of approval went through the gathering and the first man and the king's brother both backed down.

'It is decided,' the old man said. 'Spread the word.'

2. Morality

'That,' Ernest said, 'was almost it.'

Jon gasped for breath.

'Did you hit anyone?' he asked.

Ernest shook his head.

'It was too dark,' he said. 'Where are we?'

Jon looked around them, at the bright lights, the new buildings, at the rows of glowing pubs and restaurants.

'Temple Bar,' he pronounced.

Ernest nodded.

'I thought so,' he said.

They collapsed in a heap in the small synthetic square.

'I hate this place,' Ernest reflected as he looked around him. 'All supposed to be so young and hip. I don't feel young and hip when I'm in this place. I feel old and out of touch.'

'And poor,' Jon said. 'The new Dublin. For the rich. For the tourists. Our dole would not last too long round here.'

Ernest sighed.

'We have no money,' he said. 'We have no drink. I'm sober and the trauma of recent events has rid me of all obnoxious chemicals.'

'We still have this,' Jon said, holding up Drake's acoustic guitar.

'Where did you get that?' Ernest demanded.

'I was holding it,' Jon said, 'when we began to run. I simply did not let go.'

'Good man,' Ernest said. 'Well, go on then. What are you waiting for? Start playing.'

'What shall I play?'

Ernest sighed.

'Anything,' he said. 'The Beatles. We need money. We are in a desperate situation. This would never have happened if you'd stuck to your task.'

'No use blaming me,' Jon said. 'You're the one everyone wants to maim or kill.'

Ernest nodded bitterly.

'They'll be sorry,' he said ruefully. 'What about ABBA?'

'What about them?'

'Do you know any?' Ernest asked. 'Everybody loves ABBA. They are pure pop.'

'Well, I don't know any,' Jon said.

'What about "Fernando"?'

'No,' Jon said. 'I'm sorry if I was vague, but when I said I did not know any, I meant I did not know any ABBA songs. Not a one.'

'It's my humble opinion,' Ernest said, ignoring Jon, 'that "Fernando" by ABBA was the pinnacle of all musical creation until this moment. Nothing's been the same since then. I mean, think about it. It was all so glorious. The cheesy smiles. The sequinned outfits. The names: Bjorn eh . . . Bob, Anastasia, Alice, something like that anyway. And they were all married. How much more perfect could it get?'

'Yes,' Jon said. 'But I don't know any ABBA. I don't know "Fernando".'

'Perhaps that's where music went all wrong,' Ernest said. 'Perhaps that's when everything went wrong. When they all got divorced. Perhaps ABBA themselves were the height of human existence, the perfect married musical foursome, and it's all downhill from here.'

'I don't know any!' Jon repeated in frustration.

Ernest came back down to earth. He looked at Jon.

'Just play anything,' he said. 'I can't take being sober any more. I'm beginning to get nostalgic, which is never a good sign. It shows the end is close. It's cold and late and I want to go home, but we have no home, so I at least want to get enough money to get drunk.'

'All right,' Jon said. 'I just have one small problem.'

Ernest sighed. 'What is it?'

'I don't really know any songs as such,' Jon explained. 'I can't play anything. I mean, apart from "Faith" by George Michael and I only know one verse of that.'

'What?' Ernest said. 'Why were you asking me what to play then?'

'I thought I might get lucky,' Jon said. 'You never know.'

'Jesus. We can't make any money with one verse of "Faith".' Ernest moaned. 'We couldn't even make money with the whole of "Faith".'

'I agree,' Jon said. 'It does not lend itself to busking.'

'Because it's crap.'

'Yes,' Jon nodded.

'Why didn't you learn something worthwhile? What sort of a person learns the guitar only to play one verse of "Faith"?'

'I don't know,' Jon said. 'Someone who could only ever afford the free introductory lessons?'

'Well, go on then,' Ernest sighed. 'Start.'

For ten minutes Jon played the first verse of "Faith" over and over again. Finally Ernest could not take it any more.

'Shut up!' he instructed. 'Not only are you not making any money but you are making me want to kill you.'

Jon stopped playing.

'Right,' Ernest said, standing up. 'I'm going to get us all the money we need by simply reciting one of my poems.'

Jon nodded.

'It won't work,' he said.

'Shut up.'

Ernest retrieved the manuscript from his bag, selected a page, cleared his throat and began to read.

> 'What words
> Left bare
> Can control the situation?
> What light
> Kept still
> Can keep this picture bright?
> What . . . '

'A tosser,' a passerby said.

'Philistine,' Ernest yelled after them. He sat down grumpily.

'Bastards,' he said. 'They don't deserve to hear my words.'

'I did tell you,' Jon said. 'Nobody wants to hear original poetry. They don't have the patience for it. They want famous Irish names.'

'Right,' Ernest said, clasping his hands together and standing up. 'I've had enough. I'm going to make us some money.'

'Poems!' he yelled. 'Famous Irish poems! Famous Irish historical verse. The story of Tír na nÓg. Fionn and the seven dwarves. Cúchulainn and the dragon. Poems! Famous Irish poetry!'

A fat American couple appeared as if from nowhere. The fat man stood staring at Ernest for a long while, as if he were in the distance.

'Poems!' Ernest yelled into his face. 'Famous Irish verse!'

'Do you do poems?' the American man asked.

'Yes,' Ernest answered.

'Irish poems?' the American man asked.

'Ask him if he does Irish poems,' his wife added helpfully.

'I do Irish poems,' Ernest yelled. 'They are my speciality.'

'Shush,' Jon said. 'You don't have to yell when they're close.'

'But they're not hearing me,' Ernest said.

'Say,' the American man said. 'My wife and I'd like to hear a poem from one of your big shots, you know? All these guys thaa' they got plaques of all over town.'

'Of course,' Ernest said, nodding vigorously. 'Plaques.'

'Honey,' the American man said, turning to his wife. 'Honey wha's that fella . . . they gottatt thaa . . . at thaa . . . the waterway. The guy with the statue.'

The American lady pursed her podgy lips.

'Kavanagh?' Ernest suggested. 'Patrick Kavanagh?'

'Yeah, that's him,' the American man said. 'You know eh, any of his stuff?'

Ernest smiled bashfully.

'Actually,' he said. 'I did my thesis on Patrick Kavanagh. Oh yes. At the prestigious Trinity College Dublin which, if you walk straight on there, will be the large, old building bang ahead.

Wonderful place. A positive palace for poetic patronage. Spent my best years there. A must for tourists. They have a wonderful book there the eh, "Book of Elves". Oh, it's a treat. A wonderful thing. It's a historical account you see. It details the great war of the 1700s between the leprechauns and St Patrick. St Patrick hated the leprechauns. Absolutely despised them. And, of course, the leprechauns hated St Patrick because he was French. There was no other reason. They just hated him because he was French.

'Oh, of course, historians have speculated. A lot of people think it might be because the French ate frogs' legs and that the leprechauns were worried that St Patrick might eat their legs because they were small and wore green.'

'Really,' the American man said. 'Well, that is absolutely fascinating.'

'Yes it is, isn't it?' Ernest said. 'In fact Patrick Kavanagh wrote a poem on this very theme and eh, I'd like to recite it for you now.'

Ernest cleared his throat.

> 'The green the green
> The boys the boys
> Stuck fast
> Hold tight
> Don't bite
> You'll be all right.'

With that Ernest took a short bow.

'Very minimalistic,' the American woman said, nodding her head approvingly.

'That's very perceptive of you,' Ernest said. 'Kavanagh was, indeed, an advocate of the minimalistic form. Or, as we say in Latin, the *formus minimus*.

'Have you studied poetry?' Ernest asked, leaning towards the American woman.

'Oh yes,' she said. 'Well, no. No, not really.'

'Of course, of course,' Ernest said. 'How true.'

He held out his hand in readiness for his reward. The fat American man looked from the hand to Ernest's smiling face.

'What about thaa . . . what about the poems in Irish?' he said. 'Do you do poems in Irish?'

'*As Gaeilge*?' Ernest said.

'No,' the American man said. 'In Irish. You know? What's it you call it, hun?'

'Irish,' the American woman said helpfully.

'Oh Irish,' Ernest said nodding his head gravely. 'Of course. I am entirely fluent in the Celtic tongue. The mother tongue, excuse my French. Yes, it's like a second language to me. In fact it is a second language. A language of its own. There are things you can say in Irish that sound completely different if you were to say them in English. Oh yes, I love it.'

The American man squinted and pointed his nose at Ernest.

'Well, we'd like to hear one of your poems in Irish,' he said. 'Wouldn't we, hun?'

The American woman nodded her head and for a moment Ernest was transfixed by the sight of her many wobbling chins swelling upwards and downwards in waves of flab. He set about trying to count them. He was interrupted at number six by the American man.

'Say, eh . . . are you gonna say it then or what?' he said. 'Cause we gotta get back to the hotel sometime this week.'

'Of course,' Ernest said, nodding gravely.

He cleared his throat. He took a step forward. He took a step back. He cleared his throat. He took a step forward and put his hand to his chest.

> '*Chuaigh mé*
> *Go dtí an siopa*
> *Cheannaigh mé milseáin*
> *An bhfuil cead agam dul* .
> *Go dtí an leithreas?*
> *Níl, níl, níl.*'

'That was beautiful,' the American woman said, a single tear rolling down her cheek.

Ernest nodded sadly. He held out his hand in readiness for its reward.

'What'd it mean?' the American man demanded.

'Mean?'

'Yeah. Translation. What was it in English?'

'Oh,' Ernest said. 'Oh, oh it's difficult. Yes, it's difficult you see because there can be no . . . there can be no . . . real translation. At least, no direct translation to em, to eh, to do it justice. The words . . . the words just wouldn't be . . . wouldn't be right.'

'Try,' the American man said, flashing the wad of bills he had in his wallet.

'Right,' Ernest said. 'Fine.'

He cleared his throat. He took a step forward. He took a step back. He cleared his throat. He took a step forward and held his hand to his chest.

> 'Love can't live
> In a vacuum
> It wouldn't have any air
> If I were to live
> In a vacuum
> Would anybody care?'

A single tear rolled down the American woman's cheek.

'That was beautiful,' she declared.

'I don't get it,' the American man said.

'Well,' Ernest said, 'you see, the vacuum, represents the transfixion of the unhealthy . . . '

'No, no,' the American man interrupted. 'I'm not talking about the meaning. I get the meaning. I just don't get, seeing as how you said the words weren't the same.'

'I see what you mean,' Ernest said. 'What are you talking about?'

'It rhymed,' the American man said. 'I don't get how it could possibly rhyme, if you had such . . . ahh . . . difficulty in translating it.'

'Coincidence?' Ernest said hopefully.

'But the first one,' the American man said, 'the one in Irish, didn't even rhyme.'

'Ah,' Ernest said.

He was beginning to feel that he was not going to make any money. Jon, sensing the outcome, resumed playing the first verse of "Faith" over and over again

'What I'm saying is,' the American man went on, 'I don't see how, when you say it was so goddamn difficult to translate it, how then, in a matter of seconds, not only could you translate it, but you could get it to rhyme as well.'

Ernest stared from the American man to his wife and back again.

'I don't believe this,' he said, shaking his head. 'I mean, I work my ass off for you. I tell you the Book of Elves story for free. You want a Patrick Kavanagh poem, I give you one. You want an Irish poem, I give you one. I do all of this and then, when you ask me to translate, I manage, through sheer intellect and strength of will, to give you a translation that not only rhymes, but effectively translates the meaning, the truth, the inner core of the poem. I do all of this for you and what am I met with? Hostility. Hostility and distrust. Accusations. I ask you, is it any wonder? Is it any wonder?'

Ernest held his head in his hands for several seconds. When he removed them he saw the American woman was in tears and her husband was staring sorrowfully at the ground.

'Is it any wonder?' Ernest whispered softly and devastatingly.

'Son,' the American man said, his great big John Wayne voice choking up, 'son, I owe you an apology. You did a beautiful thing for us tonight. You did a wonderful, holy thing, and I'm ashamed to say that all I could do was doubt you. I tell you, I'm feeling pretty low right now. I'm feeling pretty small. Here, son, take this.'

The American man took a clutch of notes from his wallet.

'No,' Ernest said. 'No, I can't. It's too late.'

'Son, please,' the American man begged. 'Don't be a fool. Now there's a lot of money there. Don't let your pride get in the way. Come on, now, take it. The Lord knows you deserve it.'

'I'm sorry,' Ernest said. 'You have broken my heart. No amount of money could fix what you did to me.'

The American man nodded sadly and he and his wife walked slowly away.

Jon stopped playing the first verse of "Faith".

'That,' he said, 'was an awful lot of money.'

Ernest looked at him.

'Oh my God,' he said. 'What have I done?'

He looked down the street but saw no sign of the Americans.

'An awful lot of money,' Jon repeated.

'I never had a chance,' Ernest said desperately. 'It was a matter of pride you see. I got caught up in my own act. I never had a chance. I tried. I tried to reason with my brain. I tried to be greedy.'

'Shall I resume with "Faith" then?' Jon said.

'Oh it's hopeless,' Ernest said, slumping down beside Jon. 'It's hopeless. Our one clear chance of making money and it's gone. I sent it away. I think I must have a self-denial complex. I need to deny myself the things I most want. I don't know why. Ever since I was a child it's always been the same. If someone offered me a toy I liked I'd pretend I didn't want it. If I liked a girl I'd pretend I couldn't care less. If I wanted a puppy I'd drown it in the river.'

'Really?' Jon said.

Ernest nodded.

'Yes, really. Apart from the puppy which I made up to make the story interesting.'

'Shall I resume playing?' Jon said.

'No,' Ernest said. 'Nobody will ever do anything but smack you in the mouth for playing the first verse of "Faith" over and over again and with my luck they'd probably smack me.'

'Perhaps we should call it a night?'

'Do you think that would help?'

'It can't make it any worse,' Jon said.

'Where will we go?'

'I don't know,' Jon said

'Then we might as well stay,' Ernest said. 'And stick to the plan.'

There was silence for a long while.

'What is the plan?' Jon said.

'A taxi,' Ernest said. 'We need to get a taxi to Paul's. First an off-licence. Then Paul's. He'll provide us with food and warmth and a roof over our heads and if he doesn't we'll cut his throat.'

'Money,' Jon said. 'We need money for a taxi.'

'Right,' Ernest said. 'We'll just have to rob a tourist. Any one will do.'

Ernest began looking for tourists. Jon sighed. He put the battered old guitar on the ground and stared at Ernest as he wandered up and down the street asking people if they were tourists.

'I can't find any,' he said finally. 'They're in hiding.'

Jon picked up the guitar again and began strumming sadly to himself.

'Didn't you hear me?' Ernest said frantically. 'I can't find any tourists. This is a crisis. We're going to freeze to death out here. I'm going to be eaten alive by rampant travellers. Don't think they'll spare you. You're as much a meal as I am. In fact you're more of a meal. You're fatter than me. They'll go for you first.'

'I am not,' Jon said as he strummed. 'I'm underweight for my height.'

'Look at those cheeks,' Ernest said. 'And those flabby arms. They'll feed off you for weeks. They'll slowly sauté you with herbs and spices. Don't think you're not involved because you are.'

Jon ignored Ernest and concentrated on playing the open E-note of the guitar intermittently like a morose church bell.

'Are you listening to me?' Ernest said. 'We're going to be eaten alive. Don't just sit there, you bastard. Do something.'

'I am doing something,' Jon said. 'I'm playing the guitar.'

Ernest stared at Jon, shaking, for a few furious seconds. He slowly walked over and plucked the guitar from his hands.

'We're having a crisis,' he said, raising the guitar high in the air. 'Fuck your music!'

Ernest brought the guitar smashing down onto the pavement. It shattered immediately into a scatter of splinters. A thick silver object flew from the bowels of the guitar as it smashed. Ernest watched it floating in the air for a long time before reaching out and grabbing it. He stared at the shining silver package in his hand, smelled it, turned it upside down, turned it right side up.

'What is it?' he asked finally.

'Why don't you open it and find out?' Jon suggested.

Ernest sniffed the package again.

'Strange,' he said. 'It smells . . . strange.'

'What sort of strange?'

'Strange,' Ernest said helpfully. 'Oh Jesus.'

'What's wrong?' Jon asked.

'What if it's a bomb?' Ernest said suddenly, holding it away from him. 'It smells like it might be a bomb. Gunpowdery.'

'Is it ticking?' Jon asked.

'Of course not,' Ernest said. 'If it was ticking I would have thrown it in the air and ran.'

'That wouldn't have been very considerate.'

'Bombs don't tick,' Ernest said, 'necessarily. Just because it doesn't tick doesn't mean it's not a bomb. In case you hadn't noticed there have been several advances, such as metallurgic batteries and digitalisation. What do you think? Do you think the British army all keep very quiet and still when faced with suspect packages and if they don't hear a ticking they all go home?'

'You smashed it on the ground,' Jon pointed out. 'I think if it were a bomb it might have exploded at that point.'

'He might very well have been an agent,' Ernest said, not listening. 'Drake. You heard his accent. He had an English accent.'

'He didn't deny he was English,' Jon reasoned. 'He told us he was.'

'Well, of course he told us,' Ernest said. 'To gain our trust. To catch us off our guard. Oh God. I don't even care about the North and here I am going to die over it at such a young age.'

'I really don't think it's a bomb,' Jon said. 'Why don't you open it?'

'You open it, you bastard,' Ernest said. 'I'm about to be blown into several hundred million pieces because I was born in the wrong country. I don't even believe in the afterlife. Why should I die? There's plenty of people out there who want to die for their country. Let them. Why me?'

'Give it to me,' Jon said.

'Are you mad? I'm not moving.'

Ernest shut his eyes tightly and stood like a statue, with his arm extended. Jon sighed. He stood up and walked over to Ernest. He walked round the extended arm and removed the package from his hand. Ernest moaned slightly and kept his eyes firmly shut. Jon opened the packet. He shook it, sniffed it, turned it upside down, turned it right side up and sniffed it again.

'Hash,' he pronounced.

'What?' Ernest said, opening his eyes.

'Hash,' Jon said, motioning with the package.

Ernest took a step backwards.

'Don't point that thing at me,' he said. 'What are you talking about? Form sentences.'

Jon sighed.

'This silver stuff is tinfoil,' he said. 'Wrapped in several layers around this brown stuff, which is hash. This is an extremely large piece of hash which Drake must have been concealing in his guitar.'

'It is?'

Jon nodded.

'Give me that,' Ernest said, grabbing the hash. 'This is . . . this is it. This is what we've been looking for. The sign. The gift. The luck that has been so sorely missing from my life. Do you realise what this means? Do you realise what we have here? This is the biggest lump of hash I have ever even seen. It's enormous. This is worth money. Lots of it.'

Jon nodded.

'Yes,' he said worriedly.

'Right,' Ernest said. 'We must sell it. Immediately. I am so sober it hurts.'

'Sell it?'

'Sell it,' Ernest confirmed, looking round for potential customers.

'I'm not sure about this,' Jon said.

'Good, good,' Ernest said, as he looked up and down the street.

'I mean, if we sell this, we'll be drug dealers.'

'So?' Ernest said impatiently. 'What's your point?'

'Well,' Jon said. 'I'm not sure I want to be a drug dealer. I'm not sure I could live with myself. I mean, it's a bit of a leap. Morally it leads to several difficult questions. Plus the fact that it doesn't actually belong to us. The guitar belongs to Drake and therefore everything in it. Not only would we be drug dealers, but we would be drug dealing thieves. Which is, moreover, a bit of a leap from what we were before which was, after all, a couple of fairly harmless if somewhat self-abusive unemployed disaffected youths.'

'Right,' Ernest said, clasping his hands together. 'Morals is it? That's no problem. I did my thesis on morals. I am an expert. I can shoot down any theory you like. I will quell all your moral qualms in one foul swoop.'

Jon nodded but did not look convinced.

'What, exactly, is your problem?' Ernest asked.

'Well,' Jon said, 'as I say, it's a leap. I mean, I know we lead fairly meaningless scrounging existences, taking pleasure only from illicit substances and poor taste humour, but drug dealing? I have no moral problem with drug taking. I'm happy to oblige. But to inflict it on others? To actively inflict? It's not safe. Clearly drugs are not safe. They are addictive, if only because excitement is addictive and life without drugs is rarely all that exciting. Not that there's anything particularly wrong with that. I stopped trying to be happy within myself a long time ago, like most ordinary human beings do.

'When you are a child you can be happy with a small, red, car shaped piece of plastic, but, as you grow, you slowly lose the ability to find wonder in small things. You learn to give up, as your parents and peers have given up. To consume alcohol to be social. To consume it to be humorous. To be loving. To consume it just to pass the time.

'When you're young, you don't see the harm in other drugs, such as hash, because they are not, necessarily, any better or worse than the ones they have commercials for, and there is nothing wrong *per se* in choosing to use them.

'But there is something fundamentally wrong in encouraging others because, after all, there might be people out there, however unlikely, who can find happiness without drugs. There might be a meaning to this existence and just because you and I have not found it nor ever will find it does not mean we have the right to encourage others to give up.

'Plus, again, there is the health issue. I did not make or grow what is contained in that package. I don't know who did. I don't know what chemicals it contains. There are no ingredients on the sides of these things and no guarantees. Taking drugs can often result in death and I don't want to kill anybody. Let them kill themselves if they want to but I won't assist.'

Ernest sighed.

'Okay,' he said. 'Firstly, you are saying you do not wish to deflect people from a course which, however unlikely, may result in them finding some meaning or truth or spiritual enlightenment. Fair enough. I propose a simple solution. I propose we sell the drugs to people who are already smoking drugs and will continue to smoke drugs whether or not it is our drugs or somebody else's they are smoking.'

'How do you propose that?'

'Simple,' Ernest said. 'We will merely find a suitably poor area. Where drugs and crime and hopelessness are rampant. We simply offload the drugs in this area where they will have no real ill effect and only serve the community by taking money out of the pockets of the real drug dealers and into our own.'

'That seems a little cynical to me,' Jon said. 'You are proposing to take advantage of a destitute community who are ignored by the wider elements of society, by the government and by the police.'

'No, no,' Ernest said. 'I'm helping them. Listen to me, drugs will be taken? Yes? You're not saying that we're going to introduce drugs into these communities?'

'No,' Jon said. 'No, I'm not saying that.'

'Well then, which is better? That the locals buy from a drug dealer, who will probably use the money to buy more drugs, to enlarge his empire, to kill off rivals, to encourage minors and pregnant mothers to use hard drugs, to increase their stranglehold on the community, or, that they buy from us, who, once we have offloaded this *soft* drug will disappear from their lives forever and use their money to buy alcohol so that the community, the off-licence, in fact the Irish economy as a whole will benefit.'

Jon nodded.

'I suppose,' he conceded.

'Right,' Ernest said. 'What was next? Ah yes, safety. Well, to be honest, Jon, this one is no challenge at all. In fact, it is laughable. What, in the name of all that is reasonable, is safe these days? There's hormones in chicken, testosterone in pork, and mad cow disease in beef. Fruit and vegetables are treated with noxious chemicals that make your muscles melt and your mind mush. The fluoride in the water and in the toothpaste makes your bones brittle and break. There's radiation from mobile phones and microwaves, nuclear power plants and overhead power lines, all causing cancer. The exhaust fumes from cars, buses, trucks and planes make your lungs black, can lead to asthma, more cancer, ruin the atmosphere and melt the polar caps, leading to more smog, pollution and death and possibly a mini ice age that will kill millions. Mercury fillings in your teeth release toxic vapours that accumulate in your tissue and in organs and cause Alzheimer's, Parkinson's, arthritis and candida. Every week some new warning comes out about something that we have been using or consuming every day in the misguided belief that it is without risk or threat. Half the medical profession argue with the other half about what is nutritious, dangerous or deadly. Multinational corporations pay for phoney studies saying everything they're doing is *just fine* and *perfectly healthy*.

'What is safe? Who the fuck knows anymore? Can you seriously tell me that this stuff is any more harmful than the crap we are breathing into our lungs right now?'

'No,' Jon said, shaking his head. 'And I see your point, but it's not enough. I don't make or sell any of those products you talked about and I can't do anything about the exhaust fumes or the multinationals. What I can do, however, is opt *not* to sell something when I have no idea whether or not it is going to result in sickness or death.'

'Fine,' Ernest said furiously. 'I'll test it.'

'That,' Jon said, 'would not be wise.'

'I don't care,' Ernest said, taking out his lighter. 'I'm willing to die if necessary.'

Ernest broke off a piece of the tinfoil and hurriedly burnt some hash into it.

'You don't appreciate life enough,' Jon said. 'I think it would be good for you to develop a major illness.'

'What's to appreciate?' Ernest said, burning away. 'You're born, you're miserable, you die.'

'If you had been in hospital,' Jon said, 'as I have, if you had to rely on others, to be totally helpless, you might appreciate some things. The ability to walk, for instance, the ability to breathe without assistance.'

'Right,' Ernest said. 'It's ready. I propose to inhale the smoke directly, because we have no tobacco or skins or anything. If I don't die in ten minutes, we will sell the stuff, agreed?'

Jon sighed.

'Agreed.'

Ernest leaned his head over the tinfoil and began burning and inhaling the hash.

'I sometimes wonder,' Jon said, 'if it weren't a blessing. Developing asthma. In fact, sometimes I wonder if there isn't a meaning to this life after all. I mean, it's not inconceivable. It's not so hard to imagine things happening for a reason. Maybe there is a God. Maybe I developed asthma and spent so long in hospital so that I could appreciate my health when I had it again. So that I could appreciate my freedom. The ability to do things without a nurse's or doctor's permission. Not to have to take drugs to breathe easily.

'And yet, while I sometimes wonder about such things, in reality, there does not seem to be much actual purpose to my being alive. Here I am, still unemployed, still with few prospects and now without a home. If there is a God he's probably more than a little sick.'

Ernest fell over onto his side.

'Are you all right?' Jon asked him.

Ernest nodded.

'Strong,' he said through clenched teeth.

'Perhaps that's it,' Jon said. 'Perhaps God's grown senile. If we're created in His image I don't see why He couldn't go senile as much as the next person. Maybe He went mad long ago and the world has been left unchecked for centuries. Maybe that's why human beings have developed and overrun the planet when it probably would have been a better idea all round if we had never happened.'

Ernest sat up.

'Am I alive?' he asked.

Jon stared into Ernest's glazed eyes.

'Just about,' he said.

'Right. We can sell it then.'

Ernest thought a moment.

'What is it we're selling anyway?' he asked.

'What do you think?' Jon said. 'It seems unlikely to me that there could be any cosmic significance to you and I being thrown out of our flat, to wonder through these cold streets.'

'Cosmic,' Ernest gurgled.

'I didn't think so.'

'Hoy!' a distant angry voice shouted.

Jon and Ernest turned to see the figures of Drake and Gladys, running towards them, shaking furious fists in the air.

'Are they real?' Ernest asked.

'It's hard to tell,' Jon replied, mesmerised by the two strange figures.

Drake seemed to float in his long dressing gown as he moved rapidly towards them. Ernest suddenly snapped out of it.

'We have to run,' he said, gathering up the hash. 'Escape. The drugs. We must flee.'

Ernest stood up and ran into a wall. Jon sighed. He picked him up from the ground.

'Thank you,' Ernest said, holding his nose.

'Hoy!' Drake shouted.

'Run!' Ernest screamed, and both men took off as fast as their short legs would carry them.

'Where are we?' Ernest asked, when they finally stopped to regain their breath.

Jon looked around them, at the huge open street and the rows of shops and department stores.

'O'Connell Street,' he said.

Ernest nodded.

'What are we going to do now?' Jon asked.

'Repent,' a woman's voice said.

Ernest and Jon turned around to see an old woman dressed from head to toe in black walking towards them, holding a huge wooden cross in the air with both hands. Round her neck she wore a heavy silver cross. Behind the woman there was a large group of young people, dressed casually in jeans and t-shirts. All of them were carrying placards with various slogans written on them, like *God is love,* and *Praise Jesus: Protect the Unborn.*

The old woman and the group approached Ernest and Jon in slow advancing steps.

'Repent!' the old woman said. 'Repent.'

She stood beside Jon and yelled into his face.

'Repent,' she yelled, her whole face glazed over and expressionless.

Jon was surprised, when she stood next to him, to see how small she was. She had looked so tall from a distance.

'What exactly is it you'd like me to repent?' Jon asked.

'Hello,' said one of the young people, a girl in jeans and a t-shirt that read *There is no Pro choice. There is only Pro life or death.* 'My name is Suzanne. We are members of the Catholic Youth United organisation. Would you like to talk to us for a minute or two?'

'No, thank you,' Jon said.

'She doesn't look very young,' Ernest pointed out. 'For someone in Catholic Youth United.'

'She is the founder of our organisation,' Suzanne said, staring at the old woman admiringly. 'She inspired us. Watching her walk up and down O'Connell Street, day after day, night after night, with her cross and her words of wisdom. It inspired us all.'

'Repent!' the old woman screeched.

Jon shook his head.

'Yes,' he said. 'Very inspiring.'

'She can only say that one word,' Suzanne said. 'And yet she puts so much feeling into it. She had a stroke you see. She carried on though. She says more, in that one simple phrase, than any of us could in whole conversations.'

'Now, that I do believe,' Jon said.

'Would you like to sign here in support of Jesus?'

'Why?' Ernest asked. 'Is he in trouble?'

'Yes,' Suzanne said, not noticing the sarcasm. 'We believe His message is under great threat. From all these card carrying liberals, murdering our children and distorting the message of our Lord Jesus Christ.'

'I don't believe in God,' Jon said. 'Especially not your kind.'

Suzanne shook her head sadly.

'Jesus forgives you,' she said. 'I want to tell you something. I love you. All of us here love you, isn't that right?'

She turned to the assortment of young people in t-shirts and they all smiled warmly at Jon and nodded their heads.

'Well I don't love you,' Jon said. 'I don't even like you very much.'

'But *Jesus* loves you,' Suzanne said, pleading with him, her voice strained, as though he were being unreasonable. 'And that's what's truly important, isn't it? I mean, look at the cross. Just look at what He did for us. He died on that cross so that all mankind could live, so that we could all live eternally.'

'That's all fine and dandy,' Ernest said. 'But my friend and I have important business, so, if you'll excuse us.'

'Well, Jesus will forgive you,' Suzanne said. 'Remember that. And we forgive you too.'

'That's very generous of you,' Ernest said. 'Now we must go.'

'So that's it, is it?' Jon said. 'That's your most important symbol, the cross?'

Suzanne nodded.

'Of course,' she said. 'He died for us.'

'You know,' Jon said. 'I've often wondered about something . . . '

'We have to go,' Ernest interrupted.

'One second,' Jon said. 'I've often wondered about this theory of mine. How somebody like yourselves might take to it.'

'We're open to all new theories,' Suzanne said. 'As long as they don't contradict the laws of the Bible and the Catholic Church.'

'Good,' Jon said. 'I'm glad to hear it. See, my theory concerns the Bible. In particular it concerns that cross that everyone, including you, carries around with them everywhere. I mean, don't get me wrong, it's a wonderful marketing tool. Like all great marketing tools, it's simple and direct. But one day, in any case, I kind of came up with this theory. About the Bible.

'This theory of mine centred around this question: what would have happened if Jesus, the son of God, the Messiah, whatever name he went under, what would happen if, after the few years' teaching he did, the few years wandering around through the deserts, the hillsides and small villages with his troupe of merry men, you know, not eating well, constantly being followed, never having a moment's peace, having to perform little miracles left, right and centre, what would happen if he just got sick of it? Like a lot of people in his line of business, what if he had a couple of really good years on tour and burned out? Or maybe he just decided that enough was enough and that he'd said just about everything he had to say. He'd done all the parables he could think of, he'd given out so much advice in neat easy metaphors that he was bored out of his mind with them.

'So, having done what he set out to do, having accomplished all he felt he could accomplish, he returned to the simple, ordinary life. Retired. Maybe even taking over his daddy's carpenting business and settling down and having two point four kids.

'Occasionally of course, somebody might call in, one of the old disciples maybe, and ask him to do one last speech or miracle or hotel conference but he'd just shake his head and say, "Those days are over. Don't get me wrong, I don't regret them, but I was young, full of energy. I'm happy being anonymous."

'So, and here's where we get to the crux of my theory, despite his early retirement, maybe even because of it, Jesus's message became more and more popular. It started to catch on. Some of the disciples carried on preaching and they in turn inspired new members, who went on to teach in new and distant lands.

'And, some time later, I think it was about seventy years in fact, after Jesus's preaching days, a few of the newly converted decided they would write a book, setting down all the teachings of Jesus and trying to persuade people what a good guy he was and that their religion was better than all the other ones going round at the time.

'But when they had it all set down, when every bit of information was right there in front of them in print, something was missing. Something wasn't right. They read it and re-read it and, of course, they liked the message, and the parables. It conveyed all their beliefs well. It was concise, catchy, but *something* was missing.

'Finally, one of the guys hit on it and when he did, he realised immediately that it was the one final thing missing from the book.

'"An ending," this guy said. "It needs an ending."'

Jon stood staring into Suzanne's eyes for a long while.

'What do you think?' he asked her finally.

Suzanne stared at him wordlessly. Her left eye began to twitch. Her white teeth began to show as she tried to smile. Her lower lip began to shake. Her breathing intensified.

'Let's get them,' she said finally, grabbing the old woman's huge cross and stepping forward.

Jon took a step backwards. He looked around the group. Every one of their expressions had changed to pure contempt. They stared at Jon and Ernest with a steady focused hatred. It was at this point that Jon realised that if they did not get out of there very quickly, they would be beaten to death by the group.

'Run,' he shouted at Ernest as the group advanced upon them.

Jon and Ernest took off down O'Connell Street as fast as their short legs would carry them. Catholic Youth United followed seconds behind, screaming at the tops of their lungs.

'Blasphemers!' they yelled.

'Atheists!'

'Protestants!'

Jon and Ernest ducked down Talbot Street and out onto the

Liffey quays. They ran for several more minutes before they realised the members of Catholic Youth United were no longer behind them.

'I think their crosses slowed them down,' Ernest, said, through gasps of breath.

Jon nodded.

'I must admit,' he said, 'whatever reaction I had expected, it was not being beaten to death by crosses.'

'Never mind,' Ernest said. 'We have far more important matters to concern ourselves with.'

'Where are we going?' Jon said, as they continued to walk along the quays.

'Where do you think?' Ernest said. 'To sell, to sell. I know the ideal place.'

'I don't know,' Jon said. 'Maybe we shouldn't. Drake seemed very angry.'

'Bah!' Ernest dismissed. 'Finders keepers. He shouldn't have been so trusting. He'll have learnt a very valuable lesson tonight.'

'Where are we going?' Jon repeated.

Ernest stopped and turned around.

'To an area,' he said, 'so poor and vanquished that we will have next to no trouble at all off-loading these drugs.'

Ernest turned around and resumed his walking.

'Where?' Jon called.

'Brewers Street.'

'*Brewers Street?*'

'Yes, Brewers Street.'

'You can't be serious,' Jon said.

'Why not?'

'Brewers Street?'

'Look, what is the matter with you? Did you hit your head in the chase?' Ernest asked.

'I am not going to Brewers Street,' Jon replied. 'I'd sooner cut my own throat and save time.'

'It's not that bad.'

'Yes,' Jon said. 'Yes, it is. In fact, it's worse. It is the worst.'

'Okay, so it's bad. But this suits our plans better. The worse the area, the better for us.'

'We're going to die,' Jon said. 'Not even the riot police go in there.'

'Exactly,' Ernest said. 'So no chance of getting caught.'

'No chance of getting out alive.'

'No, no, no,' Ernest said. 'Risk is a relative thing. You have to look at our goal. You have to keep focused. Financial reward. If we stick to our task we will not go far wrong.'

They turned off the quays and walked along the desolate dark grey streets until they came beneath the shadows of the tall thin high-rise flats of Brewers Street.

A cold wind picked up, throwing a collection of empty cans noisily against a wall and nearly giving Jon a heart attack. Ernest began shivering from the cold.

'We're going to die,' Jon said.

'I'm not so sure I like this,' Ernest said, staring around him. 'It's very quiet.'

'We are two posh Southsiders from privileged backgrounds,' Jon said. 'These people will tear us to shreds.'

'Ha,' Ernest said. 'No they won't. Ha. We'll be fine. We'll just . . . just sell our drugs and eh . . . and eh . . . oh fuck it let's get out of here.'

Jon nodded in agreement and both men turned around and began walking back the way they had come. Just then, from around a corner ahead of them, a crowd of boys appeared and blocked their path. The boys ranged from the very young to the late teens. They had tightly shaven heads and stared with a menacing directness at Ernest and Jon.

'Ha,' Ernest said, turning around again.

A crowd of boys were already coming at them from the opposite direction. They seemed to come from everywhere. From side streets, from the stairwells of the flats, from surrounding walls, from beneath the streets themselves.

They gathered and then stood quite still, on either side of Ernest and Jon, and stared at them wordlessly. Finally, a small blond haired boy stepped out from behind one of the groups and walked, quite slowly and calmly, up to where Ernest and Jon stood.

'What are youse doing here?' he said in a soft, menacing voice. Ernest swallowed hard.

'We have something,' he said. 'Something to sell.'

'Where are you from?' the young boy asked.

'I can't remember,' Ernest said.

The blond haired boy nodded. He reached into his trouser pocket and pulled out a small white plastic object. He pressed a small switch on the plastic and a silver blade flicked out from its centre.

'Where are youse from?' the boy asked again.

'We're from the Southside,' Jon said. 'We got lost. We were just on our way out.'

The boy nodded again. He looked back at the group he had come from for a few seconds before turning back around.

'What are you selling?' he asked Ernest.

Ernest looked at Jon, who, with the slightest of movements, shook his head.

'Hash,' Ernest said, turning back to the boy. 'Of the finest quality. Not . . . not the crap stuff. That's why we came here, because . . . because we know this is a place that appreciates quality.'

The boy nodded.

'Show us it,' he said.

Ernest fumbled desperately in his bag. He took out the thick package wrapped in tinfoil and held it up.

'It's lovely stuff,' he said. 'I've tried it myself. I knew I'd find an . . . an appreciative palate here so . . . '

The young boy took the package out of Ernest's hand. He opened a small bit of the tinfoil and smelled the hash.

'Where's it from?' he asked.

Jon shook his head.

'We don't . . . '

'Jamaica,' Ernest interrupted. 'Directly imported from Jamaica by one of my contacts. A dried fish exporter and a Rastafarian by the name of Drake . . . Drake. Drake Drake.'

The young boy nodded.

'What are you selling it for?'

'Ah,' Ernest said. 'Well . . . it's . . . it's obviously very fine quality, you know, unlike anything you will have had in your lungs before. It's mind blowing. It's . . . '

'Fucking answer me,' the boy said quietly.

'Two hundred pounds.'

The young boy laughed.

'Are you fucking serious?' he said.

'Well,' Ernest said. 'You know, we're open to offers . . . '

'This,' the boy said, pointing to the package, 'is worth a lot fucking more than two hundred pounds. It's worth at least a grand. Why are you selling me something for two hundred that's worth a grand?'

'I like you?' Ernest tried. 'I mean . . . I like the area. I mean . . . I feel sorry . . . no. No I . . . I need money, fast, you see, I'm dying. I need an operation. I need a valve put in my heart.'

'For two hundred quid?'

'It's a very small valve,' Ernest said. 'Look . . . look I'll be honest with you. Me and my friend here, we're selling this for somebody. The money's for him. He's in jail you see. Busted. His flat was raided. They caught him with the lot: hash, acid, weed, speed, methadone, coke, dope, crack, heroin, smack. He needs the money for bail. This is his only asset. We're not really drug dealers you see, my friend and I, this is all just, for a favour.'

The boy sniffed loudly.

'I don't give a bollocks about your friend,' he said. 'He can rot in jail.'

Ernest nodded.

'Okay,' he said.

The boy motioned for the two groups either side of Ernest and Jon to close in. As the boys walked forward they took out a variety of sticks and knives from their pockets. Ernest could not stop nodding. He turned to Jon and nodded. He turned to each advancing knife-wielding group and nodded. He turned to the young boy and nodded.

'So,' he said. 'I take it you're not interested.'

'Shut your face,' the boy said. 'You're going to to get a bating. For ignorance and lack of respect. You're going to wish you were never born. You're gonna wish you never seen me. You're gonna wish you never heard of Brewers Street.'

With that he took a small cigar from his jacket pocket, cut off one end with his flick knife, and lit it up.

He shook his head as he exhaled the smoke.

'You don't come in here,' he said, 'with your Dublin 4 accents and your bullshit fucking stories about your friends in low places. You must think I'm thick. You're going to learn.'

The two groups were almost upon them now. The young boy took a step backwards and smiled as he sucked on his thin cigar. He exhaled, turned around, and began walking through one of the advancing groups. Boys at either side moved to make a way for him.

'Wait,' Jon called after the boy.

The young boy stopped. He turned around and stared at Jon.

'Listen,' Jon said. 'My friend here has a bit of an active imagination. He's prone to delusions of grandeur.'

The young boy simply continued to stare at Jon without moving.

'We are in fact, not drug dealers,' Jon explained. 'Nor friends of drug dealers. We just found this lump of hash somewhere and decided to come here and sell it. We had no idea how much it was worth. We just wanted money because we were thrown out of our flat today and wanted to drown our sorrows a little bit.'

The young man walked forward. He looked from Jon to Ernest.

'Is that true?' he asked.

Ernest nodded.

'Well,' the young man said. 'Then things are different.'

He reached into his pocket and took out a thick roll of twenty pound notes. He counted out two hundred pounds' worth and handed it to Ernest.

'Here,' he said. 'Two hundred. Now you'll fuck off if you know what's good for you.'

Jon and Ernest nodded.

'Thank you,' they said to the young boy.

A gap appeared in the middle of one of the groups and Jon and Ernest backed out through it, thanking the young boy the entire way.

'Tell your friends what you saw tonight,' the young boy said, pointing with his cigar. 'Tell them what you've learned.'

Ernest and Jon nodded and kept backing away as the group of boys got smaller and smaller till finally they were on a different street bereft of people and sound.

'Where are we?' Ernest asked.

Jon stared around them, at the graffiti, and at the collection of tower blocks looming overhead.

'I don't know,' he said. 'I've never been here before.'

'We must get out,' Ernest said. 'We have money. Cash. We have to find a taxi. An off-licence.'

Jon nodded.

'Fine,' he said. 'But which way?'

They were at a crossroads. Huge tower blocks spun out in every direction for as far as the eye could see.

'We must be close to a way out,' Ernest said desperately. 'We must be. This is town. We must find a taxi rank. We have the money.'

Ernest began walking off down one of the streets. Jon sighed and caught up with him.

'I am beginning to think,' he said, 'that this luck you were talking about is a double edged sword.'

'It's fine,' Ernest insisted. 'We have the money. We just need to get out of here. Everything is okay.'

Suddenly they heard the sound of footsteps.

'What was that?' Ernest said, stopping.

'I don't know,' Jon said. 'Footsteps.'

The two men listened. Nothing. They walked cautiously on.

'Money, money,' Ernest said. 'I used to be so stupid. I didn't appreciate it. I had idealistic notions. Idealism is for the birds.'

Suddenly, from out of nowhere, a group of men dressed in black jumped down onto the road in front of them. Jon and Ernest screamed. The men in black screamed. They ran at Jon and Ernest and threw a large black blanket over them. Jon and Ernest were engulfed in darkness and their screams were muffled into cloth filled gasps.

'Ahhh!' Ernest screamed through the cloth.

'Quiet,' they heard a voice say. 'You are being abducted. Walk quietly and quickly with us and you will come to no immediate harm.'

The word *immediate* did not inspire confidence and Ernest began screaming again.

'Shut up!' the man instructed.

Ernest continued to scream until one of the men hit him over the head with a heavy object, knocking him unconscious.

Jon was ordered to continue walking as one of the men put Ernest on his back and carried him. Jon was continually pushed and shoved as he walked through unseen streets before finally being ordered up a flight of stairs. He climbed what seemed an endless number of steps, falling every few minutes only to be picked up by one of the men and told to keep moving.

Eventually, Jon and Ernest, who was still unconscious, were brought into a darkened room and sat in two chairs. The blanket over Jon's head was removed and he squinted into a harsh bright lamp that was pointed directly at their faces. He couldn't make out any of the figures behind the light but he could tell there was a crowd of people from the amount of mumbling. He turned to look at Ernest, who was propped up against his shoulder and looked for all the world as if he was sleeping peacefully.

'Order!' someone called. 'Can we have order please? First Superintendent.'

'Thank you, Second Superintendent,' a second voice said. 'Prisoners, you are now in the headquarters of the People's Society for Justice, Retribution and Maintenance of Social Order. You are here to answer charges of violations of civil and local law in accordance with the constitution of the PSJRMSA.'

'O,' another voice said.

'What?'

'O,' the voice repeated. 'PSJRMSO. You said PSJRMSA.'

'Right,' the first man said. 'You are here to answer a charge of violations of civil and local law in accordance with the constitution of the PSJRMSO. The penalties for such offences are: ten lashes, a beating by ten men, a beating by twenty men and twenty lashes, or hanging. How do you plead?'

'What are we accused of?' Jon asked.

'You should have said that,' the second man said.

'I was coming to the charge,' the first man said. 'It is customary to tell the prisoners who we are as an organisation and what their potential punishment is before reading the charge.'

'What's the point?' the second man said.

'What?'

'Well,' he went on, 'what's the point if they don't know what they're charged with? I mean, it could be anything. You're supposed to tell them who we are, what they're accused of and *then* tell them the possible punishments.'

'Look, Second Superintendent Hughes,' the first man said, 'we are not here to discuss policy. Policy meetings are on a Tuesday. This is a Thursday. And never in front of prisoners.'

'They could be here for littering,' the Second Superintendent grumbled.

'Shut up!' the first man said. 'I'm in charge here. I am invoking my right by Rule Four, Section Seven of the constitution, as First Superintendent, to conduct judicial trials any way I see fit, providing it does not contravene any other points laid out in the constitution, right?'

'Excuse me?' Jon said.

'What is it?' the First Superintendent yelled, turning furiously on Jon.

'Superintendent?' a female voice said.

'What is it Vice Chancellor?'

'First Superintendent, it is not my wish to bog down proceedings,' the Vice Chancellor said. 'But I think the tone of your voice while addressing the prisoner contravened Rule Seven of the prisoner's charter.'

'Quite right, quite right,' the First Superintendent said impatiently. 'I hereby admit that, in accordance with the terms laid down in the constitution, to all assembled members, my own culpability in that, while acting as First Superintendent of the court, I did woefully allow negative emotions to enter my tone of voice while addressing a prisoner.'

'Excuse me?' Jon said.

'What?' the First Superintendent shouted, turning angrily.

'Superintendent . . . '

'Shut up,' the First Superintendent yelled. 'Everyone shut up. Right, you, what's your question?'

'I just wanted to know what the charge was,' Jon said.

'Right,' the First Superintendent said. 'You are charged with selling illicit substances not twenty minutes previously, that you knew those substances to be illicit, that you sold these illicit substances to gain financial or personal reward, and, that you are not a member of this area and came into this area without prior notice or written permission.'

'Not a member of this area?' Jon said. 'Is that a crime?'

'Of course,' the First Superintendent said. 'A very serious one. This organisation has determined that, since Ireland, and therefore Dublin, and therefore the city centre, is not, according to results written and published in the features section of the organisation's committee on drug information and research's bimonthly leaflet, suitable enough a climate in which to grow illicit substances, therefore, we have reasoned that all drugs must come in from the outside and have implemented into the Constitution a rule whereby all people who are not resident in this area or have members of their family who are resident in this area, must apply in writing three weeks prior to any visit.'

'I see,' Jon said. 'Well, we didn't know.'

'Yes, well,' the First Superintendent said. 'It's no good complaining. You should have read the leaflet.'

'Where is it available?'

'At the committee headquarters, of course.'

'Which is here?' Jon asked.

'Yes.'

'How are we supposed to read it if it's only published in an area we're not allowed into?'

'He's right,' the Second Superintendent said. 'How could they?'

A few other voices began to murmur in agreement.

'Quiet!' the First Superintendent yelled. 'Take a note please, Chief Records Officer: amendment to be added to Rule Fifteen, Section One of the constitution, to be debated next policy meeting, Tuesday next.

'Fine, we'll drop that charge. Which leaves us, in any event, with the more serious charges, namely that you sold illicit substances, you knew them to be illicit and that you sold these substances to gain financial reward.

'How do you plead?'

'I'd like a recess.'

'Shut up,' the First Superintendent said. 'How do you plead?'

'My friend is unconscious,' Jon protested.

'You'll have to plead for him then. Guilty or not guilty.'

Jon thought a moment.

'Not guilty,' he said.

'Fine,' the First Superintendent said mockingly. 'Second Superintendent, if you could read to the court the account of the incident which the Vice Chancellor witnessed.'

'We'll need the swearing in first,' the Second Superintendent said.

The First Superintendent sighed.

'Is it really necessary?'

'I'm only following the rules as laid down . . . '

'Oh God. Fine, fine. Just hurry up.'

The Second Superintendent cleared his throat.

'Is the witness here present?'

'Yes,' the Vice Chancellor answered.

'Are you a member of the PSJRMSO?'

'Yes.'

'Do you believe in the constitution as laid down by the High Committee and as maintained by all members and implemented by our leader, his most Catholic, the First Superintendent?'

'Yes,' the Vice Chancellor answered.

'And do you claim the purported statement is true in all regards?'

'Yes.'

'Right,' the Superintendant said. 'The statement reads as follows: "I, Vice Chancellor, while on official watch on the roof of the Security Committee's number two look-out tower, do solemnly swear that I, while acting as an agent for the Security

Committee's binocular offensive, did witness through said binoculars, two males of unknown origin handing over illicit substances to known users of said illicit substances in exchange for monetary reward. Signed Vice Chancellor.'"

'Very good,' the First Superintendent said, nodding approvingly. 'Proceed.'

'Very well,' the Second Superintendent said. 'Vice Chancellor. You got a clear view of these men, is that correct?'

'Objection,' Jon said.

'Silence,' the First Superintendent said. 'The plaintiff will remain silent throughout the proceedings or will have to be restrained.'

'Where's my lawyer?' Jon asked.

'You don't have one,' the First Superintendent said. 'Now shut up.'

'What's going on?' Ernest said, waking up. 'Are we in jail?'

'Silence!' the First Superintendent screamed.

For a while, there was silence.

'Right,' the First Superintendent said. 'Mr Hughes, proceed.'

'Second Superintendent.'

'What?'

'Second Superintendent. You called me Mister.'

'Just get on with it, will you.'

The Second Superintendent sulked for a minute before proceeding.

'Vice Chancellor,' he said, 'did you or did you not get a good look, with the aid of your binoculars, at the two men perpetrating the aforementioned crime.'

'Yes.'

'Very good. Do you see the men anywhere in the room?'

'Objection,' Jon said.

'Objection,' Ernest chorused.

'Silence!' the First Superintendent shouted.

'It was them two,' the Vice Chancellor said.

'This is a kangaroo court,' Jon complained.

'Shut up,' the First Superintendent screamed. 'One more outburst and you will be restrained. You should be bloody grateful.

You should think yourself lucky. Most vigilante organisations, you wouldn't even get a trial.'

'What's the point?' Jon said. 'If we don't have a defence?'

'Silence!'

'Excuse me.'

'What is it, Vice Chancellor?'

'It was just that you called us vigilantes,' the Vice Chancellor said. 'I thought the aim of the society was not to be a corrupt vigilante group.'

'Of course,' the First Superintendent said.

'That we were going to create a new police force because the real police won't come here.'

'Of course.'

'Except that we were going to be a democratic police force, devoid of corruption and abuse.'

'Exactly,' the First Superintendent said. 'Which is what we are.'

'No, we're not,' the Second Superintendent said, addressing the crowd. 'I told you. I told you all this would happen. First, everyone had an equal vote. Then, only the upper chambers and committees, with his as the casting vote. I told you, but you wouldn't listen. If you had elected me as the First Superintendent instead of him, none of this would be happening. We'd still be a democracy.'

'Arrest that man,' the First Superintendent shouted.

There was a scuffle and the next thing Ernest and Jon knew there was a man sitting next to them.

'You see,' he shouted. 'You see what's happening? He's gotten too big for his boots. It'll be you next. You wait and see.'

'Silence,' the First Superintendent said. 'You are charged with insubordinance and treason.'

'I told you,' the Second Superintendent yelled. 'I would have created a truly democratic force. One member, one vote. One member one vote!'

A few other people in the room began chanting along with the Second Superintendent. Ernest and Jon began chanting too.

'One member one vote! One member one vote!'

'Silence!' the First Superintendent screamed. 'Look, I want democracy as much as the next person. But it doesn't work. Not in a police force. Do you think the dealers have democracies? Of course not. You've got to fight fire with fire.'

'Fight fire with fire,' the Second Superintendent said mockingly. 'He's insane. He's probably on drugs. He's probably in league with the drug dealers.'

A disquieted murmur went through the gathering.

'I am not on drugs,' the First Superintendent insisted. 'I founded this organisation to combat drugs.'

'What better way to hide the truth?' the Second Superintendent yelled.

The murmurs grew louder.

'Shut up!' the First Superintendent screamed. 'Be quiet will you. I'm trying to convict these two men.'

'Three men,' Jon said.

'Shut up!'

'First Superintendent?'

'What is it now Vice Chancellor?'

'Well,' the Vice Chancellor said. 'It's just that you continue to have negative emotion in your voice while addressing the defendants. I don't want to bog down proceedings but it's expressly forbidden. Plus, you said you were *trying* to convict these men. I thought we said we were going to have fair trials where guilt or innocence would be established by the evidence. I don't see how that could happen if you're setting out to convict them.'

'What difference does it make?' the First Superintendent said. 'They're guilty. We all know they're guilty. You saw them yourself.'

'I thought it was them,' the Vice Chancellor said defensively. 'It could have been anyone.'

'What?'

'Well, if the funds committee had agreed to pay for the longer range binoculars which I made a request for months ago I wouldn't have a problem recognising them.'

'Right,' the First Superintendent said. 'Arrest that woman.'

There was another short scuffle and a middle-aged woman was

seated next to Ernest, Jon and the Second Superintendent.

'What have I done?' the Vice Chancellor asked.

'Perjury,' the First Superintendent sneered. 'Perjury and constantly interfering with the First Superintendent's God-given right to convict drug dealers. And contempt of court.'

'Did you hear that?' the Second Superintendent said. 'He think's he's a god. Who'll be next? Ask yourselves.'

'Silence!' the First Superintendent screamed. 'Or you will be restrained.'

'I want to go home,' the Vice Chancellor said. 'I thought we were going to have a proper police force. One that believes in values. One that has the integrity and moral standing to defeat those people out there, killing our kids, because the real police are too afraid to come. I want to go home.'

'Ah, let her go, Pat,' a man's voice said.

'Right,' the First Superintendent said. 'Who said that?'

There was silence for a few seconds.

'Come on,' the First Superintendent said. 'Step forward. Who was it? One of you called the First Superintendent by his first name.'

'He's mad,' the Second Superintendent interjected.

'Shut up! Step forward whoever it was. Come on, or I'll arrest every single one of you. It's my right. You people. You don't know how lucky you are. Most of you lot are too bloody ignorant to appreciate just how lucky you are to have a leader like me.'

'Fascist,' someone whispered.

'I heard that,' the First Superintendent yelled. 'Step forward. The pair of you. Whoever called me Pat and whoever called me a fascist. Come on.'

There was total silence for a few seconds.

'Right,' the First Superintendent said. 'Arrest that group.'

There was another scuffle and one by one about twenty men and women were led in front of the light. After the fifth person, they ran out of chairs.

'Have them sit on the floor,' the First Superintendent instructed. 'You ungrateful bunch of neanderthals. Before I started this organisation you were a mess. A totally pathetic mess. Beating up the odd heroin addict. Stringing up an occasional dealer. I gave you discipline. Order. A chain of command. Ideals. Truth. Wisdom. And what do you do? You start getting wafty bloody notions.

'I am the First Superintendent. All of you, each and every one of you are subservient to me. I decide what's in the constitution. I wrote the bloody constitution.'

'He's loopy,' the Second Superintendent said.

The First Superintendent began going through and every each one of the glorious achievements of the organisation since he had been elected leader.

'Excuse me,' Jon whispered to the Second Superintendent. 'But how many guards are out there?'

'Three,' the Second Superintendent answered.

'Well,' Jon said. 'I'm no mathematician, but I'd say that would give us a numerical advantage.'

'He's right,' the Second Superintendent said. 'There's only four of them.'

All twenty-four people, including Jon and Ernest, stood up as one.

'What's going on?' the First Superintendent said. 'Who gave you permission to stand up?'

Nobody said a word.

'Guards,' the First Superintendent said. 'Restrain those criminals.'

Again there was total silence.

'Guards?'

At that precise moment the Second Superintendent held up his hand and yelled charge and the twenty-two arrested members of the PSJRMSO surged towards the First Superintendent. Jon and Ernest stepped out from behind the light and slowly tiptoed around the group, who were all massing around one shivering, quaking, middle-aged man with a beer gut and balding hair.

'Please,' the man begged. ' I'm your leader. You can't do this. Guards!'

Jon and Ernest exited the flat as the group descended upon the

First Superintendent. They walked down a dirty urine-smelling hallway and into the stairwell.

'Power corrupts,' Jon observed and his voice echoed up and down the stone stairwell and in every floor of the tower block's corridors.

3. The Litter

When they arrived back down in the street Ernest and Jon were faced, once again, with the fact that they were lost.

'We're still lost,' Ernest observed.

'I never remember it being such a large area,' Jon said.

'Perhaps we died long ago,' Ernest said, 'and this is not in fact Brewers Street at all but some unknown place between heaven and hell where we must rack our consciences and repent our lively sins.'

'There's the Liffey,' Jon pointed out and the two men began walking towards the dirty city river.

When the PSJRMSO had beaten their former leader to an unrecognisable pulp, the Second Superintendent looked up.

'Where are the prisoners?' he asked.

Everybody stopped and looked around. They looked in cupboards, under tables and beds and under the First Superintendent himself, but could find no sign.

'Right,' the Second Superintendent said. 'I will now formally take over the First Superintendent position in accordance with the corruption amendment to Section One of the constitution.'

'Aren't we going to disband?' the Vice Chancellor said.

'What for?'

'Because we were corrupt and undemocratic.'

'That was under First . . . that was under Pat. The organisation under me will be a whole different kettle of potatoes. I will make it democratic, equalitarian, just and honest.'

'I'm not sure,' the Vice Chancellor said.

'You, of course, will be my second in command.'

'Oh, thank you,' the Vice Chancellor said.

'Now,' the new First Superintendent said. 'I propose we go now immediately to search for the prisoners so that we can beat them within a millimetre of their lives.'

'Shouldn't we have a vote?' the new Second Superintendent said.

'Not now,' the First Superintendent said. 'There is no time.'

Jon and Ernest were drained and weary as they walked.

'I'm not as spritely as I used to be,' Ernest remarked. 'I used to be able to jump entire buildings in great bounding leaps.'

'It's only going to get worse,' Jon said nodding. 'Maybe we should start out old and weak and gradually get fitter. Maybe we would appreciate our youth more that way.'

'Then we would have to experience birth backwards at the end of life,' Ernest said. 'I think I'd prefer death.'

'All we are is a collection of soft and flabby layers stuck onto wiry bones,' Jon observed.

'When I was younger,' Ernest said, 'I always wanted to be big and strong. To be muscular. I'd happily settle right now for something that doesn't break down after five minutes of running.'

'That's lack of fitness,' Jon commented. 'Today's society is too inactive. We have everything done for us.'

'We don't have anything done for us,' Ernest said.

'Yeah?' Jon said. 'When's the last time you went out and hunted any of the meat you cooked?'

'Last Tuesday,' Ernest said.

The two men heard a terrible screaming behind them. They turned to see a large number of the PSJRMSO running towards them wielding knives and brushes and pieces of wood.

'Drugs out!' they screamed. 'Give us back our streets!'

Ernest and Jon sighed and ran as fast as their short legs would carry them. It became very clear very soon that they were not going to make it. The crowd were almost upon them and they had only made it as far as the river. The two men looked into its icy black waters and contemplated which death would be the more unpleasant.

'I've always had a terrible fear of a drowning sensation,' Ernest said as the crowd closed in. 'Trying to breathe through gasping hopeless waterlogged lungs.'

'Personally,' Jon said. 'I've always had a fear of being kicked to death by a marauding mob.'

Ernest nodded. Both men looked back into the Liffey and then towards the crowd. Just as the new First Superintendent was about to take Ernest's head off with his metal bar a bright yellow taxi appeared from out of nowhere, a few yards away from the two men.

Ernest and Jon leapt away from the First Superintendent and began yelling and screaming for the cab to stop. They managed to jump into the cab just as the First Superintendent took another swipe. As they sat in the back seat, the crowd gathered round the cab and began shaking it violently up and down so that it only ever rested on two wheels.

'Where to?' the taxi driver said, as the taxi rose and fell.

'Em, Bray,' Ernest said. 'If you could hurry too, because we're in a rush.'

The taxi driver sniffed. He revved the car.

'In a rush are youse?' he said as backed the car over several members of the PSJRMSO.

'Everyone's in a rush these days,' the taxi driver said as he slammed down the accelerator, driving over several members of the group in front of them.

Minutes later they were clear of the crowd and Jon and Ernest began to breathe easy.

'I feel very positive about things,' Ernest said. 'Our luck is holding.'

'Is it luck,' Jon asked, 'to have come close to death and escaped, or to have never come close to death at all?'

'That's semantics,' the taxi driver said. 'Luck is what you make of it. Take death for instance. Some people see it as a terrible thing. For me now, it would be a release. I have lived in this taxi for fifty years. I sleep in it, I eat in it, I spend every waking hour in here.'

The taxi driver broke three pairs of lights and took a right turn violently without indicating.

'It's a lonely life,' he said, as they sped. 'A tiresome, lonely life.

Nobody wants to hear what taxi drivers have to say. Nobody is interested in their opinions because, they feel, they offer them too readily. There's the old joke made by a man whose name I can't remember, "What a pity it is," this man said, "that all the people who know exactly how the country should be run are too busy driving cabs and cutting hair."

'Perhaps he's right. Perhaps we are tiresome and repetitive. Opinionated without thought. But we have feelings too. I bleed just as readily as the next man even if my bleeding can never result in my death.'

The taxi driver drove up onto the kerb for several minutes sending pedestrians flying before driving through a public park and breaking three more sets of lights.

'When I said we were in a hurry,' Ernest said. 'We would like to be in one piece.'

'It's the boredom,' the taxi driver said. 'I've always had a problem with it. And now it is my sentence. You see, I could never sit still as a child. I always had to be doing something. Walking, running, constructing something, beating up my brother. They even brought me to the doctor. He prescribed beating me but it didn't work. Nothing worked and I grew from a bored frustrated child into a bored frustrated teenager, constantly chasing girls and never satisfied.

'I loved to drive, though. I would drive for hours. It kept my mind occupied, you see. So many things to look at. If things seemed uninteresting all you had to do was press down on the accelerator. It was wonderful. Physically it kept me occupied too. I don't like these modern cars. Automatics. Things shouldn't be automatic because, if they are, then there is no way *not* to do them and the ability *not* to do something in a car, I find, is one of the most important abilities of all.

'I thought, as a youth, that I would never grow tired of driving. I thought I had found my perfect match. I lost all my friends. I wouldn't even slow down for girls. I was too busy. It's addictive, you see. Interest. Keeping the mind constantly occupied. It's not a healthy thing after all and now I've learned too late. There is a world outside this cab that I will never exist in and that is why I cannot live or die or grow old or crash the car, because I'm too focused, and being focused is not always such a healthy thing.'

The driver slammed on the brakes. The car skidded and rested, finally, two inches from a huge tree. They had arrived.

'How much?' Ernest asked, as they got out of the cab.

'Sit quietly,' the cab driver said. 'Sit still in silence and revel in boredom because if you are bored then you are alive.'

With that the driver drove off down the street, backwards, and disappeared into the mist.

'Where are we?' Ernest asked.

Jon looked around them, at the large houses, the big shining cars, the alarm systems, the tasteful gardens, the furniture shops, the restaurants, the pubs.

'Bray,' he said.

Ernest shook his head.

'I hate these small communities,' he said, 'with their residential associations. Towns that win tidy town competitions. Interfering small-minded upper-middle class values. I mean, I don't see why Marx was wrong and everyone has not just overrun these bastards.'

'Did you ever wonder,' Jon said, 'whether Marx himself destroyed any chance of his own prophecy by mere prophesising alone? I mean, he believed he could predict the future, yet by predicting it, he led certain people to pre-empt it, when the conditions were not suitable as laid out by Marx himself. People such as Lenin, and scores of short-lived communist dictators.

'Perhaps the future is meant to happen naturally and by creating an accurate blueprint for what would come to be Marx ensured that it could never come to be.'

'Having said all that,' Ernest said, 'since we have gotten this money I have decided to be a capitalist because I don't want to share.'

'Your dedication to your principles is inspiring,' Jon said.

'Good,' Ernest said, not listening.

He was growing increasingly impatient.

'Beer,' he said. 'Money converts to beer. Where is the off-licence? Off-licence first, then Paul.'

Jon looked at his watch.

'My watch has stopped,' he observed.

'How can you tell?'

'The seconds don't move.'

'How do you know it isn't time that has stopped and not your watch?'

'Well,' Jon said, 'the battery has fallen out. It would be some coincidence.'

'I did my thesis on time in Trinity,' Ernest said. 'It's a fascinating subject. One which I could discuss with you in detail but, having come so close to the end of my existence on so many occasions on this night, I feel I must avail of the next half hour to get completely rat arsed.'

'Do you suppose he was mad?' Jon asked. 'The taxi driver. It reminded me of the old Chinese curse: May you live in interesting times.'

'Shut,' Ernest said, staring at the shutters of the off-licence. 'How can it be shut?'

'My watch stopped at half past twelve,' Jon observed. 'That's an hour past closing time already.'

'We must find drink,' Ernest said, wandering off.

Eventually they found a 24-hour shop and Ernest went inside.

'Ah,' he said, heading towards a stand with several rows of gleaming red wine bottles.

'Wine,' Ernest said. 'The nectar of the Gods. The blood of angels.'

He turned to Jon.

'Red or white?'

'I'm partial to red myself,' Jon said.

'Good,' Ernest said. 'Me too. Any year or country of origin of preference?'

Jon shook his head.

'Well, we'll take the most expensive then,' he said. 'That's usually a good indication. We'll take two. No, three. One for each of us and one for Paul, as a gift, even though he doesn't deserve it.'

Ernest brought the wine to the checkout till.

'We'll take all these,' he said to the thin spotty teenager behind the till.

'You can't,' the thin spotty teenager said.

'Can't?' Ernest said.

'It's too late. It's half past one. We can't sell wine past eleven.'

'What's he talking about?' Ernest said.

'I think he's saying we can't buy the wine,' Jon said.

'Can't buy the wine? Nonsense. Of course we can buy the wine. We have all this money.'

Ernest threw the twenty pound notes up into the air. The thin spotty teenager was mesmerised for a few moments by the sight of the money floating lazily back down again.

'What's going on here?' a middle-aged balding man, with eyebrows that met in the middle and a manager's badge on his shirt, asked as he appeared from nowhere. 'Who's throwing all this money around?'

'I am,' Ernest said. 'It's for the wine.'

'Wine,' the manager said scowling. 'It's half past one. We can't sell wine at half past one.'

'Why is it on display then?' Jon asked.

'Look here my good man,' Ernest said, putting a twenty pound note into the manager's shirt pocket. 'My friend and I's watch stopped so we didn't realise. What say we keep this schtum?'

'Schtum?' the manager said. 'Schtum! How dare you? I don't want your money. I don't take bribes from vagrants. What do you think this is? Where do you think you are? This is a Cheapeasy 24-hour convenience store. We have rules in this store. Guidelines. Guidelines that we expect every one of our semi-permanent staff to live and die by.

'You make me sick. Coming in here, flashing your money at this poor boy, who probably won't make this amount of money in a month, in a year. Do you know how long I've worked here? Fifteen years. Not at this chain, obviously. No, we only opened in March of this year. But I started out like this young man is starting out. At the till, as an assistant, and I worked my arse off. Slowly being promoted from the till to sandwiches, from there to fruit and vegetable supplies, from fruit and vegetables to assistant general manager of quality control, from assistant general manager of quality control to assistant general manager of personnel, to general manager of personnel, to assistant general retail manager, back down to general manager of personnel for a minor indiscretion that I was later entirely cleared of by an independent judiciary, back up to assistant general retail manager to manager itself.

'I slaved through every working day, eight am, to eleven pm. I had no life. I had no friends. I lost my hair. I developed several ulcers and a facial tic and now you have the gall to come here with your cheap bribes and expect me to keep things schtum! Me! Schtum! Get out! Get out of here, before I break Rule Fourteen of the Cheapeasy management guide to customer relations and break every bone in your worthless body!'

Ernest sighed. He gathered up the twenty pound notes and slowly left the shop with the manager frozen in a furious pointing shake.

'I still don't see,' Jon said as they walked away from the store, 'why they had the wine on display when they weren't allowed sell it.'

'Cruelty,' Ernest said. 'Plain and simple.'

He sighed.

'People don't like me,' he said. 'I don't know why. They're not willing to do me any favours. Plenty of people, happy, smiling, chirpy, well adjusted people, they get away with things. Favours. From total strangers even. Not me. Total strangers hate me. They hate me immediately. People at tills I've never even seen before. They put the change on the counter even though my hand is outstretched because they don't want to touch my infected hands.

'I can see it in their eyes. From people walking by me in the street. They hate me. I don't care. I hate them back. You hear me you bastards? I hate you back!'

'Who are you calling a bastard?' a stocky young man said, approaching, as his giggling girlfriend looked on.

Ernest sighed.

'You,' he said. 'You're a worthless, snivelling, insignificant, lowly, neolithic plonker.'

'Oh dear,' Jon said.

The stocky man nodded. He turned away, turned swiftly back and punched Ernest hard in the stomach. For a few seconds Ernest could not breathe. No air would enter his lungs. No air would leave them. They were stuck, as if burst and deflated. The stocky man kicked him once in the leg as his girlfriend giggled before walking off with her, his hand immediately fastening itself to her arse.

'Why did you do that?' Jon asked, standing over Ernest.

Ernest was too busy trying to breathe to answer. After a few seconds he had recovered enough to speak.

'I wanted to know what it felt like,' he answered. 'Not to be punched, so much. In fact, I could have done without that part, to be quite honest. I wanted to know what it felt like, not to run away. Not to run away after I insulted somebody. To stare them in the face like all those men with brains the size of peas do when they fight.

'Why was I born so weak? I often think that, had we been living in the wild like we used to, I would have been the runt of the litter, and that I would never have survived. That we are living in unreal circumstances and that I don't belong in the world because people like me aren't supposed to be around. It's no wonder. It's no wonder everyone wants to punch me. I'm not supposed to be here. I'm the runt of the litter and everyone can spot it in me a mile away because, after all, we're just animals living in concrete cities and pretending we're civilised when all we want to do is eat and kill and have sex.'

Jon sighed.

'I wouldn't be alive,' he said. 'Not without my inhaler. I would have died long ago. My lungs would have tightened up so that not enough oxygen could get in and not enough carbon dioxide could get out and not nearly quickly enough.

'Sometimes, I thought that maybe I wasn't suppose to be alive. That technology had interfered with Mother Nature, who was just trying to do her job of getting rid of all that's weak. That if I'd been born one hundred years ago I wouldn't be standing here now because that technology would not have existed.

'But you have to resign yourself to relying on it. Maybe we are runts of the litter. It doesn't make much difference. Things change. Things beyond our control. The temperature of the planet rises, killing off one species and making another one flourish. We are just products of modern society.'

'I don't want to be a product of modern society,' Ernest said gloomily. 'I want to either fit in or not. I'm sick of being shunted from one dark hole to another. I'm tired of carrying this manuscript around with me hoping somebody will recognise my genius and give me the blank cheque I need to live a life of ease. More than that, I'm tired of the constant rejection. Hundreds of rejection letters, all in printed apologetic politeness. Phrases like shows promise and certainly interesting and do keep sending your work. I'm sick of it. I'm sick of it all.'

Ernest sighed

'I don't feel like getting drunk any more,' he said.

'No,' Jon agreed. 'Neither do I.'

Ernest began walking off.

'Let's call on Paul,' he said, 'and either he'll put us up or not.'

Jon rang the top doorbell of the large Georgian house.

'It's been a long time,' he reflected, as they waited.

'Success,' Ernest said. 'That's what it does to you. It makes you forget who you really are. Who your friends are.'

A young man, wearing a dressing gown over pyjamas, opened the door and stared at the two strange figures in the doorway.

'Jon,' he said. 'Ernest.'

'Paul,' Ernest said.

Paul rubbed the sleep out of his eyes. He looked at his empty wrist and thought of his watch, sitting by his bedside table.

'How are you?' he said vaguely. 'I mean, what time is it?'

'We're fine,' Ernest said, 'and it's very late. Are you going to let us in then, or not?'

Paul laughed a little and stood aside.

'Of course,' he said. 'Sorry I was . . . I was in bed and . . . '

'That's all right,' Ernest said, walking into the hall. 'I like your pyjamas.'

Paul reddened as he shut the door and followed Ernest and Jon up the stairway.

'I like these old Georgian houses,' Jon reflected as they climbed the stairs. 'I mean, I think I'd like to live in one, one day. Not to rent. But to own one. They make me think of James Joyce.'

'Yes,' Paul said. 'Well, they are expensive enough. I've just been doing refurbishments. Some of the quotes I've been getting . . . Anyway, how are you two? How's the eh . . . how's the form?'

'Good,' Jon said.

'Terrible,' Ernest said.

'Good,' Paul said.

They got to the open door of Paul's apartment and Ernest walked right in. He sat down grumpily on the couch and looked around him.

'New stuff,' he said.

'Yeah,' Paul said, shutting the door. 'Do you like it?'

'Not really.'

'Great,' Jon said. 'It's very modern.'

'Yeah, yeah,' Paul said, nodding. 'That's the look right now. Very minimalistic, you know? Very modern, very . . . '

'Uncomfortable,' Ernest said, shifting up and down in the couch to no avail.

Jon sat down on the couch beside Ernest, elbowing him as he did so.

'Tea anyone?' Paul asked. 'Coffee?'

'We're fine,' Jon said. 'Thanks.'

Paul nodded. He sat down in one of the Foko chairs and tapped his foot on the floor.

'So,' he said. 'What's up?'

'Nothing,' Ernest said. 'Can't we just call in on an old friend?'

'We've been thrown out,' Jon said. 'Of our flat. By our landlord.'

'An evil bastard,' Ernest said. 'He used to walk in without knocking. Sometimes I'd look up from the TV and he'd be standing there, watching.'

'What did he throw you out for?' Paul asked.

'Refurbishments,' Ernest replied.

'Oh I see,' Paul said with a knowing smile. 'You were doing a few, refurbishments, and he didn't take too kindly to it.'

'No,' Jon said. 'He wanted to do the refurbishments. He said he was upgrading the flat and that it would no longer be within our price range. He gave us 48 hours to get out.'

'You're joking?' Paul said. 'But, that's illegal.'

'I told you it was illegal,' Ernest said.

'He can't do that to you,' Paul said. 'You have rights.'

'That's what I told him,' Ernest said, pointing to Jon. 'We have rights.'

Jon shook his head.

'We had no rights,' he said.

'Of course you did,' Paul said. 'You have rights as a tenant. You're protected by the law. Did you have a lease?'

Jon shook his head.

'But still,' Paul said. 'You still have rights. You're still entitled to four weeks' notice. At least four weeks' written notice.'

'No,' Jon said. 'No, we're not.'

'Of course you are,' Paul insisted. 'It's the law.'

'No it's not. The law is, if you have enough money, you can do whatever you want.'

'Oh I see,' Paul said. 'You're talking figuratively.'

'No,' Jon said. 'I'm talking reality. We have no money other than the dole, therefore, if we wanted to get our deposit back, which was our only commodity, we had to comply with all the landlord's requests.'

'But he has to give you the money. He's required by law.'

'No,' Jon said. 'No he isn't. He can do whatever he wants. All he had to do was tell us to get out and we had to.'

'You could bring him to court,' Paul said.

'No, we couldn't. He'd have more money and more time.'

'You're entitled to free legal aid,' Paul pointed out.

'And he could afford better.'

'No,' Paul said. 'No, you're being naive. A person can't just treat someone like that. It's the law.'

'Why not?' Jon asked.

Paul opened and closed his mouth. He flapped his arms, shifted up and down in his seat, and opened and closed his mouth again.

'It's the law,' he said finally.

'They have him brainwashed,' Ernest said sadly. 'There's no hope for him.'

'What?' Paul said.

'You're as good as dead,' Ernest told him.

'What's he talking about?' Paul asked Jon.

'We wanted the money,' Jon explained. 'We would have needed it to put another deposit on a new flat. We even thought that's what we were going to do, for a while, instead of spending it all on expensive drink. But we wanted the money and even if we hadn't we would have had to leave.'

'The law protects the tenant,' Paul said.

'A walking corpse,' Ernest said.

'No,' Jon said. 'It doesn't. It protects people with money. If we had decided to stay in the flat he would have called the police and forced them to remove us. He'd invent some reason why. Like we had damaged property, or made threats, or, if necessary, he could plant drugs and accuse us of being drug dealers. And when it came to any trial he'd have a dozen witnesses and we'd have none, and he'd have a team of shrewd lawyers and we'd have one who was uninterested.'

Paul nodded vaguely.

'So what are you going to do?' he asked.

'Drown our sorrows was the original plan,' Ernest said. 'But it's not going too well.'

'We thought,' Jon said, 'that you might be able to put us up for the night.'

'Ah, I'd like to,' Paul said. 'But I haven't really got the room.'

There was a long silence as Ernest and Jon looked around the spacious living room and back at Paul.

'I have some workmen coming in the morning,' Paul said. 'To finish work.'

'We'll be gone by then,' Ernest said.

'Just tonight?' Paul said. 'I really can't have anyone staying while the work is going on. I'm not insured for it.'

'Insured?' Ernest said.

'We'll be gone by tomorrow,' Jon said.

Paul nodded.

'Where are you going to go?' he asked.

'The gutter,' Ernest said. 'But at least we'll be staring at the stars.'

Paul nodded solemnly.

'You really ought to get yourselves organised,' he said. 'I mean, you can't go on living the way we did three years ago.'

'What's wrong with the way we lived our lives three years ago?' Ernest demanded. 'You seemed happy enough then.'

'I was,' Paul said. 'But, come on. You've got to grow up some time. Be responsible.'

'Bah!' Ernest said.

'At least I can stand on my own two feet,' Paul said, suddenly remembering he was, after all, in his own home. 'At least I don't have to rely on the kindness of other people who *are* responsible.'

There was a long silence. Paul reddened slightly.

'Do you want us to go?' Jon asked.

'No, no,' Paul said. 'Look, Jesus, it's just . . . I was asleep. It was just a bit of a shock. I haven't seen you in . . . Here, why don't we have a drink?'

Paul got up and began looking through a small wooden press filled with bottles.

'Celebrate old times.'

Ernest began salivating.

'Drink,' he said.

'Yes,' Jon agreed.

'You know,' Paul said, as he picked up and put down a variety of bottles of spirits and wines, 'I really shouldn't be doing this. I have work early in the morning.'

'You're a true martyr,' Ernest said sarcastically.

'We appreciate it,' Jon said.

'How's the banking?' Ernest asked.

Paul emerged with a bottle of red wine.

'This all right?' he asked. 'Rest of the stuff's a bit heavy. Oh, the banking. Em, it's fine, yeah. The usual. Well, I say that but it's . . . it's actually extremely busy right now.'

Paul opened the bottle of wine with effortless ease and poured three glasses.

'Yeah,' he said. 'I'm in at about six am every morning.'

'I see,' Jon said, sniffing the wine.

Ernest picked up his glass of wine and knocked it back in one.

'More please, sir,' he said.

'Steady on,' Paul said, trying to appear jovial. 'This is good stuff. You won't appreciate it if you drink it like that.'

'I remember,' Ernest said, 'when you drank your first bottle of wine. You threw up inside your sleeping bag. You slept in a large pile of sick.'

'Why do you have to get up so early?' Jon intervened.

'Oh,' Paul said, smiling. 'It's the markets. It's the nature of the business really. Hong Kong closes at eight am our time. I deal mostly in foreign currency, you see. The early hours are just par for the course.'

'What do you mean, you deal in foreign currency?' Ernest asked, as he helped himself to a third glass of wine.

'It's speculation,' Paul explained.

'Gambling,' Ernest said.

'No, no not really. You see, if you're good at it, you can predict the way the market's going to go. You can smell it. It's absolutely instinctive to some people. You can't learn it. I'm just good at predicting. I can tell what's going to happen as far ahead as two years with a great deal of accuracy.'

'So,' Ernest said. 'Basically, you predict whether markets will boom or fail or be just middling.'

'Well, in crude terms,' Paul said, 'yes.'

'I'll put it cruder still,' Ernest said. 'You profit from the misery of others.'

'What?' Paul said. 'Look Ernest, don't lecture me, all right? What is your problem?'

Ernest shook his head silently and sipped his wine.

'So,' Jon said. 'Are you playing much at all?'

Paul shook his head.

'I don't have a spare minute,' he said. 'After work everybody goes for drinks. It's pretty-much mandatory. I could do without it a couple of nights a week

to tell you the truth but . . . '

'Has anybody seen *East of Eden?*' Ernest interrupted.

'Yeah,' Paul said. 'So what?'

'James Dean,' Jon said.

'That's right,' Ernest said. 'James Dean. James Dean plays the son of an entrepreneur who is so upset when he sees his father sink his savings into some harebrained ahead-of-its-time scheme that goes horribly wrong, that he sets out to recoup all the money for him by borrowing money and investing it in some crop that he knows will somersault in value if the war in Europe happens.

'The war happens and Jimmy makes his money and more and he's deliriously happy because he's always been the bad seed wild child who never made his father truly happy or proud and now here's his chance. His chance to show his dad that he's not such a waste of space after all.

'But Jim's dad happens to be the head of the local draft board and it's his job to chose who will and who won't go to the war from the town's eligible men and it's something he deeply regrets having to do but at the same time something which he feels is his sorrowful duty.

'So when Deano presents his father with the money and explains how he got it, his father gives him the most terrible heart-broken look and tells him that he could not, not for one minute, even contemplate taking anything that had profited from a war, a war in which hundreds of thousands of boys and men had died. Men from that very village. Men he himself had sent to their deaths.

'And so of course James Dean remains the outcast and for all his efforts his father is only more deeply disappointed in him because, whereas before, his attitude towards him had been one of mild ambivalence, of silent disappointment in his young son, he is now almost repulsed by him. He shrinks away from the terrible truth that any son of his could seek to profit from the misery of others.'

There was a long silence. Paul slowly and methodically poured a glass of wine for himself and knocked it back in one.

'I feel he was overrated,' Jon said. 'James Dean. Oh, he had potential. But he was prone to melodramatics if you ask me.'

'You know, you think you're so fucking clever,' Paul spat out at Ernest. 'You think you're so fucking smart. You're not, you know. You're a fucking idiot. I make money because I'm smart. I'm good at my job. I get paid because I'm good. And if I wasn't making the money, somebody else would be.

'It's real easy to criticise when you have no life. It's real easy to take the moral high ground when you never have to deal with reality. When you opt out of everything. I pay taxes, do you? No. Of course you don't. You're still on the dole. I give to charity, do you? Of course you don't. You probably still carry your fucking poems around with you hoping some nonexistent publisher's going to make all your dreams reality.

'Well, I deal in the real world. In the real world you have to make money. You have to go out there and get it. So, don't lecture me. Don't come round here with your hard luck story, looking for help, and then lecture me.'

There was a long uncomfortable silence during which all three men sipped nervously on their wine.

'I wonder who's living in the old place now,' Jon said after a while.

Ernest smiled.

'They must have knocked it down by now,' Paul said, trying once again to sound lighthearted. 'Place was falling to bits.'

'Remember that piece of wood in the hallway?' Jon said.

Paul laughed.

'Holding up the ceiling,' he said, nodding. 'Or at least that's what we thought. Nobody ever quite had the guts to check.'

'I think everyone must have had a kick at it though,' Jon said.

'It's still there,' Ernest said. 'The place.'

'How do you know?' Jon asked.

'I walked by,' Ernest said. 'The other day.'

'You never said. '

'I forgot,' Ernest said. 'I was delivering something in the area, actually it was to a publisher, and I just happened to walk by. I didn't even remember where I was till I was right outside.'

'How did it look?' Paul asked.

'The same,' Ernest replied. 'The exact same. Same rundown old house. Same crap in the driveway.'

There was a long silence as all three men thought of their old home.

'God,' Paul said finally. 'When I think of it . . . We'd kill each other now.'

'We got on quite well,' Jon said. 'Considering.'

'Well there was that time I threw Paul out the window,' Ernest said.

Paul giggled and rubbed his ribs.

'If I hadn't been paralysed with pain,' he said, 'I would have killed you.'

'I still maintain there was a gust of wind,' Ernest said.

'Too many cigarettes,' Jon said, 'and too much coffee.'

Paul nodded and reached into his dressing gown pocket. He took out a packet of cigarettes and offered them to Ernest and Jon. Both men shook their heads.

'You still smoke then,' Jon said.

'You have to,' Paul said. 'In my line it's practically the law. What about you two, given up?'

'Can't afford it,' Ernest said matter of factly. 'They keep on raising the price of cigarettes by far more than they ever raise the dole.'

'I got asthma,' Jon said. 'Two years ago. It kind of scared me a little.'

'No?' Paul said. 'I didn't think you could catch something like that. What was it? I mean, how did you get it?'

'They don't know,' Jon said. 'I wouldn't say *catch* exactly. I don't know. It could be anything causing it, pollution, exhaust fumes. Who knows?'

Paul nodded.

'We're out of wine,' Ernest observed.

'Oh, fuck it,' Paul said, going back to the drinks cabinet. 'I've gone in pissed before.'

He took out another bottle of wine and fumbled for a little while before opening it and pouring into the three glasses.

'So,' he said. 'What are you two doing these days?'

'I'm wandering around with my manuscript,' Ernest said. 'Hoping some nonexistent publisher will make my dreams reality.'

'And I,' Jon said, 'am still auditioning for every role going and getting none of them.'

Paul laughed.

'You haven't changed at all,' he said

'Oh yes,' Ernest said. 'We are now extremely bitter and I'm losing my hair. We're all the more bitter because one amongst us has got a decent job and is doing well, which means we can't blame our age or society for our circumstances.'

'It's not so decent,' Paul said, finishing his glass. 'I often think of those days. Hanging out in the flat. Smoking drugs. Watching bad TV. They were good times. I miss them.'

'There's nothing to miss,' Jon said. 'You tire quickly of drugs and bad TV. We're getting too old. We're getting to the age when we should be serious and dedicated but both of us are interested in careers where it doesn't help to be serious or dedicated.'

'But you're free,' Paul said, waving the hand which contained his glass of wine. 'You can do whatever you want. You don't have to go to work. If you want to get drunk, you can.'

'No,' Jon said. 'We're not free. We're trapped. I'd rather not get drunk. I'd rather be boring and have a steady job. I just don't think I could do a steady job.'

'You don't want to,' Paul said. 'They're crap. Steady jobs are crap.'

'I'm lazy, that's my problem,' Ernest said. 'I want an income as much as the next person. But I don't want to do manual work and I'm not qualified to do anything that isn't manual work. And I can't do service jobs because I hate people. It would eat me alive.'

'You see,' Jon said. 'We're trapped between a rock and a hard place. We want money. We're sick of signing on. It's not exactly as much fun as it's made out to be. People are mean. It wears you down. Our only hope is that we'll manage, through supreme luck, and perhaps a sliver of our own talent, to succeed at the things we want to succeed at, and there's not much chance of that.'

'I think you're great,' Paul said, knocking back another glass. 'I don't know what happened to me.'

'You lost your soul,' Ernest said.

'You did the right thing,' Jon said. 'You weren't happy in the flat. You weren't happy signing on. You weren't happy being a broke musician.'

Paul nodded.

'I haven't played in years,' he said.

'More wine,' Ernest said.

Paul nodded silently, stood up too soon and nearly fell over. He came back to the table with a bottle of tequila and set it down on the table with a thud.

'Tiqi,' he said.

Ernest nodded in approval and poured everyone drinks.

'I hate my job,' Paul said after his second tequila. 'All this fucking pressure. Constantly. Buy, sell, buy . . . I couldn't give a fuck. I'd give it all up in a minute. Like that. Snap of the fingers. This fucking flat, the overpriced car . . . everything. It's a pile of shit.'

'You're drunk,' Jon said. 'You're lucky. You like your job.'

'I don't,' Paul insisted. 'I swear to God I don . . . I don't. Pile of shit.'

He stood up. Held up his glass in a salute to the room.

'Pile of shit!' he yelled and knocked back the drink.

For five full seconds Paul laughed to himself then brought his fists beating down on the table.

'You spilled my drink,' Ernest said.

'Sorry,' Paul said. 'I just . . . I just wish I could go back, you know? I should never have left you guys. I was going to be a musician. I swore to myself that, no matter how long it took, I was going to be a musician. I wrote it down.'

'You were very good,' Ernest said. 'We could have used you earlier.'

'I was, wasn't I?' Paul said. 'Probably couldn't even play the fucking thing any more. Gathering dust. Fucking bank!

'I used to look at guys like me. Guys in suits with mortgages and I'd say, what is he like? How can he live like that. Bein' told what to wear. No freedom.'

'You weren't happy,' Jon said. 'It was obvious.'

'I didn't know how lucky I was,' Paul said, shaking his head. 'So stupid.'

There was a silence for a long while as all three men concerned themselves with their tequila. Finally, Paul looked up at Ernest.

'I'm sorry about what I said.'

'Tosh,' Ernest replied. 'I've said far worse to you.'

'No,' Paul said. 'No, I had no right. You live the absolute way I want to live. I was just jealous. I tell you, if you wanted to trade I'd do it in a minute. No . . . no of course you wouldn't.'

Paul stared at the floor for a long time.

'It's my fault,' he said finally. 'It's my fault you two have no home. I want you to move in here.'

'We couldn't,' Jon said.

'We could,' Ernest said.

'I insist. You must.'

'There's no room,' Jon said. 'You have workmen coming in the morning. It's not your fault or responsibility that our landlord has no morals.'

'It is my fault,' Paul insisted. 'There are no workmen coming. I was afraid you might stay, you see. I was afraid. Ha! My two truest friends and I was afraid. I even thought you might steal something. It's true. But I don't think that now.'

'I had thought about it,' Ernest admitted. 'Only liquor though. I'm not an animal.'

'You'd deserve it,' Paul said, spilling tequila everywhere as he pointed with his glass. 'You see . . . you see if I hadn't left the flat in the first place, none of this would be happening to you now.'

'Yes it would,' Jon said.

'No,' Paul insisted. 'No, it wouldn't. If I hadn't left the flat then you wouldn't have needed to find a smaller place so, you see, you wouldn't be in the jam you are in now.'

'He's right,' Ernest said.

'Come on, Paul,' Jon said. 'Who knows what would have happened? It's not your fault. How could it be?'

'I have all this,' Paul said, sweeping his arms around the room. 'And what do you have? Nothing. Nothing. It's my fault.'

'Maybe a little,' Ernest said.

'No!' Jon said.

'I am always keen to blame others for my predicament,' Ernest said. 'Mrs Brown wrote that in red ink on my Second Class report card.'

'Here have some money,' Paul said, going over to a small cabinet and taking out a clutch of notes.

'No need,' Ernest said, taking out the two hundred pounds. 'We have plenty.'

Paul nodded and shoved the money back in the cabinet.

'I must do something,' he said. 'For abandoning you. For abandoning myself.'

'Hadn't you better be going to sleep?' Jon said. 'If you have to get up early.'

'I'm not going in,' Paul said. 'I'm not going in ever again. You've made me see the error of my ways. You made me remember what . . . what I really want to be.'

'Whatever happened to Audrey?' Ernest asked suddenly.

Paul blinked in quick succession for several seconds.

'She left,' he said.

'I used to call her Yoko,' Ernest said. 'Behind your back.'

'You did?' Paul said.

Ernest nodded.

'Jon didn't like it, though. He thought it should have been Linda, seeing as how your name was Paul, but I always thought Yoko suited her better.'

'Bitch,' Paul said. 'Bitch, bitch, bitch.'

'I always liked her,' Jon said.

'Me too,' Paul said, as he took out another cigarette. 'Why don't we go somewhere? Just the three of us? Go off for a drive. Like we used to. Go up to Killiney Hill and smoke drugs.'

'I know just the place to get them,' Ernest said.

'No,' Jon said. 'No, no.'

'What we need,' Ernest said, 'is a get rich quick scheme. That way you wouldn't have to do your banking. You could start your own record company. I'd publish my own damn book and Jon could make any film he liked and put himself in it.'

'Wouldn't you rather get there on merit?' Jon asked.

'Why?' Ernest said. 'The people who are there aren't there on merit. Why should we care?'

'I'm just not sure I'd want to buy success,' Jon said.

'I'm not talking about buying success,' Ernest said. 'The success part would still be up to us. People would still have to buy the book. They'd still have to pay into the movie. Nobody is anywhere on merit. Merit is something that comes after the fact, after the people with money and power agree to endorse something. They don't agree to it because it has merit, they agree to it because they think it'll make them more money.

'It is all to do with who you know. How much money you have. Which family you are born into.'

'Yes,' Paul said bitterly. 'The bastards have it all tied up.'

'I would still like to think,' Jon said, 'that if something is meant to be, it's meant to be.'

'I'd like to think that too,' Ernest said. 'But it's not very fucking likely is it? I mean, I'm as patient as the next guy. All right, I'm not but still, I don't want to be patient. I don't want to wait for things to happen naturally. Sometimes things don't happen that way. Honourable, talented people die cold lonely deaths in damp-filled bedsits while shallow pricks get on.

'I need some money. I need just a little bit of success. Before I'm swallowed up by all this hatred.'

'There's no such thing as a get rich quick scheme,' Jon said.

'Yes there is,' Paul said. 'I see it every day. Every day on the market people become instant millionaires. I've seen them. Most of them don't even know the market very well. With most of them it's pure blind luck.'

'It's like Paul was saying,' Ernest said. 'You've got to reach out and grab it. Look at this. We made two hundred quid in one night. All we need to do is multiply that by a thousand and we'll be going places.'

'It's sad,' Jon said. 'Sad that we have to resign ourselves to such shallow aims.'

Ernest ignored him.

'I propose the quickest get rich quick scheme there is,' he said. 'Theft.'

'Theft is difficult,' Paul said.

'It depends,' Ernest said. 'Mine is simple and without moral qualms.'

'No theft is without moral qualms,' Jon said.

'My one is. Well, almost. I'm willing to live with my qualms. In fact, I plan to have plenty of space for me and my qualms. Like a small island somewhere off Hawaii.'

'Banks are very hard these days,' Paul said. 'My one is virtually impossible, if that's what you're thinking. My being an insider wouldn't help much at all. They have fail safes for such things.'

'No,' Ernest said. 'I propose nothing quite so daring. I propose to rob one of the evilest bastards alive.'

'Michael Winner?' Jon suggested.

'The very man,' Ernest went on, 'who has us where we are right now.'

'My father?' Jon said.

'Mr Dorfel?' Paul said.

Jon nodded.

'He was an evil bastard. I had him for two classes.'

'Oi,' Ernest said. 'Here I am having the biggest brainstorm of my life and you will not even listen. I'll have to get it out before I explode so be sure and shut up and listen. My friend, here seated to my left, and I were discussing, at some unknown time many hours ago, the plausibility of a scheme I had to rob some rich uncle of his in America.

'My head was not so clear then and, in my confusion, I had not considered the strong possibility, pointed out by my good friend here seated, that his Yankee uncle might not keep his money in the house in convenient cash, thereby making any attempt to rob from him useless and puerile, witless and dumb.

'But, what if I were to tell you that I know a man, a man so evil, petty and conniving, so mean-minded, that he would not part with his cash even for an instant, let alone keep it in a bank. A man so selfish and obscene that I am extremely confident that he keeps all cash, if not on his person, then hidden somewhere about his home.'

'Who?' Paul said.

'Who?' Jon said.

'Copper Downey,' Ernest answered.

'Who?' Paul said.

'Copper Downey,' Jon said. 'Our landlord. I should have known.'

'How do you know?' Paul said to Ernest.

'How do I know what?'

'How do you know he doesn't keep his money in a bank?'

'He told me,' Ernest said. 'He told me his very self and, at the time, I thought nothing of it. In fact, at the time, I was far too busy being nervous that he'd start shouting at me because, not only were we two weeks late with the rent, but I had just lost my rent allowance money in a midnight game of poker.

'I learnt my lesson though. I learnt that people who can't help but giggle when they have a good hand should not play poker. A terrible game in any case. A terrible masculine po-faced farce of a game for men who don't know what a game is.

'Anyway, I had no rent, no hope of rent and had spent Jon's half on drugs to steady my nerves so that I could face the landlord. So, I made up a story. A story involving a bank clerk who would not cash my rent allowance cheque because they had spelt my name wrong on the cheque. I had not, in fact, been holding out much hope of sympathy but when I told him, old slipshot Cop began a fuming tirade of abuse, not at me, but at the bank and at all banks.

'"You can't trust the bastards," he said, in his own inimitable country style. "They're too cute for their own good. And what do they do with your money, in any case, but gamble with it? Your money. And if they go bust it's your tough luck.

'"And if you come to them asking they're not so quick to hand it out. Oh no. By God, they're not too quick to hand it out. They're as good as thieves and they won't see any of my money. I'll keep it to myself any day, than have the likes of them get their filthy hands on it."'

Jon nodded.

'He always took cash,' he said. 'He never wanted cheques. Cash or nothing, he would say. I think I remember him saying, when I tried to hand him a cheque: "I'm not cashing that." Yeah, I remember now. "I'm not cashing that. You can go into them fellas and cash it yourself and I'll take it then. You won't catch me in there in a hurry."'

'He owns at least five different houses in Dublin,' Ernest said. 'And at least twenty flats in each. The amount of cash that man must have stored away would feed several Third World famines over.'

'So what?' Jon said. 'What are we going to do about it?'

'Simple,' Ernest said. 'I propose we rob him, relieve him of his money.'

'You're drunk,' Jon said.

'Yes,' Ernest agreed. 'I am drunk. I am drunk and pissed off. Why shouldn't we? Why should we take this lying down? I know his address. I know where he lives. What's stopping us?'

'Galway some place isn't it?'

'No,' Ernest said. 'Not some place. Skriel. I don't know the specific road or number or anything, but we can find that out when we get there.'

'While I agree,' Jon said, 'that few people would deserve it more, I am not traipsing across the country on some whim of yours that will never bear fruition.'

'I like it,' Paul said.

'Not a whim,' Ernest protested. 'It's been building up inside me. I almost died tonight. Unseen forces are moving against me. There must be a reason things have progressed the way they have progressed. Something has drawn me to this solution. It is a way out. If I don't follow it, something is going to happen to me.'

'You think he keeps it in his house?' Paul asked.

'Undoubtedly,' Ernest said. 'Well, not undoubtedly, but close. He keeps it in Galway some place. That much is sure. He hates Dublin. He comes here to make money. It's perfect. Every Friday he goes home for the weekend. We simply find his home, make him tell us where the money is, slit his throat, take the money and jump the next ferry to God knows where.'

'Brilliant,' Paul said. 'Fucking brilliant.'

'Flawed,' Jon said. 'Deeply flawed.'

'What else have you got to do?' Ernest asked. 'What, have you a soap ad audition to go to?'

'No,' Jon said. 'Not this week.'

'Well then.'

'I'm in,' Paul said deliriously. 'I'm in, I'm in. This is wonderful. This is just like old times. Except we never really did anything back then. This is even better.'

'I suppose I wouldn't mind seeing a bit of the West,' Jon said. 'It would make a change.'

'From the East, yes,' Ernest said. 'Almost completely opposite.'

'I'll get the keys to the car,' Paul said, getting up.

'He's in no shape to drive,' Jon said when he had left.

'I'll drive,' Ernest said.

'You're in no shape to drive,' Jon said. 'Plus you have the added disadvantage that you can't drive.'

'Oh, yes,' Ernest said. 'Well then, he'll drive. Somebody must drive. We'll go very slow. We have all weekend.'

'Very slow,' Jon said, nodding his head backwards and forwards and making himself slightly nauseous.

'It is engendered,' Ernest said. 'Hell and fury shall bring this beast to light.'

'Yes,' Jon said.

Ten minutes later all three men were sitting in Paul's large expensive car.

'It's good to be finally under way,' Ernest said, as the three stared straight ahead. 'Why aren't we under way?'

'Because we're not under way,' Jon said, turning to Paul. 'You've to turn the key.'

'Oh,' Paul said. 'I wondered why the pedals weren't working.'

He started the car and pulled out into the grey deserted streets. While they were driving down the main street in Bray Paul took his hands off the steering wheel and began grabbing for the seat belt.

'Safety first,' he said, finally clutching hold of the seat belt as the car veered dramatically to the left.

'Should we be heading straight for that church?' Ernest asked as the car rode up onto the footpath.

Just as the car was about to slam into the church wall Jon reached out and grabbed the steering wheel, straightening the car back out onto the road.

'Oh,' Paul said, as he finished clicking his seat belt in. 'Okay. You do the wheel thingy and I'll do the pedals.'

On they drove and Jon steered and Paul worked the pedals while Ernest drank more tequila and giggled on the numerous occasions that they almost crashed.

'Twenty thousand pounds this car cost me,' Paul said, as they drove. 'I don't even like it very much. Twenty thousand pounds. Status symbol.'

He picked up his mobile phone.

'The car and the phone,' he said. 'Go hand in hand, don't you know? It's all front. My balls are bigger than your balls.'

Paul began dialling on the phone.

'Keep with the feet,' Jon said.

'What?' Paul said as he finished dialling. 'Oh, yeah.'

He resumed driving the car with his feet and didn't notice that the person on the other end of the line had answered the call. 'Who is this?' they were yelling.

'Oh,' Paul said, finally noticing. 'Who is this?'

'Who is this?' the person asked.

'Who is this?' Paul said.

'You rang me,' the person said. 'What's going on?'

'What are you talking about?' Paul said. 'I did no such thing. I am driving in my car which cost me one million pounds. I sold my soul. Of course, I could only get one pound fifty for that.'

He began giggling and slumped down onto the steering wheel.

'I can't steer,' Jon complained.

'Of course, of course,' Paul said, sitting back up.

'Paul?' the person at the other end of the line was saying. 'Paul is that you?'

'Malcolm,' Paul said. 'How the derve . . . how the darva . . . how the devil are you?'

'I'm . . . I'm fine Paul,' Malcom said. 'Look, Paul, what's going on? It's the middle of the night.'

'On?' Paul said. 'I don't know. My friends and me . . . I beg your pardon, my friends and I are in my car and my good friend Jon has hold of the wheely thing and I am doing the pedals.'

'Paul, if this is your idea of a joke, I'm not laughing.'

'Joke?' Paul said. 'I don't joke, man. Oh yes! I remember now, I called you.'

Paul giggled for a little while. He cleared his throat.

'I am sorry to have to infray . . . I am sorr I have to infer . . . I am sorry I have to tell you I won't be coming in tomorrow or any other day.'

'You're drunk,' Malcolm said. 'Ring me in the morning.'

With that the line went dead.

'No,' Paul said. 'No, quite the opposite. I am soberererer than I have been . . . Well, okay, I am a teencey bit pissed but I mean it. I won't go in. It's no use. I have rediscovered the important things in life.'

Paul waited for a reply.

'Hello?' he said, shaking the phone. 'Hello, operator? Hello operator, somebody seems to have cut us off. Could you . . . Oh well, never mind.'

Paul threw the phone out of the open window.

'You know, I can't help wondering if this is such a good idea,' Jon said, turning to Ernest. 'I think Paul may have just quit his job and I am certain he has just thrown his mobile phone out the window.'

'Good,' Ernest said. 'He wasn't happy. He's a musician, aren't you Paul?'

'Musician,' Paul said. 'Whatever happened to Baby Jane?'

'A good question,' Ernest said. 'You see? He's fine.'

Jon turned back round in the seat and considered their options.

'I would like to see more of Ireland,' he mused. 'I could never afford the insurance for a car. I always thought it unfair that it's more expensive if you have a long term, potentially life threatening illness, such as I do. I mean, who's going to be more careful, those who have confronted their own mortality, or those who are young and full of cum and think they are immortal?'

Paul suddenly slammed on the brakes.

'Where are we going?' he asked, when the car had stopped skidding.

Ernest, who had banged his head from the suddenness of the stop, looked down at the bottle of broken tequila on the floor of the car and almost cried.

'Tequila,' he said. 'My one true friend. Do you suppose it would be unhealthy to lick?'

'Where are we going?' Paul asked again,

'I can't remember,' Ernest said.

'Galway,' Jon answered.

'Where are we now?' Ernest asked.

'Dublin,' Jon answered.

'We'll need some petrol,' Paul said. 'Some petrol and a map because I don't know the way.'

'You don't need to,' Ernest said. 'Jon is steering.'

'Well, I don't know the way either,' Jon said.

'How hard can it be?' Ernest said. 'Just go west, directly, and we'll get there.'

'Well, which way is west?'

'I don't know,' Ernest replied. 'Where is the sun?'

'It's the middle of the night,' Jon pointed out.

'Well, where is the sea?' Ernest asked.

'How should I know?' Jon said. 'Where it always is. All around us.'

'Well, where's the moon?'

All three men looked out of the windows of the car.

'Behind the clouds,' Jon said.

'Well,' Ernest said. 'Then, we shall need a map.'

They pulled into the next available petrol station and for a long time sat in the car and did nothing.

'Where's the attendant?' Ernest asked finally.

'They don't have them,' Jon said. 'Especially not at night. At night they sit in special bullet-proof booths and conduct transactions through microphones.'

Jon and Ernest got out of the car while Paul giggled a gurgling spitting laugh and continued to press down on the car's various pedals with his feet.

'A map,' Ernest said to the figure in the bullet-proof glass booth.

'Anywhere in particular?' the girl's strange echoing microphone amplified voice came back. The sound continued to echo as Ernest's eyes met hers for the first time. For several moments he was so transfixed he could not speak.

'Ireland,' Jon intervened as he returned from filling the car's tank. 'A road map.'

'Okay,' the girl said and left her booth to go into the shop that was now vacated and shut to the public.

'This all right?' the girl said when she came back, holding up the map.

'Has it got Galway?' Ernest asked, wanting to be a part of the conversation.

'I think it does,' the girl said. 'Seeing as it is a road map of Ireland and Galway is in Ireland.'

'You'll have to check,' Ernest said, not wishing their relationship to have to end. 'Someone might have surreptitiously cut it out or eaten it as a symbol of their absolute hatred or love for it as a county.'

The girl looked from Ernest to Jon, who shrugged his shoulders. She sighed and opened up the map. Ernest pressed his forehead against the cold glass.

'Rebecca,' he said, reading the girl's name tag. 'Rebecca.'

Rebecca looked at him for one brief second before, with a slight shudder, focusing her attention back on the map.

'Galway,' she said, pointing to the area on the map. 'Meet with your satisfaction?'

'Lovely,' Ernest said. 'I do so admire your ability to manipulate a map. It's a gift. I myself am unable to open a map without tearing off some large portion or other so that, usually, after only a very short while, I am left with a kind of paper jigsaw puzzle.'

Rebecca nodded solemnly.

'It was brave of you to admit that,' she said.

'I am a giver,' Ernest said.

At that point Paul began beeping the horn of the car to the annoyance and frustration of Ernest who felt he was finally getting somewhere. When Jon and Ernest turned round they saw Paul merely waving at them, quite happily.

'Just saying hello,' he shouted. 'I felt lonely.'

'We'll take that then so,' Jon said, anxious to hurry proceedings.

'And a packet of crisps,' Ernest said.

'A packet of crisps?' Rebecca said.

Ernest nodded. Rebecca sighed and left the booth again to retrieve the crisps from the empty locked-up shop.

'Now,' she said on her return. 'That will be ten pounds fifty please.'

'And one of those watches,' Ernest said, pointing to a row of luminous Mickey Mouse watches on a stand in the shop.

Rebecca nodded and walked back into the shop. She picked up one of the watches and held it up for Ernest. Ernest nodded approvingly and she brought the watch back out.

Ernest tried the luminous orange watch on.

'What do you think?' he asked.

'Lovely,' she said. 'Twelve pounds fifty please.'

'And a can of coke,' Ernest said.

'Look,' Rebecca said. 'I'm not going in and out of that shop for you all night. If you want me to get you something, I'll get you something, but I'm not making any more trips, so just make up your mind exactly what you want, okay?'

'A can of coke,' Ernest said quietly.

'A can of coke,' Rebecca repeated. 'Nothing else? Some chocolate perhaps? A magazine for your journey?'

With that she turned and stormed back into the shop, murmuring under her breath that she was not a bloody air hostess.

'I'm in love,' Ernest said, turning to Jon.

Jon nodded.

'Wonderful,' he said.

When Rebecca returned she slammed the coke can down so hard she almost burst the aluminium.

'Thirteen pounds,' she said.

Ernest took a twenty pound note from his pocket.

'Plenty more where that came from,' he said, winking.

'Oh God,' Rebecca said as she opened the till.

'Rebecca,' Ernest said. 'How would you like to escape from this miserable ho-hum dull existence and leave with us on a mystical journey across Ireland to seek clean air, spiritual enlightenment, a king's fortune and do battle with the wicked witch of the west?'

'I'll pass, thanks,' Rebecca said, putting the change through the narrow slot below the bullet-proof glass.

'Let's go,' Jon said to Ernest.

Ernest was still staring at Rebecca.

'You don't understand,' he said. 'You don't know what you're passing up. Excitement, enlightment, romance, mystery, financial gain. I am offering all of these things and more. You can't tell me you're happy here, in this petrol stinking world. It can't be a choice you're happy taking. Come with us and I guarantee you will not regret it.'

'Look,' Rebecca said, 'you strange little man, I've had more drunk propositions than you've had or are ever likely to have girlfriends. My job is to serve you, I have done that. Now, please go away.'

Jon took Ernest's arm. Ernest shook his head. Tears welled up in his eyes.

'All right stay then!' he screamed, as Jon dragged him away. 'Stay here in your safe, artificially created, bullet-proof world! In your risk-free existence! We don't need you!'

With that he turned around and walked voluntarily away.

'It must have been lust,' Ernest said as they stepped inside the car, 'but it's over now.'

'Did you get my cigarettes?' Paul asked, as they pulled out of the station.

'You didn't ask for cigarettes,' Jon pointed out.

'Oh yes,' Paul said. 'That was what it was. Instead I ended up waving.'

'You know,' Ernest said, 'I've never been very lucky with the opposite sex. For some reason, even though I am a moderately handsome man, they are repulsed by me. Pretty soon I will be bald and there'll be no chance.'

'Don't talk to me about women,' Paul said.

'I wasn't,' Ernest said. 'I was talking generally about their reaction towards me. Perhaps it is the same impulse that makes men want to be violent towards me. I'd even settle for a woman who wanted to be violent towards me.'

'Audrey wanted to be violent towards you,' Paul said. 'She said from the minute she first met you she wanted to punch you in the teeth.'

'You're just saying that to cheer me up.'

'No,' Paul said. 'I'm with you all the way. Women are not worth the paper they're printed on. You give them everything. You do what they want. They're not happy. I want you to move out of there, she said. I want us to get our own place, she said, and I did. I did. Was she happy? Of course not.'

'Perhaps,' Jon said, 'it was because your relationship was not on an equal footing to begin with that it did not work out. Perhaps you were each looking for different things. Perhaps that's why it didn't work out and therefore blaming one person or the other is nonsensical.'

'Bitch,' Paul said.

'Bitch,' Ernest agreed.

They drove on flat smooth motorways and behind them the grey of Dublin faded away into green open fields.

'Hitcher,' Paul said slamming on the brakes.

The hitcher was dressed in a long black overcoat. His hair stuck out in various directions from his head, and his thumb extended from his tightened fist. He stood and watched the car as Ernest, Jon, and Paul debated the merits of letting him in.

'No men,' Ernest said, regarding the hitcher.

'No women,' Paul said.

'This is not a good idea,' Jon said.

The hitcher slowly walked over to the car and stuck his pale white face in front of Jon's window. Ernest and Jon stared at him through the glass.

'We don't need another man,' Ernest pointed out. 'We have

enough. What we need, if anything, is a female dimension.'

'No, no,' Paul said. 'We must be charitable. I've never picked up a hitcher before. I've always been terrified.'

The hitcher knocked on the window once and then resumed his patient waiting.

Jon slowly rolled down the window.

'Where are you going?' he asked the hitcher.

'Anywhere,' the hitcher said, getting into the car without further invitation.

'Cold,' the hitcher said as he clapped his hands in front of Ernest's unimpressed gaze.

'When you say anywhere,' Jon said, as they resumed their drive, 'did you have a specific spot in mind?'

'I will go as far as I need to,' the hitcher replied.

Jon nodded.

'But you don't know where we're going.'

'I will go so far and no further,' the hitcher said.

They drove on in silence for a few miles. The hitcher closed his eyes the entire time and kept one hand on each knee. Ernest watched him curiously for a while before getting bored and deciding to stick his head out the window. It was beginning to rain slightly and he stuck out his tongue attempting to catch some of the rain drops. Paul looked out his window at Ernest's tongue and began giggling.

Suddenly the hitcher's eyes opened. He pointed to a field on the right, where there was a great stone castle.

'Do you see that place?' the hitcher said.

All three men turned and stared out the window at the huge grey mass of stone, with a giant spiralling tower jutting out from its centre.

'That place,' the hitcher said, 'is known as Connolly's Folly. Connolly was an Irish MP, in the time between the Act of Union and the Dáil, when MPs of Irish constituencies were represented in the British parliament. Connolly was a rich man. One of the richest in Ireland. People say the gap between the rich and poor is widening. They should have been around in Connolly's time when the rich owned all the land and peasants had to pay them for the right to live and work their land with the money from the spoils of their endless labour.

'Connolly, along with all his money, had property all over the country, but Dublin was his home and it was here that he owned most of his many houses. Although he had plenty of land, he had no country residence and, as it was the fashion of the time to live away from the city, he set about building one for himself and his wife, in the style they were accustomed to.

'He had but one problem. His wife was a deeply paranoid woman who greatly feared the peasants living on Connolly's land. She was afraid they would one day uprise against them and storm the house and kill and steal and rape and pillage.

'So Connolly built this great house, befitting an MP and his wife, and at the very centre of its spiralling chaotic stone he built a tower, with a small round hole at the very top of its many stairs, with a view of his entire land.

'And from that day on, and every day after that, his wife would climb the winding steps to watch for foaming peasants and not one did she ever see, and the place became known by everyone thereafter as Connolly's Folly.'

Paul began clapping.

'Wonderful,' he said.

'Stop the car,' the hitcher said.

Paul slammed on the brakes. The hitcher stepped out of the car.

'I know when I am not welcome,' he said before walking off into a nearby wood.

'What an unusual man,' Ernest said. 'I am glad he's gone.'

They resumed their long straight course on the darkened motorway. Ernest looked out of the window. He shook his head.

'This is all wrong,' he complained. 'Nothing's new. Everything's the same. I amn't seeing anything.'

'Yes,' Jon agreed. 'It is disappointing. But then, that's the trouble with these motorways. You don't get to see anything except other cars, petrol stations and crappy one-stop cafés.'

'I want to see something,' Ernest said. 'This is not an adventure. Stop the car.'

Paul slammed on the brakes.

'Go there,' Ernest said, pointing to a small stony road, leading off the motorway.

'Where does this lead?' Jon asked, as they bumped along the road.

'I don't know,' Ernest replied. 'It wasn't on the map.'

'I see,' Jon said. 'So why, may I ask, are we here?'

'Because we are,' Ernest replied.

'It may be going to Kathmandu for all we know,' Jon complained.

'Do you want to see Ireland or not?' Ernest asked.

'I'm not sure any more,' Jon said as they drove on.

4. Moo!

Jon dreamt that that he was the Connolly of the hitcher's story, living in the twisting castle. He dreamt he was chasing up and down the grey stone steps of the tower as his wife stared calmly through the small round look-out hole.

'They're coming,' his wife said, in a low monotone.

Jon was busy running up and down the steps, carrying as much gold and silver with him as he could.

'Do something,' he would say to his wife as he walked by her.

'There is nothing *to* do,' she would reply. 'They're coming.'

And in the distance he could hear the yells and shrieks of the peasants, the anger of a thousand years of pain and persecution burning towards the castle.

On and on it went, Jon panicking and continually searching for gold and jewellery to hide and his wife calm and reserved and quite resigned to their terrible fate, with the screams gathering closer and closer.

Jon awoke, with a start, to the sound of Ernest and a cow mooing.

'Mooo!' said the cow

'Moo!' said Ernest.

Jon rubbed his aching head and stared from Paul, who was either unconscious or dead against the steering wheel, to Ernest, who was sticking his head from the rear window of the car and happily mooing.

'We're having a conversation,' Ernest said, when he noticed Jon was awake.

'I see,' Jon said. 'Could you tell it to perhaps conduct it a little quieter? It's just I'm not having the best of luck keeping my brain from lolling about my head and shattering against my skull in tremendous painful bursts.'

'Moo!' Ernest said.

'Mooo!' the cow said.

'He seems quite willing,' Ernest said.

'Thank you,' Jon said.

'I should warn you, however that, while I have been attempting to study the intricacies of the language, thus far I am considerably short of a breakthrough.'

Jon nodded.

'I understand.'

Paul began to stir. He sat up in the car and stared lazily around him as he opened and closed his mouth. He looked from Ernest to Jon, giggled slightly, then seized his own forehead with both of his hands. He then stared back at Jon and Ernest and, suddenly in panic, all around him.

'What the . . . ' he said.

He stared at the steering wheel, at the country road, back at Ernest, at the cow, from there to Jon and at his reflection in the mirror.

'Oh my God,' he said. 'OhmyGodholymotherfuckingshit! Oh Jesus. Oh Jesus. Oh Holy . . . Jesus.'

'Morning,' Ernest said.

Paul put his head in his hands.

'This is not . . . This is . . . This cannot be real.'

He looked at his empty wrist and felt his stubbled chin.

'What happened?' he said. 'Where are we?'

'You don't remember?' Jon asked.

'No,' he shook his head. 'Well, yes . . . no. I don't know. Bits. I remember bits. We were sitting . . . we had a drink . . . Oh my God . . . '

'Coming back?' Ernest asked.

'Jesus Christ,' Paul said. 'I called my boss. Did I call my boss?'

'Em . . . ' Jon said. 'Is your boss's name Malcolm?'

'Oh Christ no! What did I say?'

'You quit,' Ernest said. 'You told him where he could stick his soulless pursuit of money.'

'No,' Paul said. 'No, no, no, no, no, no. Jesus.'

Jon looked guiltily at Ernest, who had already turned his attention back to the cow.

'Moo!' he said. 'You know, I think I'm beginning to develop a basic structure for their language. Basically, as far as I can work out, moo means everything.'

'I've got to call him,' Paul said. 'I've got to apologise. Jesus. Where are we?'

'The road to Galway,' Jon said. 'Actually, it could be anywhere.'

'I resent that,' Ernest said.

Paul began looking round the car.

'Where's the phone?' he asked. 'The mobile phone. Who's got it?'

'You threw it out the window,' Ernest said.

'You're joking. Why didn't you stop me?' Paul shouted. 'You fuckers! You conniving low life pricks! How could you do this to me? What did I ever do to you? What the fuck did I do to deserve the pair of you?'

'Could you lower your voice?' Ernest said. 'You're upsetting the cow.'

'Fuck the cow!' Paul screamed. 'I'm talking about my life. I should have been in work four hours ago. Instead I'm sitting here with the two most idiotic, least grounded in reality people I know. I've lost my phone, probably my job. I have no idea where we are or how I'm going to get back.'

'Back?' Ernest said.

'I'm a lot more grounded,' Jon said, 'since I spent a month in hospital for my asthma . . . '

'I don't give a flying fuck about your asthma,' Paul said. 'Or anything either of you have to say, unless it's an apology, and even then.'

'Nobody twisted your arm,' Jon said. 'You said you were miserable. You said you didn't want to go to work ever again.'

'I was drunk,' Paul said. 'You say crazy things when you're drunk.'

'I don't,' Ernest said.

Paul started the car.

'We're going back,' he said.

'Back?' Ernest said. 'I'm not going back.'

'Fine,' Paul said. 'Get out.'

'Could we talk about this?' Jon said.

'Talk?' Paul said. 'What for? You're quite obviously both insane.'

'We made a deal,' Ernest said. 'We are going to rob Copper Downey and share the spoils.'

'Lovely,' Paul said. 'But I'm due back on planet Earth so you'll have to excuse me.'

Paul pressed down on the accelerator and the car began reversing up the path. Ernest opened the back door of the car. It slammed into a tree and was shorn completely off. Paul screeched on the brakes. He turned and stared at the gaping hole where the door used to be. He turned and stared at Ernest, who smiled guiltily.

'Oops,' he said.

'Get out,' Paul said. 'Before I do something I *might* regret.'

Ernest stepped out through the open doorway. Jon sighed and got out with him. Both men stood in a small ditch as Paul furiously got out of the car, picked up the crumpled door and shoved it onto the back seat.

'I thought you hated your job,' Ernest said, as Paul sat back into the car. 'I thought you wanted to be a musician.'

'I'm a banker,' Paul said. 'I feed off the misery of others.'

With that he stepped on the accelerator and reversed, at high speed, down the narrow path.

Ernest and Jon stood and watched the car drive off into the distance, until it was a tiny speck and then was gone. Neither man moved or said anything for a long while.

'Mooo!' the cow said, finally breaking the silence.

Jon sighed.

'Oh well,' he said.

Ernest stepped out of the ditch and began walking down the path. A few seconds later Jon followed him.

'This is not the way to Dublin,' Jon pointed out.

'No,' Ernest agreed.

Jon nodded.

'So,' he said, 'am I to presume that, unlike Paul, you have not come round, with sober morning, to the view that what we are planning is both foolish and folly.'

'It doesn't matter,' Ernest said. 'We have begun. What else do we have? I'm never going to get this manuscript published and you will never become a successful actor.'

'You're probably right,' Jon said, and the pair walked on.

They wandered in silence down the narrow path. Jon began rubbing his temples. The cold of the morning seemed to seep in through his ears and worsen the pounding in his head.

'I won't be drinking again for a fair while,' he said. 'My head feels like it's been slammed into a freezer door over and over again for several hours.'

'I used to get great migraines when I was a kid,' Ernest said.

'Really? I didn't know.'

'I try to avoid talking about my childhood,' Ernest said. 'If I talk about it I have to think about it. But I used to get wonderful migraines. Positively the highest class of migraines available. Migraines that made you want to die just to stop the endless pain. My mother thought it was chocolate. I don't think she had any hard evidence. I think she was just looking for something to blame and she picked chocolate. Myself, if asked, I would probably have chosen something green, like broccoli or spinach, or cucumber or peas or any other damn vegetable. I don't know if you picked it up, but I don't like them too much. It's not that I don't like vegetables so much, I wish them no ill will. In fact, if it were left up to me they would be allowed to run free in sun-drenched fields of green with all their other disgusting tasteless friends.'

Jon nodded soberly and wondered to himself whether it was such a wise thing being stuck in the middle of the countryside on a small road with a friend who might or might not be verging on the edge of insanity.

'My aunt got migraines,' Ernest went on. 'She got them from dairy products. But the flaw in the argument was that I would get migraines regardless of whether I ate chocolate or not. I'm no lawyer or anything but I see this as a distinct weakness in my mother's case. I remember though, and it's one of my most vivid memories of my childhood, rolling around on the floor, an intense burning pain behind my eyes, and crying so much that my dog kept coming over and licking my face, and for a couple of seconds I would laugh, and then I would start screaming again.'

Ernest and Jon walked in silence for a while, Jon not wanting to talk too much because of his headache and Ernest lost in memories. The pair of them walked on down the long narrow country road and as they did so the sounds of the cars rushing along the motorway, already far in the distance, gradually faded till they couldn't hear them any more and there was a silence that neither man had experienced in a long while, living in the rattling city.

After walking down the seemingly endless road for two hours both men heard a low menacing rumbling sound. They stopped dead in their tracks.

'What was that?' Jon said.

'I don't know.'

'It sounded like thunder.'

'I thought it sounded like a wolf,' Ernest said.

Both men listened silently for a long while. There was no more sound. They walked on. Once again they heard the rumbling and froze.

'I think it's thunder,' Jon said.

'I think it's a wolf,' Ernest said.

'Great. Rain or a wolf. Wet or dead. I don't know which I'd choose at this moment.'

'Yes,' Ernest agreed and they walked on.

Again they heard the rumbling.

'I know what it is,' Ernest said this time.

Jon stared at him.

'My stomach,' Ernest explained. 'I hadn't realised.'

Jon sighed.

'I thought it sounded close.'

'It's not my fault,' Ernest protested. 'I'm hungry. It does that when I'm hungry. I don't think I ate at all yesterday. I didn't even get to have that bag of crisps.'

Jon looked around them, at the miles of green nothingness with the road at its centre.

'There is never a convenience store when you want one,' he said.

'But I have money,' Ernest said desperately, taking out a clutch of twenty pound notes. 'I have money. I must be able to get food.'

'That doesn't quite follow,' Jon said. 'Not in the country.'

'Follow? Of course it does. I need food. I have money. This is so unfair. It's all this walking. It's not good for a person.'

They came to a rusted gate by the side of the road.

'Let's cut through this field,' Ernest said.

'To where?'

'How should I know?'

'Stick to the path,' Jon said. 'If children's stories and horror films have taught me anything it is never veer from the path. Didn't you see *An American Werewolf in London?*'

'It's daytime,' Ernest pointed out. 'Besides, it's not a wood. It's a green open field. If anything tries to attack us we'll be able to see it twenty miles away.'

Jon nodded but did not look convinced.

'We will die without food,' Ernest said. 'I don't want to die from starvation. It seems to me it would be a rather painful death. If I am to die young I want to be hit by a two ton truck as I happily cross some street without looking, whistling till the impact. I don't want to know I'm going to die. I don't want to see death looming over me as my stomach expands and my immune system begins breaking down my fat cells because it has no other source of sustenance, sending toxins throughout my body that lead to a gradual slow decay of every organ.'

'Who's to say,' Jon said, 'that if we stick to the path we won't come to some small village? Who's to say if we start crossing fields that we might end up more lost and more remote. I mean, that's the thing: paths lead somewhere. Paths always lead somewhere.'

'But I can't walk much longer,' Ernest said. 'I'm unused to all this exercise. My body has not developed for exercise. It has developed to fit smoothly on a couch and stare at television. There is too much countryside, I have a hangover, I want to go home but we have no home. Just let me cross this field, not for any rational reason but because I'm sick of walking along this miserable little path.'

Jon nodded.

'Fair enough,' he said quietly.

They climbed over the rusted gate because it would not open. They walked through one field and then through another. When they walked through the third field they came to a fourth. This field was unremarkable, in fact quite similar to the previous three, but closer inspection revealed hundreds of small brown mushrooms sprouting just beneath the blades of grass.

'Food,' Ernest said.

He lay down on the grass and stared, up close, at the little brown mushrooms.

'Not safe,' Jon said. 'We can't eat them.'

'Why not?' Ernest demanded. 'Not safe! Death is not safe.'

'They might be hallucinogenic.'

'Your point being?'

'However much drink I was willing to take,' Jon said. 'however much hash I was willing to smoke, I was never willing to take anything that messed with your mind. I don't want something affecting my brain in that way. I don't trust my brain enough. I have some fairly unpleasant thoughts in a day and I would not like to blur the lines of reality.'

'Food,' Ernest repeated, plucking up the small fungus.

'I am as hungry as you,' Jon counselled. 'I just feel we should think about this. It's highly questionable.'

Ernest put the mushroom in his mouth. His face screwed up and he chewed quickly before swallowing.

'Well?' Jon said.

'Disgusting,' Ernest said. 'Really, really, disgusting.'

He picked up another mushroom and devoured it whole. He scooped a whole collection and began swallowing them one by one.

'The trick is,' he said after a little while. 'Not to have them in your mouth too long. So that your taste buds can get hold. The trick is to swallow quickly. Not giving them a chance.'

Jon was salivating as he watched his friend gorge on the mushrooms.

'Not safe,' he repeated aloud.

Ernest finished eating some moments later. He had managed to clear almost half the field in his ravenous hunger.

'Anything?' Jon asked. 'Any strange sensations?'

'Nothing,' Ernest said. 'Just the sweet contentment of a man who has eaten and eaten well.'

Jon nodded. He paused and tried to regain his composure. He could not. He dived into the collection of mushrooms and began eating. He did not even pause for breath. A few moments later he had cleared the other half of the field.

Both men lay on the soft grass and held their full stomachs in their hands.

'Glorious,' Ernest said.

'Wonderful,' Jon agreed.

The sun had risen high into a clear mid-morning sky and it shone down at them as they lay in their contentment.

'It's not so bad,' Ernest said. 'The countryside. I feel closer to nature.'

'It's certainly quiet,' Jon reflected. 'You get used to background noise in the city. A constant drone of several automations strangely absent.'

Ernest plucked a long grass and began chewing it.

'It's a pity,' he said. 'that you can never remember such glorious feelings as we are having now. Such utter contentment and relaxation. If your body could only store these feelings inside of itself you could call on fragments of them when feeling defeated, depressed or suicidal.'

Jon nodded. He was thinking how silly he had been to worry about the mushrooms, how he was always so sensible and that sometimes he would like to be more like Ernest. How easy it had been to give in to wanton abandon. He was thinking about this when, suddenly, he began to giggle. He looked over at Ernest and noticed that he was suddenly miles away in a distant field with hundreds of fields between them. Jon smiled at Ernest and thought he could see Ernest smile back, despite the distance.

'Are you all right?' he heard the remarkably close-sounding Ernest say.

Jon giggled at how close Ernest sounded despite the distance. He giggled at Ernest's confused face which he could just make out. He giggled at how reserved he always was compared to Ernest. He giggled at the fact that he could not stop giggling. The more he giggled the lighter he began to feel. He felt his body fill with helium starting from his head and shooting through his arms, twisting down to his stomach and down each leg.

Suddenly he could barely keep himself fixed onto the ground. He felt his body in a struggling drift away from gravity and giggled again. Jon decided to stand up at this point and, so light was his frame, that he did so with no effort at all.

'Where are you going?' said the far away figure of Ernest.

Jon was going to reply but felt it was not necessary. He found the question quite hilarious and decided to jump in the air for joy. He crouched down in a sitting position and, using his legs as springs, leapt up into the air. He flew up like a rocket into the bright blue sky.

As he flew he watched the shrinking figure of Ernest far below in the field. In no time at all Ernest was little more than an ant in a model craft miniature world. Soon he could not make out Ernest at all. He was so high by now he could see all of Ireland below him. Its strange uneven shape seemed so ridiculous to Jon as he watched. He thought how silly all his problems were as he climbed. Looking at Ireland, at all of Europe, from his high vantage point, he began to realise how minuscule it all was. How insignificant his own petty neurosis. How stupid the whole thing was. Life. That these tiny creatures running around the pockets of green land on a planet of great blue oceans could cause so much trouble. That they could argue and fight and kill each other in the deluded notion that they could keep or win the land on which they scurried.

Jon looked up and realised, with a start, that he was approaching the edge of Earth's atmosphere and that he was still not slowing down. In fact he was moving faster than ever, hurtling towards the edge of sky. He tried to scream in horror but found he had no voice. The atmosphere thinned so much that he found he could no longer breathe. He gasped for air that was not there. He flapped his arms to try and stop his flight but it was no use. Soon he would break the atmosphere entirely and go hurtling forever into space. Jon closed his eyes and prayed to a God he was sure did not exist.

Ernest stared at Jon and scratched his chin. His friend was standing, with his eyes closed, flapping his arms, with a look of terror on his face. Ernest had been yelling at him for twenty minutes to no avail. He sighed and wondered what could possibly have made Jon go so suddenly and entirely mad. It could not have been the mushrooms. After all, he had eaten them first and he felt fine.

Ernest looked at Jon and giggled slightly. After all, he did look ridiculous. It was funny really, he decided, giggling more. He had always thought he would go mad first. Jon had become so sensible of late. Ernest stood up, and began walking away from Jon, into the next field. He was filled with a sudden and immense desire to move. He waved happily at Jon, before realising Jon's eyes were closed and giggled again.

'I am a traveller,' Ernest reflected aloud, 'roaming through the countryside in search of silver truncates. In search of cantabulous crayons to gargle down the sheep. Freely fashioned frillocks form a funny fulsome face. Dedi Dedi. Did I? Did I?'

Ernest stopped because he did not know the answer.

'What was the question?' he said aloud.

'How should I know?' somebody answered.

Ernest looked around him but could not find the source of the voice. The only thing in this field was a lone grey donkey tied to an old oak tree. Ernest approached the donkey cautiously.

'Careful now,' he warned the donkey. 'I know shujitsu.'

He began demonstrating to the donkey his prowess at the martial arts. The donkey seemed quite unimpressed. He chewed some grass then spat it out again.

'I hate this bloody tough grass,' the donkey said. 'It's hard enough finding anything decent this time of year, let alone being restricted to the length of this bloody rope.'

Ernest nodded solemnly. He punched the air with his fist then turned back to the donkey.

'What?' he said.

The donkey stared back at him blankly.

'Did you say something?' Ernest asked.

'Not something,' the donkey said. 'I was making a complaint.'

Ernest nodded.

'Good,' he said. 'Good. I didn't know donkeys could talk. I suppose I never tried to engage them in conversation before. I was talking to a cow earlier.'

'A cow?' the donkey said. 'Don't be daft. You can't talk to a cow. Cows communicate through telepathy. Like trees.'

Ernest nodded solemnly.

'Of course,' he said.

The donkey picked up another tuft of grass with his teeth and then spat it out.

'It is a terrible year for grass,' the donkey said. 'We're not getting the right kind of rain, you see. Summer rain is all wrong. Winters are too mild. I remember a time when donkeys of the whole world would talk about the grass in this country. Now it is not much better than the continent. A yellowy mush. My father used to talk of a time before pesticides. He used to say that the whole soil was contaminated. That grass was not safe any more and that it had lost all taste. I don't know about all that.

'Some say he was not right in the head. He pulled a cart for most of his life and had two very cruel owners. Some say his mind went under the pressure. I cannot taste the chemicals. But it would not surprise me if he were right, after all.'

Ernest sat down in front of the donkey and stared into its large brown eyes. It had a very wise face, he reflected.

'And now I'm condemned to this second rate stuff,' the donkey said, motioning to the grass around the tree. 'Bereft of moisture lost to this old oak. All for a sin against man.'

'Sin?' Ernest said, keen to hear more.

The donkey nodded.

'I killed a human child, you see. Terrible thing. One of the neighbours' children. Used to come around, pretending to like me and, when nobody was looking, kick me for no reason. Well, not for no reason. He kicked me because his owners did not love him and treated him poorly. So one day, when it was gearing up to kick me it made the fatal mistake of wandering behind me.

'My hind legs struck him so fast he never knew what hit him. It is a wonderful feeling, that kick back, leaning forward on my front legs and pushing back with that tremendous leap of strength. Of course the child was killed instantly. I was pronounced mad by a vet psychologist and dangerous by a city judge. I was to be put down forthwith and my meat made into animal feed.

'But my owner was a bitter man who hated the courts and his neighbours with equal contempt and, to thwart them both, he took me to this field filled with grass, where they could not find me and carry out their barbarous justice, and he tied me to this tree.'

Ernest stood up and wiped a tear from his eye.

'I can release you,' he said.

The donkey shook his head sadly.

'Where would I go?' he asked.

'You could find another field,' Ernest said. 'Perhaps a field full of better grass. A field with other donkeys. You must get lonely.'

The donkey nodded.

'You learn to live with loneliness,' he said. 'We are all alone with our guilt. It is kind of you to offer, young man, to release me, but it is not within the power of you or I. The truth is more binding than this rope and the truth is I killed that boy, and even though he was unpleasant, he was still a child and did not deserve such a fate. It was instinct, you see. Terrible instinct. He was a threat and he was within my range. I tried to resist but found I could not. It was imprinted within me. I could do nothing more or less than kick. And now I must live out my punishment. I am lonely, but I deserve it. I complain but I know that it is right. I sometimes wonder if it had not been better that I was turned into animal feed.'

The donkey picked up some more grass and this time, with great effort, swallowed.

Ernest drifted sadly away from the field. He returned to the spot where Jon had been standing, only to find him lying out on the grass, his arms flailing about his sides.

'Space,' he was saying. 'Infinite nothingness.'

Ernest sat down beside him. All at once Ernest realised they were sitting on a yellow sand island in the middle of a deep green sea. Ernest smiled as, all around them, tiny fish jumped out of the water wearing hula skirts and singing Minnie the Moocher in high pitched falsetto voices.

Hours later Jon awoke to find the field cloaked in darkness. He felt a strange sensation in his stomach. A kind of numbness.

'What happened?' he said aloud, but before he even uttered the words he remembered.

He remembered everything. He looked down at the figure of Ernest who lay sleeping beside him, a serene smile on his face.

'Mushrooms,' Jon said, shaking his head.

He remembered every minute detail of his ordeal. An ordeal that had started out so pleasantly and soon turned into a nightmare. As he drifted through space he had felt the very real sensation that he could not breathe, and yet he did not die. Every second was spent gasping and praying for an end to the infinite black. His space had no stars. It had no light. It had no planets or friendly aliens. It was an endless night. Jon sat and stared at the dark grass and wondered to himself what possible demons could have stirred up such a horrible fantasy.

Ernest began to stir. He yawned, opened his eyes and sat up suddenly.

'Catfish,' he said.

'What?'

'Oh,' Ernest said, recognising Jon. 'Nothing.'

They sat in silence for a long while, each man contemplating the experience he had just been through, wondering should he tell the other. Several times one or the other almost spoke but could never quite find a beginning for what he wanted to say. Finally Jon stood up.

'We had better go,' he said. 'We'll need to find some more food.'

Ernest nodded and stood up. They walked off into the adjacent field. Ernest waved at the old grey donkey as they passed by, but the donkey ignored them as it chewed solemnly on the grass.

'I don't remember it being this dark,' Ernest said.

'It's winter,' Jon said. 'It happens early.'

'Not this dark, though,' Ernest said. 'Never this dark.'

'I think,' Jon said, 'you must be thinking of the city.'

Ernest nodded.

'I suppose you're right,' he said and the pair walked on.

They walked for miles through endless open fields till finally they came to a small and stony road that looked identical to the one they had strayed from.

'Do you suppose it is the same one?' Ernest asked.

Jon looked up and down the road.

'There's no way to tell,' he said. 'It looks the same.'

Suddenly, from out of nowhere, a small hunched figure began walking towards them. Ernest jumped and Jon almost screamed.

The hunched figure stopped as it noticed them.

'Are you there?' he called out.

Ernest and Jon looked at each other.

'Are you there?' the figure repeated.

'Yes,' Jon said, tentatively.

'Good,' the hunched figure said, walking on.

Ernest and Jon looked at each other.

As the figure came closer, Ernest and Jon saw that he was an extraordinarily ugly looking old man with a split lip and cabbage ears and a black cloak wrapped around his shrunken frame, from top to bottom, over and over again.

'I'm not in the mood for the others,' the old man said, standing beside Jon. 'Not on a night like it is.'

Jon nodded solemnly.

'Could you tell us where we could find a main road?' he asked.

The old man shook his head fiercely.

'Not on this night,' he said. 'The mist comes down and takes them away. Keep on this road. If the others come, give them one of these.'

The old man handed Jon a potato, and winked a knowing wink

at him before heading off down the road. Ernest and Jon stared at the potato, which seemed entirely unremarkable. They looked back towards the old man and saw he was already a considerable distance down the road and almost out of sight.

'He moves quickly for an old man,' Ernest reflected. 'And for someone who's clearly mad.'

Jon put the potato in his pocket and they resumed their journey.

As they walked the road got narrower and narrower and the evening got darker still. Trees began sprouting up on either side of the path till finally they were completely surrounded by them and the sky was entirely blocked out.

Three strange figures emerged suddenly out of the darkness in front of them.

'Travellers,' the figure at the front, a scraggily dressed man with shoulder length hair, said.

'Travellers,' a small round figure agreed, smiling gleefully.

'A spoon and a carrot,' the third figure, a tall, thin, elegant-looking man, said bitterly.

'Which is which?' laughed the first man.

'Which is which?' the round man repeated gleefully.

They were dressed in old-fashioned peasant clothes, as if they had come from the set of a film about the Middle Ages.

'We're not travellers,' Ernest explained calmly. 'We are from the city.'

'And how did you get here?' the first man asked. 'My guess would be that you travelled?'

'Well, yes,' Ernest conceded.

'Forfeit,' the fat man said, clapping his hands excitedly.

'Forfeit,' the tall man agreed. 'They walked right into it. They are as blind as they are ignorant.'

'Forfeit,' the first man agreed sombrely.

Ernest took a twenty pound note from his pocket.

'Look,' he said, slipping it into the long haired man's pocket. 'We don't want any trouble. We'd like to get by.'

The long-haired man took the twenty pound note out of his pocket and stared at it with a mocking grin. He gave it to the fat man.

'A painting?' he said.

'Poor quality reproduction,' the fat man said.

The third man snatched it from his hands. He stared at the bill for a long time. He looked from the bill to Ernest.

'Worthless,' he said, rolling the twenty pound note into a ball and throwing it at him.

'Forfeit,' the fat man began squealing over and over again.

The tall thin man took out a small silver knife.

'Why don't we disembowel them?' he said. 'We'll spill their guts and make them walk around a tree.'

'Messy,' the long-haired man said. 'But entertaining.'

Jon reached a shaking hand into his pocket. He took out the potato and held it up uncertainly.

'This is all we have,' he said.

All three men turned to see what other ridiculous offer the travellers would make. Their faces went completely white when they saw what Jon was holding in his hand. All three fell on their knees at once.

'Forgive us,' the long-haired man said, bowing his head.

'Forgive us, forgive uss!' the round man said, kissing their feet as he begged.

'Please,' the thin man said. 'I have never seen these men before in my life. They tricked me. They are holding my children hostage.'

'Letch!' the long-haired man said contemptuously.

'Traitor,' the fat man said.

Ernest and Jon looked at each other. Ernest decided to try something.

'Forfeit,' he said, to the thin man.

'Forfeit,' the long-haired man agreed.

The thin man nodded.

'Of course,' he said. 'Of course.'

He took something out of his pocket and offered it to Ernest. It appeared to be a small old-fashioned musket gun.

'Here,' he said. 'It was a dying gift to me by my first wife just before she passed away giving birth to my only child.'

'Ha!' the long-haired man said. 'He stole it from a whore, who stole it from an officer.'

The fat man laughed hysterically at this.

'Lies!' the thin man said. 'Contemptuous lies. These men are thieves. They are natives of this rotten place.'

Ernest nodded.

'If we give you this,' Jon said, holding out the potato, 'you will leave us alone?'

All three men bowed their heads.

'Of course,' the long-haired man said. 'What else could we do?'

Jon nodded. He placed the potato on the ground in front of the men, turned to Ernest and nodded. They walked around the three kneeling figures and further down the path.

When they had walked a little distance away they heard a scuffle from behind them. They turned to see the three men flailing about the ground in a desperate struggle. The thin man held the potato in his hand while the other two were trying desperately to wrench it from his grip. Jon and Ernest turned around and hurried away from the strange scene.

A few moments later Jon and Ernest emerged from under the trees and found themselves bathed in sunlight.

'We must have walked right through the night,' Jon observed.

'It only seemed like minutes,' Ernest said.

Both men turned and looked back into the darkened path and then at each other. Once again they nearly spoke but found they could not formulate the beginnings of their sentences. They turned around again and walked on.

The path finally ended at an old grey wooden gate on which there hung a small hand-painted sign.

'O'Neill's Farm,' Jon read. 'Beware of the cows.'

'Surely that should be "Beware of the bulls",' Ernest said.

Jon looked around them.

'There is nowhere else to go,' he said. 'Unless you feel like walking back down that path.'

Ernest began climbing over the gate. Jon soon followed. They jumped down off the gate and into another green field, quite unremarkable, save for the fact that it was swamped in a thick mist. They could not make out more than a few feet in front of them because of the thick white billowing cloud.

'Where did this come from?' Ernest asked.

They turned around and stared back down the path. It was entirely free of mist.

'We are in the Midlands,' Jon said. 'Normal rules do not apply.'

Ernest nodded. Jon got out his inhaler and took two deep breaths.

'All this cold is not good for my chest,' he said as they began walking. 'It's beginning to take its toll.'

'This is all because we're poor,' Ernest said. 'If we were rich we'd never have to be cold. It's a form of oppression.'

'Perhaps human beings shouldn't be living in countries like Ireland,' Jon speculated. 'I mean, they say we come, that we all originate from Africa. The cold certainly doesn't feel right to me.'

'Think about how cold that bastard landlord kept us,' Ernest said. 'We had one half hour of central heating a day and the rest of the time we had to use that crappy gas thing that made us drowsy. It can't have been healthy, that crappy gas thing.'

'Bull,' Jon said.

'It's true,' Ernest protested. 'I used to pass out . . . '

'No,' Jon said, pointing. 'Bull.'

Ernest followed Jon's finger. He could just make out a huge bull through the mist, chewing on the grass at the opposite end of the field.

'I don't think he's seen us,' Ernest said. 'Let's run.'

'There's something wrong there,' Jon said, staring.

'Never mind,' Ernest said. 'We must escape.'

Jon continued to stare at the bull. Ernest grabbed him by the collar, and began running into the next field. There was even more mist in this field. It was so thick you could not see your hand in front of your face. Jon and Ernest lost sight of each other.

'Ernest?' Jon said.

'Here,' he heard a voice a few feet away reply.

Jon began walking towards the voice. He heard some movement behind him and turned round.

'Ernest?'

The mist cleared in front of him. Jon stared with horror into the eyes of a cow so large, it was impossible. It was enormous. The size of a truck. The cow stared at him with large vacant eyes as it chewed slowly and methodically. Jon tried to scream but could not. He reached desperately for his inhaler. He took it very slowly out of his pocket as the cow continued to stare, and inhaled three puffs of the chemical into his lungs. He felt his breathing ease almost immediately. He started to back away. The cow took a step forward. It almost crushed Jon with one of its great hooves. He took another tentative step backwards. This time the cow did not move. Jon sighed. He took another step. He took another and felt his back bang against something. He heard a familiar scream.

'Ernest?'

Ernest hugged him.

'Oh Jon,' he said. 'Thank God. Do you see that?'

He pointed to another large cow that was behind him. Jon nodded and pointed to the cow in front of him.

'Oh my God,' Ernest said. 'It's real. I was hoping it was the mushrooms. It's following me. But it can't be real. Something must have happened to our minds.'

'I remember what was wrong with the bull,' Jon said. 'He was standing next to a tree, but the tree was only half his size. I remember trying to figure out the perspective, but I couldn't.'

'I want to go back to the city,' Ernest said. 'I don't like it here at all.'

They were stuck between the two great cows.

'To the left,' Jon suggested and they began slowly edging, back to back, away to the left of the two animals. The cows did not move, merely following them with their lazy eyes as they chewed.

Ernest shrieked. They had come upon another giant cow to their left. It walked forward towards them, its hooves creating huge craters with each step. Ernest and Jon backed away, this time to the right. Once again they were met by another advancing behemoth.

'We're doomed,' Ernest said, as all four cows circled around them. 'We're cud.'

The first cow blinked slowly at them.

'Dooooed!' Ernest cried.

'Moooo!' the first cow cried setting them all off.

The strength of their cries was like a hurricane. It knocked Jon and Ernest off their feet. As they lay on the ground the four cows closed in on them. The first one sniffed Ernest's leg. A huge tongue lolled out and licked him, covering him with a thick slimy goo. Ernest began crying as one of the cows came too close and was about to crush him with a wayward hoof.

Suddenly in the distance there was a tremendous explosion and all four cows ran off in terror leaving Jon and Ernest lying still with their eyes closed, alone, waiting for their gruesome deaths.

Some moments later Jon opened a cautious eye.

'They're gone,' he said.

Ernest opened his eyes. Not only were the cows gone but the mist had gone with them.

'It must have come from their breathing,' Jon said.

Ernest nodded. He did not feel at all well. He wiped the goo from his face.

'I stink,' he said, smelling the substance in his hand.

Jon was continuing to look around them.

'I think we should run now,' he said. 'And talk later.'

Ernest nodded in agreement and the two sped off as fast as their short legs could carry them. As soon as they began running, they heard the sound of something following them. The ground shook every few seconds with each of its tremendous footsteps as the mist drew back in around them.

'Don't look round,' Jon said.

Ernest nodded. He stared straight forward. They ran for miles through the field with the unseen thing chasing them until, finally, Ernest could take it no longer. He glanced over his shoulder and the shock of what he saw made him fall over.

It was the bull. Bigger even than the other cows. Built like a small house. It was running at them with its head down, wielding its giant horns like great javelins.

Jon had not noticed Ernest fall. He turned, expecting him to be beside him. When he saw he was not, he stopped dead in his tracks and looked back. Ernest was lying on his back edging away from the bull, which was snorting viciously just in front of him.

'Get up!' Jon yelled.

Ernest shook his head.

'I can't,' he screamed. 'My body won't work. My limbs are jelly.'

The bull began beating its left hoof against the ground and tearing large strips of earth as it dragged the hoof back.

'It's counting,' Ernest said.

'No,' Jon said. 'It's going to charge.'

With one final beat of its hoof the bull put down its head and was about to gouge Ernest to shreds when another great explosion blasted. The bull looked up and saw something behind Jon and Ernest that made it turn around and run. Ernest closed his eyes. Jon froze. Neither wanted to know whatever it was that had made that thing frightened.

When they heard the next explosion Jon turned around slowly. Behind them was a giant dog, almost as big as the cows themselves. The dog barked a tremendous clapping bark and Jon realised this was the sound they had mistaken for an explosion.

'This is not good,' Jon said aloud.

'I don't want to know,' Ernest said, refusing to look round. 'I am going to lie here on the grass and pretend this is not happening. Perhaps I'll wake up in our safe Dublin flat.'

'Sit,' somebody in the distance yelled, and the giant dog duly sat.

A small tractor emerged in the distance. There was a trailer fastened to the tractor and on the trailer were several tons of doggy biscuits. The figure driving the tractor stopped beside the giant dog and got out. He stood a little way away and called out to the dog.

'Treat!' he yelled and the dog began wagging its enormous tail and tucking into the trailer full of doggy biscuits.

After regarding the dog eating for a little while, the man approached Jon.

'Didn't you see the signs?' he asked angrily.

'Yes,' Jon said, mesmerised by the sight of the dog. 'We didn't realise.'

'You are lucky,' the man said, shaking his head.

Upon hearing the normal-sounding human voice Jon was talking to, Ernest got up from where he lay and turned around. When he saw the giant dog he fell over again.

'It's all right,' the man called out. 'He's harmless really.'

Ernest cowered on the ground, repeating that none of this was real, over and over.

'You had better come back to the farm,' the man said. 'It's not safe out here.'

This was all Ernest needed to hear. The thought of those things coming back was enough to overcome his fear of the huge dog. He and Jon climbed into the tractor and, with the giant dog bounding in front of them, they made their way to a small farm cottage.

The farmer instructed the dog to sit and guard outside the door while he brought Jon and Ernest inside the house. He gave Ernest fresh clothes to wear and a basin to wash himself in.

'I'm afraid I can't offer you a shower,' the farmer said. 'We only have the well. It is still a terrible old-fashioned place despite my efforts.'

They sat at an old wooden table and the farmer took out a small pipe and a bottle of whisky. He lit a fire, heated the whisky until it was piping hot, and poured it into three mugs.

'I'd say now,' he said, as he lit his pipe, 'what you saw out there might have given you a shock.'

Jon and Ernest said nothing as they sipped on their whiskeys. Already, in the warm house, they were wondering to themselves if they had not imagined the whole thing after all.

'So few people stray down the path at all,' the farmer said. 'The locals are afraid. I would be more specific in the signs but who'd believe me?'

Jon nodded. He looked out the window and saw the shadow of the huge dog in the driveway.

'You see,' the farmer said, 'I was not born for a life of farming even though my mother had me in a room upstairs in this house, and since I was old enough to carry a pail of milk I was helping around the farm. But I did not enjoy it. It held no fascination for me. My father did not understand. My mother was more sympathetic. She was a kind woman. She said that not everyone was suited to this life. She died when I was very young.

'It was a double tragedy. Firstly, because it meant I was alone in the house with my father - I had loved her very dearly and missed her - and secondly because it meant she could bear him no more sons, which meant the farm, and the tradition, had to live on through me.

'There were very few options open to me. I could run away of course. Emigrate. But I did not want to do that. I felt guilty. I felt I owed my father a responsibility.

'My true love was always for books. For mathematics, for science. I always did well in school and dreaded having to come home to help with the chores of the farm. So, I decided that, if I were going to be a farmer, I would have to make it interesting for myself. I persuaded my father to let me go to university, on the promise that I would return and take over the heavier duties of the farm as soon as I had my degree. I lived for five happy years in England and completed a PhD in biochemistry before finally returning home.

'My father was very poorly. His back was done in from the constant work, morning, noon and night. I began to take over from him. I wanted to modernise, to use the cutting edge of agricultural technology, and I used my own knowledge of biology and chemistry to help create newer and better anti-bacterial sprays and animal feeds.

'My father was resistant. He was old fashioned. He liked to do everything by hand. When he died, finally, one Christmas, after months of arthritic agony, I decided that I would do things my way. I was not going to end up like my father. I had had to do everything for him in those last few months. He could barely move himself. When I touched him, the lightest of touches even, he felt pain. I was not going to kill myself or ruin my joints and back for this farm. I was going to use science to eradicate the need for such hardship.

'I studied all the papers, read all the agricultural magazines. I even created my own laboratory in my parents' old bedroom. It started harmlessly enough. Increasing milk yields, experimenting with hormones in the feed to make the cows a little bigger. Harmless stuff. I was making a very healthy profit for the farm, though. Healthier than it had ever been under my father. But I was not satisfied. I was beginning to get bored. I began to experiment more radically with the animal feed. I added a mixture of elements at the cutting edge of all known research added in with some discoveries of my own.

'Most of the animals I gave the mixture to died. I constantly played with the levels of the various elements and the strength of dose. Still the cattle continued to die. Eventually I was down to the last few of the herd. I came close to bankruptcy. But then, for whatever reason, one of the animals survived. Not only that but she grew, she grew and kept on growing. Finally she stopped growing, at about the size of an American buffalo.

'I was, needless to say, ecstatic. It was incredible. I mean, my mind raced with possible benefits for such a drug. Can you imagine? A herd of sheep that could clothe the entire world. A herd of cows that could feed the starving. But they needed to be bigger. I had to see how far the technology could go. I had to push things.

'And now I am left with a herd of cattle so big that I can barely control them. I had to give the feed to one of the dogs just so I could manage them. And even then I have little control over the bull. He was a mistake, you see. They weren't supposed to breed. I didn't give the food to any males. I knew the consequences were potentially devastating. But, somehow, one began to grow. He must have been stealing the ends of the other's food. And now he's out there, breeding, and I have no control over him, and every day they get more daring.'

The young farmer stared towards the window. In the distance they could hear the sound of thunder. The farmer stood up. He walked over to the window and looked out.

'You'd better go,' he said. 'While they are still wary. They get harder to frighten every day.'

The farmer picked up his coat and a shotgun.

'I'll take you to the main road,' he said.

They left the old stone farm and were driven by the farmer in his jeep along a gravel path, with huge fences and barbed wire on either side. The giant dog ran in front of the jeep as they drove, sniffing the air occasionally and pausing to urinate great waterfalls against the fence, sending sparks flying everywhere.

5. That Sinking Feeling

The farmer left Ernest and Jon on a long straight tarmacadam road before wishing them luck and heading back towards the farm with the giant dog eagerly leading the way, barking its explosive bark as it ran. When the farmer had left, Jon and Ernest were once again left to ponder silently the reality of what they had just witnessed. Ernest stared up and down the long expanse of road.

'Quiet,' he said.

'Somewhat of a relief,' Jon agreed.

'Do you think,' Ernest asked, 'that we have died and this perhaps is not the Midlands at all, but some place between heaven and Earth where we are being punished for our worldly sins?'

'I am no longer sure,' Jon replied. 'I don't remember doing anything to deserve all this.'

'Good,' Ernest said. 'In that case we shall proceed as normal. Head westwards. Revenge and fortune awaits.'

'For some people,' Jon said, 'every day is the same. They get up, have toast and cereal, go to work, come home, eat dinner, watch TV, go to bed and start all over again. As a teenager I could never understand this. I could not understand why seemingly sane people gave into such mediocrity and boredom. Right now I would appreciate some mediocrity and boredom.'

'We'll have plenty of time to be bored when we're rich,' Ernest said. 'How more bored could we get? Sitting all day in the sun. Not having to do anything for ourselves.'

'Perhaps there is a God,' Jon said. 'Perhaps He is trying to teach us something. Perhaps there is some moral to this story we cannot grasp.'

'Morals,' Ernest said. 'I know all there is to know about morals. Absolute morals. Infinite morals. Ulterior morals. I did my thesis on them.'

'No,' Jon said, 'you didn't.'

'All right, I didn't,' Ernest said. 'but I very easily could have done. College! I wouldn't give a shake of my left leg for all their learning.'

'If there is a moral,' Jon observed. 'it is wasted on the pair of us.'

Ernest read the time on his Mickey Mouse watch.

'What day is it?' he asked.

'I don't know.'

'What day did we begin on?'

'I don't know.'

'There must be a way to tell,' Ernest said.

Jon said nothing. He stared at his muddy shoes and thought of the futility of conversation.

'Some way of observing from the sun,' Ernest said. 'We need to know the day. I have the time, I just can't remember when it all started.'

'It's hard to keep track,' Jon said. 'Being on the dole. Drifting from one audition to another. It's hard to remember. One day is not much different to the next. Strange how the weekend is so important to so many people, and yet, to you and me, and to everyone else without purpose, those two days feel no different from any other day.'

'I always liked Sundays as a child,' Ernest said. 'Only the first half. The waking up and lying in. There was something horrible about the second half of Sunday. Knowing that the next morning you would have to go to school. I used to hate it. I hated every minute of Sunday evening. I resented every second that went by. And Monday morning, the sickest feeling of the week. I used to always wake up and think it was the weekend still. I would be about to close my eyes, the serenest smile of satisfaction on my face, when I would remember, and the memory would kick me in the stomach, throw me out of bed, wrap a cardboard shirt around me and squeeze me into a choking tie.'

'I wonder,' Jon said, 'did the teachers feel that way?'

'They were getting paid,' Ernest pointed out.

'Yes,' Jon said. 'But I still felt sorry for them. I felt most sorry for

127

the unpopular ones. Nobody likes to be unpopular. Some are more ambivalent than others but . . . nobody can really like it. You could see it in their eyes as they walked around the school. That they knew they were hated. It can't have been a pleasant thing. Children's hatred is so raw and unmasked.'

'They deserved it,' Ernest said. 'Who'd be a teacher? What sort of sick mind wants to teach? To share the gift of knowledge? To inspire people. It's depraved.'

'Sad to think,' Jon said, 'that children need to be scared into obedience. That every day millions sit in classrooms, quite still, and do the work because they are afraid of the consequences of doing anything else. I can't help but feel we are all a little destroyed by school. Some of us more than others.'

'What sort of a main road is this?' Ernest said. 'Not a tricycle in sight. How are we ever going to get to Galway on time with this carry on? He'll be back in Dublin by Monday and then it'll be too late. Of course, he might well leave the money in the house, but it's risky.'

'Maybe we should start walking,' Jon suggested.

'Oh no,' Ernest said. 'I'm not going anywhere. I listened to you last time and look where it got us. We are going to sit and wait and hitch a ride with a coach full of Swedish female tennis players on tour.'

At that precise second a coach appeared in the distance. Ernest rubbed his eyes in disbelief.

'Look at that,' he said. 'Look at that.'

'Yes,' Jon said.

Ernest cleared his throat and began brushing down his clothes. He steadied himself and held out his hand as the coach slowly approached. It stopped beside them and the doors were flung open.

'Silver Line Tours' was written in large letters on the side of the bus.

'Afternoon,' the plump looking driver said to them. 'Need a lift?'

Ernest nodded and the driver waved them on.

To Ernest's intense disappointment, it was not a coach-load of

Swedish female tennis players on tour, but merely a coach full of old people. Mostly old women, but Ernest took little comfort.

The coach full of old people waved as one.

'Afternoon,' they all cried with beaming smiles.

Ernest and Jon smiled fake smiles and headed for the back of the bus.

'Nice day,' an old lady next to them said as they seated themselves.

Jon nodded. 'Lovely.'

'Glorious,' the woman said. 'Couldn't get one better.'

'Yes,' Jon said, looking out the window at the dreary cloud-filled sky and back to the smiling lady.

'Where is this bus going?' Ernest asked.

'The Lord knows,' the old woman said nodding serenely.

'Good,' Ernest said, nodding. 'But, specifically?'

'I'm glad you've joined us,' the woman said, nodding her head.

Ernest turned to Jon.

'They are insane,' he whispered.

The driver of the bus seized hold of a microphone as he drove.

'Ladies and gentlemen,' he said. 'We have now amongst us two young people whom we have stopped to help on the road to redemption, just as the good Samaritan stopped. Just as Kent would stop.'

'Praise the Lord!' an old man cried.

'Thank you kindly,' the bus driver said. 'And I want to thank the Lord for giving us the opportunity to show the strength of kindness as we take this momentous journey. Perhaps we could all sing a hymn from one of Kent's albums, to help express, the shared feelings of joy we are experiencing at the glory that is awaiting us all. Hymn 14 everyone, "Not Alone".'

Music started playing from out of nowhere and the coach load of people began singing as one.

> 'As the planter plants the seeds
> That take hold in time
> So shall he bear
> The fruits divine

Not afraid
Not alone
So shall we walk
Proud and Bold
Into the warm
Embrace of Love
That is our Lord
God above!'

'Catchy,' Ernest said.

'Scary,' Jon said.

'What day is it today?' Ernest said, turning back to the old woman.

'Oh, a wonderful day,' the old lady said. 'He's known to all of us. He cares about us.'

Ernest nodded slowly. He turned to Jon.

'I think we should leave,' he said.

'There might not be another car for hours,' Jon said. 'I need to get food. Real food. These people are old. I'm sure wherever they're going there will be food.'

Ernest nodded.

'I'll have to find out where their destination is,' he said. 'What day it is.'

He stood up and delicately made his way down the aisle of the bus. He stood next to the driver, who was still smiling as he drove.

'Excuse me,' he said.

The driver turned.

'Oh, it's you,' he said.

'Yes,' Ernest said, chuckling. 'My friend and I, we were just wondering where you were going. See we have to get to Galway by Sunday.'

'Oh? You're in luck then,' the driver said.

'We are?'

The driver nodded.

'You're going to Galway?' Ernest asked.

'We're going where you're going,' the driver said.

Ernest smiled. He made his way back to the back of the bus.

'It's okay,' he said. 'Everything is okay. They're going to Galway.'

Jon nodded.

'That's good,' he said, yawning.

He put his head back on the seat and closed his eyes. Ernest stared at him for a little while. He turned and looked at the old woman, who was smiling serenely as she stared out the window. Ernest yawned. He pressed his head against the glass window and felt his eyes slowly close.

'We're here!' yelled the driver through the microphone.

The whole bus began to cheer, waking Jon and Ernest up with a start. For several seconds neither man knew where he was. They looked around the bus in total confusion as the old women and men cheered and clapped. It was only when they looked at each other that they remembered.

'Everybody out,' the driver said. 'Heaven awaits.'

Ernest stretched his arms and rubbed the sleep out of his eyes.

'Heaven?' he said.

They had to wait a full half hour before they could get off the bus, stuck as they were behind the entire coachful of decrepit and slow-moving men and women. Some of them were wheelchair-bound and had to be carried.

When Ernest and Jon finally managed to get off the bus they saw that they had arrived at a huge lone mansion in the middle of the countryside. The only feature in the entire surrounding area they could see was the small road which had brought them there.

'Something tells me this is not Galway,' Jon said.

Ernest spun around and around.

'We're nowhere,' he said in disbelief. 'Again.'

All the old people had shuffled through the doors of the mansion and were now inside. The driver was the only one from the bus remaining. He stood next to two thickset men in suits and whispered something in their ears. Jon noticed that the driver was no longer smiling. The two thickset men approached Jon and Ernest.

'Come with us,' they said.

'Where are we going?' Ernest asked.

'To meet Elijah,' the two thickset men said, picking Jon and Ernest up by the scruff of their necks and dragging them into the mansion. Jon and Ernest were brought through a huge hallway and through several large and expensively decorated rooms. Eventually they were brought into a small office area where a short, entirely bald headed man was sitting behind a black desk.

'Gentlemen,' the man said. 'Welcome.'

The two thickset men set Ernest and Jon unceremoniously down in two small chairs in front of the desk.

'I am tour director here with Silver Line,' the man said. 'My name is Elijah.'

'I am Jehovah,' Ernest said. 'This is my friend Moses.'

Elijah nodded respectfully.

'I am sorry to inform you,' Elijah said, 'that as of today I will not be allowing you to leave Silver Line Manor. If you attempt to do so, we will have to kill you. Even if you do manage to escape you will not make it anywhere on foot. We are surrounded by an extremely treacherous terrain.'

Jon stared at Elijah. He did not appear to be joking.

'What?' he said.

'It's unfortunate,' Elijah said, sighing. 'It's why we choose mostly back roads. If there are hitchers, we cannot ignore them. Our guests expect us to be charitable at all times. It's the nature of the image we are trying to put out. It's a pity, I agree, but there you are, what am I to do?'

'Why can't we leave?' Jon said. 'What are you talking about?'

'It's very delicate,' Elijah said. 'It might seem shocking if I were to blurt it out. For the moment I would ask you to trust me. You'll learn the reasons soon enough. Are you hungry?'

Ernest nodded.

'Well, you can join the guests then,' Elijah said. 'In the main dining room. In the meantime I must warn you not to try to escape. Otherwise we'll have to kill you, and we don't enjoy doing that.'

'Excuse me,' Ernest said. 'I don't mean to interrupt your threats, but, what day is it?'

'Day?' Elijah said. 'It's Saturday.'

'Of course,' Ernest said. 'Thank you.'

Elijah looked slightly confused for a moment before nodding at the two thickset men. Ernest and Jon were grabbed by the scruff of their necks and dragged through the house once again. This time they were brought to a huge pair of wooden doors and released. The two thickset men then padded and unruffled their clothes and left.

Jon and Ernest stared at the two heavy looking wooden doors. They could smell the scent of food from inside. It was impossible to resist. Ernest pushed the doors open.

Inside was a huge dining area, filled with the old people from the bus, tucking into a variety of plates and dishes. Attending every single one of the old people was a personal waiter; some waiters merely stood and watched attentively, some were serving, some were mashing up the food so that it could be swallowed by the old people with few or no workable teeth.

'What is this place?' Jon asked. 'Why was that man threatening to kill us?'

'Don't worry,' Ernest said, smiling. 'I have the entire thing figured out.'

He laughed and shook his head.

'He was very good,' he said. 'Don't you think? And the bald head, wonderful. I'm surprised he doesn't get better work.'

'What are you talking about?' Jon asked.

'Don't you get it?' Ernest said. 'This is one of those adventure weekends. You know, those murder mysteries? Where they have to guess the murderer amongst the group of hammy actors? This must be one of them. Except for old people.'

'So,' Jon said. 'That guy threatening us was an actor.'

'Exactly,' Ernest said.

'He seemed very real to me,' Jon said.

'May I show you to your seats, sirs?' a waiter, who appeared from nowhere, said.

'Gladly,' Ernest said.

'May I take your orders, sirs?' the waiter said when they were seated at their table.

'Where's the menu?' Jon asked.

'No menu, sirs,' the waiter said. 'Just order whatever you want.'

'Whatever we want?' Ernest said.

'Whatever you want,' the waiter confirmed.

'And you'll bring it?'

The waiter nodded.

'Anything?'

'Anything.'

Ernest smiled.

'So if I were to order roast duck in a strawberry jelly casing, you would bring it.'

'If that's what you wanted sir,' the waiter said, 'then that is what we would bring.'

Ernest giggled.

'So we can have anything?'

The waiter nodded.

'Anything,' he said wearily.

'Anything at all?'

The waiter nodded.

'I'll have a burger and chips,' Ernest said.

'And you, sir?' the waiter said to Jon.

Jon thought a moment.

'The same,' he said finally.

The waiter nodded and walked away, shaking his head as he did so.

'What did I tell you?' Ernest said. 'It's one of those weekends for sure. A real high class one at that. We're on a roll.'

'Isn't it funny,' Jon said, 'that when presented with unlimited options we tend to go for what we know best? We always go for what is safe rather than what we really want.'

'What are you talking about?'

'The food,' Jon said. 'We could have had anything but we chose the most common.'

'I don't know what you're talking about,' Ernest said. 'I wanted burger and chips.'

'Burger and chips,' the waiter said putting two large plates in front of Ernest and Jon.

'This is great,' Ernest said, tucking in. 'I love this place.'

Jon looked around him. Most of the old people had finished eating. A murmur of expectancy was going around the room. There was a lot of whispering. An old woman opposite Jon noticed him looking.

'He's coming,' she said, smiling. 'Isn't it wonderful?'

Jon felt extremely uneasy. He began nibbling on the food but found he had lost his appetite.

'Lovely,' Ernest said, burping loudly as he finished his meal. 'That was quite lovely. It's a long time since I have eaten so well.'

'I think we should get out of here,' Jon said. 'Something is very wrong. These people. They are too happy.'

Ernest looked around the room.

'They're old,' he said. 'They're on holiday. Old people love to go on holiday. They've probably been stuck in some crusty old home for the last fifteen years.'

'I don't know,' Jon said.

Suddenly the lights in the hall went out. A couple of the women screamed. Some people began clapping. All at once a spotlight came on at the far end of the hall.

'Ladies and gentleman,' a voice said over a speaker. 'The man you'd all die for: Kent O'Devlin!'

The spotlight began swinging around the room. Every time it stopped, there were gasps from the audience, but still there was no sign of anyone but the delighted old people.

The spotlight continued to veer around the the room tantalisingly until finally it stopped, on a podgy young man in a tuxedo, with a huge toothy smile and perfectly bouffanted hair. He was standing with a microphone in his hand and when the gathering saw him they began cheering ecstatically. Old women began crying. Old men cheered 'Kent! Kent! Kent!'

'I know him,' Ernest said. 'My gran used to love him.'

With the smallest of movements Kent motioned the crowd to

hush. He swept the entire gathering with his eyes, before smiling his huge smile again, and launching into a song. A band appeared out of nowhere to back him up. The place erupted in applause as Kent sang the first few words.

> 'Honey darling, why aren't you mine?
> Sugar sweetheart, I love you so
> And if you'll only
> Light up my life
> I won't stop trying
> My heart is dying
> But I won't . . . .stop trying
>
> Dearest beauty, where did I go wrong?
> Lovely lady, if you'd only say
> How I could
> Relight that loving light
> I won't stop trying
> My heart is dying
> But I won't . . . stop trying
>
> Oh my baby . . . '

The song seemed, to Ernest and Jon, to last forever, each verse more sickly sweet than the last. Choruses were placed randomly throughout, with no obvious sense or purpose. All delivered with that awful toothy smile and the occasional corny wink.

When the first song ended, the first old woman collapsed. Two large men in white coats immediately moved in to remove her. As the second song went on several more women and a few men collapsed. By the time the third song had ended a significant number of women and men had been carried out of the room.

'What's going on?' Jon asked, above the noise of the singing.

Ernest shrugged.

'They're swooning,' he replied.

An old woman next to Jon stood up, cried out 'Kent!' in a shriek of pleasure and collapsed onto Jon's shoulder. Jon sat there for a few moments not wishing to disturb the woman and not knowing what to do. He turned and looked at her wide open mouth and unseeing eyes.

'Ahh!' he yelled, shrinking away from the woman.

She fell from his shoulder onto the ground with a harsh crack and her jaw scattered into bloody pieces across the wooden floor.

'Ahhh!' Jon screamed again. 'She's dead.'

Ernest could not speak. He stared from the old woman's limp body to the rest of the old people around the rooms, who were continuing to collapse at an alarming rate. Immediately Ernest thought of the food.

'It's poisoned,' he said. 'Oh my God, we're going to die.'

Meanwhile Kent was really hotting up his performance. He loosened the bow tie on his tux, which sent four more women to their graves, and kicked into another soft sickly romantic song. By the end of the sixth and final song there was nobody but Ernest and Jon left in the room. Kent did not seem to notice and continued on until the end of the song, pausing afterwards, in a victorious pose, for the applause that did not come.

The lights in the hall suddenly came back on. Kent wiped the sweat from his forehead as Elijah walked into the room flanked by the two suited thickset men.

'Wonderful,' Elijah said to Kent. 'Wonderful, as always.'

Kent nodded.

'They were a good bunch, God bless them,' he said in a soft accent. 'Sure they made it easy for me.'

'I don't think we could have had more satisfied customers yet,' Elijah said, patting Kent on the back.

Kent, noticing them for the first time, looked curiously over at Jon and Ernest.

'Oh, these are a couple of hitchhikers we picked up,' Elijah explained. 'Unfortunate, but there you are. We have to be seen to be charitable.'

Kent nodded, and wiped his face with a towel.

'What's going on?' Ernest asked. 'What have you done? It's the food isn't it? You've poisoned the food.'

Elijah and Kent chuckled a little to themselves as they passed knowing glances.

'Nobody poisoned you,' Elijah said. 'Nobody poisoned anybody. All we did was help things along the way. Besides, even if you got a dosage, it wouldn't have been nearly enough to produce any effects in men your age.'

'What dosage?' Jon said. 'What did you give these people?'

'Just a little cardiac sedative,' Elijah said. 'Digitalis, they call it. It's a very beneficial drug, derived from the foxglove plant. In small doses, it can be quite effective against heart disease. In larger doses . . . it can help induce them.'

Jon shook his head in disbelief.

'You murdered all these people,' he said. 'Hundreds of people. People who thought they were here for a holiday.'

Elijah chuckled a little more. Kent shook his head. He seemed to be growing quite agitated. 'You don't understand,' he said.

'What are you going to do with us?' Ernest said. 'Look, I promise you, we won't tell a soul. They were old. They were going to die soon anyway.'

'Exactly,' Elijah said. 'But I'm afraid you can't leave. You'll, have to stay, indefinitely, I'm afraid. We can't risk news of our business getting out. You'll be given duties. A handsome pay. In a few years, who knows?'

Ernest took the musket from his pocket and pointed it at Elijah.

'Don't move,' he instructed.

Elijah grinned.

'I see you collect antiques,' he said.

'It fires well enough,' Ernest said.

Elijah nodded.

'Anybody moves,' Ernest said, 'and I'll kill them.'

Kent, who had been growing more and more agitated, finally could contain himself no longer.

'You don't understand,' he said. 'We're not murdering anybody. I love my fans.'

'Shut up,' Ernest said. 'God, I hate you. My gran used to insist on watching you whenever you were on the telly.'

'Listen to me,' Kent said. 'These old people . . . It's what they wanted. They wanted it this way.'

Ernest nodded.

'I see,' he said.

'No,' Kent said, taking a step closer. 'No, you don't. You have to understand, these people you saw here, they are my fanbase. I love them and they love me. I know I'm not liked particularly by the young. I know you find my music old fashioned and boring, but I don't care. I fill a gap in these people's lives. That's important to me. I can do something for the older population that I could not do for any other age group. I can make them feel young again. Make them remember better times.

'It started with a letter. Anne from Letterkenny. She was a darling woman. She bought every one of my records. Confined to a wheelchair she was. Riddled with arthritis. She suffered terribly. She began writing to me. I try and read all the letters. There's so many of them. But I was so struck by what Anne told me that I found myself riveted.

'She had led quite a life, dear Anne. She was, in her time, a nurse in the Second World War, a dancer in Paris, a singer in Berlin, and an actress in Dublin. The stories she wrote to me about her life! They were wonderful. You could see how vivid her life had been. How exciting.

'Anyway, she wrote that she had settled down eventually, and married a man from Letterkenny, and had an army full of kids. She was a good mother. Always there for her children. One by one though, as they grew older, the children began to move out of home, as all kids do.

'Eventually Anne's husband died, leaving her alone in the house. It was then the arthritis she suffered from got to its worst. She couldn't cope. She had thought, though, having so many kids, she wouldn't have a problem. They would look after her. But they didn't. They weren't interested. They were all too busy with their own lives. Nobody wanted a fussy old wheelchair-bound woman, full of stories and constant reminiscence.

'So Anne was put into a home, and because none of the kids were terribly wealthy or terribly generous, it was a cheap home. A home where she was treated very badly by the undertrained and underqualified staff.

'It was at this point that dear Anne wrote me the letter, and in it she told me all of this, and at the very end she told me something that moved me very much indeed. She told me the one and only comfort in life that she had left, this woman, this woman who had lived a life fuller than you or I could possibly imagine, was to listen to my records. She said that listening to me singing all those old songs, she forgot that she was an old woman, bound to a wheelchair, living in an old folks' home. She forgot everything. She even forgot that she was in pain.

'She said, in her letter, how she would like nothing more than to pass away while listening to one of my records, so that she could at least have a few moments of peace and happiness at the end of her life.

'So, a little while later, I arrived at the hospital, determined to meet the woman who had sent me this wonderful letter, and do you know, she was gone. Passed away just that morning. And I'll never forget, I walked by her room, the room in which she had died, and I saw her kids in there. There was an entire room full of her grown-up children. They were arguing, you see. They were arguing over who was entitled to what in the will.

'I don't mind telling you it made me angry. It made me very angry. They had probably never even known the woman. Not like I knew her from that one letter. If they did, they couldn't possibly have treated her the way they did.

'So, from that day, I decided I would offer a service to all who wanted it. All the old, the sick, the dying, any of my fans who wished to, could come here, to this hotel, and I would play for them in their final moments. To try and offer some peace, some contentment, so that they could forget themselves a little, before they passed on.'

There was a long respectful silence in the room. Elijah wiped a tear away from his eye.

'But it's murder,' Jon said. 'You kill them. Poison them.'

'No,' Kent said. 'These people are old. They are either dying or in constant pain. Most would not last long anyway. They know what's going to happen. They sign a contract. You saw them. You were here. Did they seem unhappy to you? Did they seem to be here against their will?'

Jon had no answer.

'What do you get out of this?' Ernest asked. 'How much money do you get out of these people?'

'That's not important,' Kent said, bristling.

'Sure,' Ernest said. 'You're as greedy as those kids were.'

'I won't have you talking to Kent that way,' Elijah said, placing a protective arm around him. 'I arrange the financial side of things. It has nothing to do with Kent. And yes, we charge for the service. So that we can maintain it. How do you think we pay for the staff? The buses? This place itself? It costs a lot of money.

'What we offer our clients is simple. They come here and whatever assets they have, in effect their will, are signed over to us. No matter how big or how small. Some people own nothing more than a few letters and a box of worthless jewellery. Some are quite wealthy. We do not distinguish.'

'So you take them for everything they have?' Ernest said.

Elijah shook his head.

'You obviously weren't listening,' he said. 'Didn't you hear what Kent said? You are typical. Typical young. Not knowing or caring anything about anyone but yourselves. If you had been listening, you might have understood our policy. You see, when people get to this age, when they are shunted off to homes by their relatives in this uncaring society, all they are to those relatives is walking inheritances. Even while they are alive, disputes arise over who is to have what.

'Now, these people, in gratitude to someone who finally treats them like human beings, choose to give us their assets rather than hand them over to their greedy relatives. What is so wrong with that? How many wills cause rifts in families that never heal? When they come here, with their money, they ensure that we are maintained and that, alone, is good enough for most of these people.'

Ernest nodded.

'If you're all so bloody charitable,' he said, 'why is it that you've threatened to kill us if we leave?'

'Because,' Elijah said, 'we cannot let word of what is happening here escape. If it did, we would be shut down and it is our moral responsibility to maintain Silver Line Tours.'

'We wouldn't tell,' Ernest said. 'Who'd believe us?'

'We cannot take the risk,' Elijah said, shaking his head sadly.

'You'll have to,' Ernest said, backing out of the room.

Jon and Ernest got to the large doors of the dining room.

'You won't get far on foot,' Elijah said. 'There is nothing out there. You should stay. We treat our staff very well.'

'If anyone tries to follow us,' Ernest said. 'I will not hesitate to shoot them.'

With that Ernest and Jon turned around and ran out of the building as fast as their short legs would carry them.

They ran for miles through mucky fields, their legs growing heavier with each step. In the distance they could still make out the house behind them.

'They don't seem to be following,' Ernest said, through gasping breaths.

Jon nodded. They walked on through the brown muddy fields as, in the distance, the sun began to set over the horizon. They came to an area filled with a firmer, deep brown substance on the ground.

'What is it?' Ernest asked,

'Bog,' Jon said. 'We are walking on bog.'

A thick mist began drifting in from the horizon with the darkness of night so that soon both men could not see where they walked. They trundled on, though their legs felt like sacks of coal, and they could barely stand upright.

'When will it end?' Ernest asked after several hours of walking through the bog.

Jon chose not to answer. He was considering a strange phenomenon. He had the vague feeling of sinking. With each step he took he was convinced it was lower than the next. Eventually, he could not move his legs at all. At precisely the same time, Ernest was experiencing the same phenomenon. For a few silent seconds both men struggled to remove their feet from the grasping earth.

'What's happening?' Ernest said as he struggled.

'I think we're sinking,' Jon said.

As if by confirmation, both men sank down in the earth to their knees. Ernest began screaming.

'Get me out!' he said. 'For God's sake I'm sinking!'

'So am I,' Jon pointed out.

For a long while both men continued to struggle but only succeeded in slipping further into the soft but thick substance below them.

'Don't struggle,' Jon said, finally. 'It's worse when you struggle. You sink quicker.'

'What am I supposed to do?' Ernest said. 'How are we supposed to get out if we don't struggle?'

'I don't know,' Jon said. 'But we will die very quickly if we continue to move.'

This was enough for Ernest. He stopped struggling.

'I suppose this is what he meant,' Jon said, 'by not getting far.'

Both men stood very still and began sinking at a slower rate.

'What is it?' Ernest asked. 'I didn't think we had quicksand in Ireland.'

'We don't,' Jon said. 'I don't know. Perhaps this is the stage in bogs before they become solid. I don't know.'

Neither men spoke for a long time. They stood in silence and tried to keep themselves warm from the freezing night as, with every hour, they sank a little further into the muck.

'I used to hate those movies,' Ernest said, finally breaking the silence. 'Those jungle movies. The American studios loved them for a short while. Where all those English and American hunters would go into the jungles to shoot some game or find some lost native treasure, or those awful Tarzan films. My least favourite thing was the quicksand parts. I hated them. I hated watching them. The looks on the men's faces as they realised their predicaments. That final lingering shot of the single pitiful hand erect, as it slipped into the sand. I don't want to die like this.'

Jon and Ernest were now immersed to their waists.

'We've got to do something,' Ernest said desperately.

'What do you propose?' Jon asked.

'What's the matter with you?' Ernest said. 'How can you be so calm? In a few minutes we'll be breathing solid muck. We'll be alive beneath this surface, for minutes probably, minutes that will seem like years.'

Jon nodded.

'It could be worse,' he said.

'How?'

Jon shrugged.

'When you have come as close to death as I have, you gain a new perspective,' he said. 'It's not such a terrible thing. I can understand those people in that place. Being in hospital. Seeing so many old people treated like they were fools. Patronised. Visited by impatient relatives. It's not such a wonderful thing, life.'

'You're insane,' Ernest said, beginning to flail his arms about the place wildly. 'I'm getting out of here.'

He only succeeded in slipping deeper into the soft muck. He was now immersed almost to his neck.

'Oh God!' he said. 'What in fuck's name have I done to deserve this? You're some miserable prick, you know that? How many prayers have I prayed to you? How many favours have I asked for? Ever since I was old enough it's been rammed down my throat by a succession of mean-spirited priests that if I want something, the first thing I should do is pray. Yet how many times have you actually done something for me? How many times have you actually come up with the goods? It's a pretty shitty ratio, I know that much for sure. Do you hear me? You're an incompetent bastard!'

'I thought you didn't believe in God,' Jon said quietly.

'I don't know what I believe,' Ernest said as his chin sank into the muck. 'I just like having somebody to shout at. It's good for the spirit.

'Perhaps you're right. Perhaps death won't be so bad after all. I mean, there are worse things than death. Muzak for instance, and chat shows. I hope there's no hell. That's been a consistent fear of mine. Those bastard priests again. I mean, what sort of a sick God would condemn someone to constant suffering?'

'I don't know,' Jon said. 'But considering your last speech perhaps it would be for the best if He did not exist.'

Ernest tried to nod. It sent him further into the ground. His nose stuck out just above the muck. Tears began welling up in his eyes.

'Try not to struggle,' was all Jon could think to say as he saw his friend's head sink below the mud.

Jon slipped into the mud up to his neck. He considered his life as a whole and began to grow quite depressed. Fairly meaningless, he thought, after all. He'd been such a stupid teenager, so bumbling and awkward. Shouting about everything but knowing nothing. He would have liked a little more time, he thought, as he sank up to his chin. He had felt, since the hospital, that he was appreciating life for the first time. Now it would be too late.

'Grab hold of this,' a sturdy voice instructed.

A thick rope was thrown an inch in front of Jon's face. He raised his heavy hands out of the muck and grabbed the rope. In a few seconds he was pulled free of the sinking mud. He lay on the turf, breathing heavily for a few seconds before looking up. He saw that he was lying beside a large caravan, of the type normally attached to a car. This one, however, was attached to two horses.

'Are you alive then?' a very large man, with a huge red face asked, crouching over him.

'My friend,' Jon said. 'He's in there.'

The large man nodded. He walked quickly over to one of the horses and tied one end of a rope onto it. He then tied the other end round his wide stomach and, without a pause, jumped into the sinking mud. Jon watched as the large man sank below the surface almost immediately.

For what felt like a long time, but could have only been a matter of seconds, there was total silence as Jon watched. The mud did not stir or move. Then there was a great tug on the rope, and the horse that it was attached to began shifting and complaining noisily. A number of seconds later, the large man emerged with a limp body covered entirely in muck in one arm.

He flopped onto the turf and laid Ernest's body out on its stomach. Jon stared at Ernest and felt sure he was dead. The large man flipped Ernest onto his back and began checking him for signs of life. He put his large head onto Ernest's chest to listen for a heartbeat. He turned to Jon a moment later and shook his head sadly.

'I don't think he made it,' he said quietly.

Jon nodded.

'You did your best,' he said.

Ernest began coughing. He sat up and coughed loudly and spit mud onto the earth.

'It's a miracle,' the large man said.

Ernest continued to cough for a few seconds more after which he paused briefly to stare from the large man to Jon, and then collapsed back onto the turf. The large man hurried over and checked for a heartbeat again.

'It's there,' he said, giggling slightly. 'It's there all right. Do you want to hear?'

Jon shook his head.

'Thank you,' he said. 'We'll have to get him to a hospital.'

The large man nodded.

'I am on my way to Clonmeg, I will deliver the pair of you,' he said.

They put Ernest gently in the back of the large man's caravan. Just as Jon was about to leave the caravan he felt Ernest grab his arm and turned.

'I saw things,' Ernest said, moving his head as close to Jon's as possible. 'Beneath the mud.'

Jon nodded.

'What sort of things?' he asked.

Ernest shook his head and looked into some far-off place.

'Lights,' he said, and closed his eyes.

Jon left Ernest sleeping and joined the large man, who was sitting on top of the caravan, holding the reins of the horses in both hands. He gave a shake of the reins and the horses started to move, dragging the caravan bumpily along the turf.

In the distance, the sun was beginning to emerge and the morning was filled with a dull expectant light.

'My name is McArthur,' the large man said.

'Jon,' Jon said. 'His name is Ernest.'

McArthur nodded.

'Did you see anything?' Jon asked, as the caravan trundled across the bog. 'While you were down there?'

'What sort of thing?' McArthur asked.

'I don't know,' Jon said. 'Lights.'

McArthur shook his head.

'I can't say I did,' he said. 'But I cannot see such things as clearly as I used to. It's possible. It's possible there were lights. I've seen some strange things across these bogs.

'You are very lucky, in fact, I was here at all. It's not often I cross these bogs, these days. I know the land well enough but it is still treacherous. They have many pools of mud such as the ones you and your friend succumbed to. They come with the rain and sometimes they are as big as lakes. You have to know how to read the horses, because the horses know the land. I can tell now, just by holding these reins, whether the horses are happy or not to cross a stretch of land.

'Still, 'tis treacherous enough, and I would not be crossing them, only I am late as it is and I must make it in time for the horse fair. I need to be there early because all the good horses go within a few minutes. There is little point in me going if I'm to be late, and I know of no quicker way than across these bogs.'

'I've never seen a horse-drawn caravan before,' Jon said.

'No,' McArthur said. 'No, they are not common. I don't know why. You don't need insurance for a horse. I'd trust a horse over a car any day now. And you don't need to buy them petrol. All you need is a field of grass and there's plenty of that around here, although you have to watch out for some of them farmers because they're not too cheerful, those people. Full of complaints, they are. They're constantly being harassed, they maintain, by everything and anything, from the birds to the bees to men like me.'

In a couple of hours of riding across the bogs, they made it to the small town of Clonmeg. Jon got down off the caravan and stepped inside to check on Ernest.

He was sitting up, with his eyes wide open when Jon entered.

'How are you feeling?' Jon asked him.

Ernest looked at him for a long time, as if the question had been asked in some unknown language.

'Where is my manuscript?' he asked suddenly.

Jon showed him the bag he carried on his shoulder.

'I managed to retrieve it,' he said. 'It's undamaged.'

Ernest nodded vaguely.

'Thank you,' he said. 'Now, we must hurry, because time is running thin. If I have learnt one thing from my experience it is to rush, because who knows when you'll fall into a pile of mud and sink forevermore.'

Ernest stood up and jumped out of the caravan. Jon rushed out after him. McArthur was busy tying the horses to a tree when Ernest and Jon approached him.

'I just wanted to give you my heartfelt thanks,' Ernest said, shaking McArthur's hand.

'You are very welcome,' McArthur said. 'Now I must hurry and buy a horse.'

With that McArthur rushed off down the street.

'He has the right idea,' Ernest said, beginning to walk off.

'We have to go hospital,' Jon said. 'You need to be checked.'

'Nonsense,' Ernest said. 'I feel fit as a fiddle.'

Jon nodded resignedly and the pair walked down the street for a while in silence.

'Do you remember anything?' Jon asked. 'About what happened?'

'Not a thing,' Ernest said. 'Quite relieved to be honest. I can't imagine it could have been a pleasant experience. I remember being dragged out. And of having difficulty breathing for several moments. Why don't we talk about something else?'

'What about lights?' Jon asked.

'Lights?'

'You don't remember seeing lights?'

'I wasn't knocked out. Why would I see lights?'

'Never mind,' Jon said.

'Perhaps there's a bus,' Ernest said. 'To Galway. We have money. That should be our next course of action. Either that or steal a car.'

'We'll look for a bus,' Jon said.

After some time wandering around the town in circles, they managed to find the small, airy building that was the town's bus station. Ernest approached a gruff looking old man, sitting behind the counter smoking a pipe.

'Do you have a bus to Galway?' he asked him.

The man nodded once and only once, so that Ernest was not sure whether it was a greeting or a confirmation.

'Bus to Galway?' he repeated.

'Yes,' the man said impatiently. 'That's what I just said, isn't it?'

'Of course,' Ernest said. 'How much?'

'Hadn't we better find out when first?' Jon said.

'When?' Ernest asked.

'Wednesday,' the old man said, looking down in consternation at his pipe which had gone out.

'What about today?' Ernest said, but the old man was not listening.

He was concentrating entirely on relighting his pipe. He lit a match with a shaking hand and held it to the tobacco, while puffing feverishly, but to no avail.

'Any buses today?' Ernest asked again.

But the old man would not listen. It was as if he would only answer questions while his pipe was lit. After several minutes and several matches he managed to get his pipe lit. He turned immediately to Ernest when he did so.

'Wednesday,' he said. 'Wednesday nine am. This being a Sunday, there is no chance.'

Ernest nodded. He turned to Jon.

'We'll just have to steal a car then,' he said.

'We could hitch,' Jon said.

'Didn't you hear him? It's Sunday. We have until tomorrow morning to get there.'

'It is only about an hour's drive,' Jon pointed out. 'If you hadn't've brought us onto that country lane we would have arrived two days ago.'

'I don't care,' Ernest said. 'It was worth it. You'll appreciate the

149

money all the more now. You have to go through hardship for genuine appreciation.'

They found a suitable corner on the road out of town and began thumbing for a lift. Two hours later, they were no closer to Galway. Not one car would stop for them. The closest they came was when a white van stopped, pulled down the window, and then took off as soon as the occupants got a good look at them.

'I think I know why,' Jon said, looking Ernest up and down. 'I don't think we're going to get a ride.'

'Why not?' Ernest asked.

'We are covered in dry mud,' Jon pointed out.

Ernest and Jon stared at their reflections in the window of an old cottage on the outskirts of town. Ernest, who had been completely immersed in the mud, looked particularly strange. The mud had set around his body in thick layers and his hair jutted out in pointed mats so that he looked like some kind of giant punk chocolate sculpture.

'We are not going to get a lift,' Ernest said, staring at himself.

'No,' Jon agreed.

They began walking back into town.

'We need a mode of transportation,' Ernest said. 'We must get underway.'

As soon as they came back into town they saw a small poster. It read: *Clonmeg: Horse Fair Today: Murphy's Square.*

'Of course,' Ernest said.

'No,' Jon said.

But Ernest was not listening. He began following the small arrows on the bottom of each poster, pointing towards Murphy's Square.

'We can't go to Galway on horses,' Jon reasoned.

'Why not?'

'We don't know how.'

'I've seen them on TV,' Ernest said. 'I've seen westerns. How hard can it be? You get up there, say Giddeeup, and off you go.'

'No,' Jon said. 'No. They are huge things. And smelly. And can be uncooperative.'

Ernest was not listening. He was thinking of riding off into the sunset on a great white horse. He was thinking of holding up carriages with a pair of silver guns and tipping his hat to goodlooking ladies who blew kisses at him while handing over jewellery.

They walked to the outskirts of the town, and finally came to a sign that read: *Murphy's Square: You have arrived.* A huge horse appeared from nowhere, as if by way of confirmation. There was a young boy on its saddleless back, clutching the horse's unkempt mane. The boy, who could not have been much older than five, stared at Ernest and Jon wordlessly as he rode across the square and suddenly the whole place was full of horses and saddleless riders.

'Oh dear,' Jon said.

Ernest was smiling as he watched the horses. In the corner a bidding war was going on between several men, conducted by a man with a red face in a tweed cap, over a huge black horse with cold humourless eyes.

'Oh dear,' Jon said.

'What's the matter?' Ernest said impatiently.

Jon shook his head.

'I didn't think,' he said.

'Didn't think? Talk English. Form sentences.'

Jon began slowly backing out of the square.

'We have to get out of here,' he said.

'What? We're buying a horse,' Ernest said.

'Ernest!' Jon said. 'These people. They're travellers.'

Ernest's smile slowly faded. He looked around the square. Sure enough, beside the many horses, were a variety of caravans and beat-up old cars. Small skinny children ran wild between the horses' legs. Huge burly men argued amongst themselves in small thick circles. And at the far end of the square was the small boy from whom Ernest had stolen the Fisher Price guitar.

'Oh dear,' Ernest said, and began backing away.

McArthur appeared from out of nowhere.

'Men!' he said, to Jon and Ernest. 'I see you've found your way. I am pleased to say I have the finest horse in the fair already. It'll be a sad thing to let dear Jenny, my oldest horse, go, but I have it organised for her to spend her last few years in a good field, with a fine stud as company.'

Ernest and Jon smiled humourless smiles and continued to back away.

'Where are you off to?' McArthur asked. 'The fun has only just begun. Stay for a drink. I will introduce you to a man I know. A wise old man. He'll know about these lights you saw. He's sure to.'

McArthur began hollering at an old man with a long beard to approach. He had such a deep booming voice that soon the whole square full of people was looking over, and everyone froze at once as they saw Ernest and Jon. Ernest and Jon froze too.

'The murderers,' the old man cried out. 'Those are the men who murdered our king.'

The entire crowd, as one, took a step closer to Ernest and Jon. Ernest and Jon looked at each other for the briefest of seconds before turning and running in the opposite direction.

Before they knew what was happening they were running on air. They ran as fast as they could but they did not seem to be making any progress. Ernest turned around and saw that McArthur was holding the pair of them by the backs of their collars, one in each hand.

'I am sorry, men,' he said. 'But this matter is of very grave importance and it will need to be cleared up.'

The crowd surged around Ernest and Jon, as they were being held by McArthur. They closed in with bats and sticks and stones.

'Kill them,' they called out. 'Beat their heads in.'

'Well done, McArthur,' the elder said. 'Now tear them apart.'

'Wait,' McArthur said. 'Keep back now. If these are the men you say they will surely die, but I must be convinced.'

'They're the men all right,' the elder said. 'Bring out young Jackie Sullivan.'

The small boy from whom Ernest stole the guitar was led to the front of the crowd. The traveller elder went over to him and lent down. Jackie whispered into the old man's ear and the old man nodded.

'It's them,' he said. 'He says they are muddier than he remembers, but it's them.'

The crowd began growling and moving forward.

'Hold it,' McArthur instructed. 'Am I right in saying that whosoever catches these men is to become king?'

The elder nodded.

'Well, if I'm king, I'll decide how they die,' he said. 'And it won't be by public beating.'

'What's wrong with public beating?' a large man said, stepping out of the crowd.

There were murmurs of approval amongst the crowd.

'We're here in this square to sell and buy horses,' McArthur said, 'and that's what we'll do.'

'You're no king,' the second man repeated. 'I demand the right of contest. I deserve to avenge my brother.'

'You'll do as I say, Tully,' McArthur said.

'The rule was, whosoever kills these men is king,' Tully said. 'All this man has done is catch them. Any one of us could have done that. It's not the right way to decide who's king. We should have a contest.'

'A challenge has been made,' the elder said. 'Regardless of what happens now, it will need to be addressed. McArthur, are you willing to fight?'

McArthur nodded.

'Let's get this over with,' he said

He threw Ernest and Jon into the clutches of a group of men to the side and began rolling up his sleeves. Tully did the same. The crowd circled around the two men and began cheering for their man of preference.

'Go on Tully! Kill the beggar.'

'McArthur will destroy him!'

McArthur said nothing. He watched Tully's eyes and stood quite still and waited. Tully danced around the stationary figure, waiting for McArthur to make a move. When he saw he was not going to, he rushed in and swung his right fist at McArthur's chin. The next thing he knew, he was being punched hard in the stomach. He stumbled to the ground, coughing, and McArthur's supporters let out a great cheer.

When he looked up, McArthur was still standing in the same position, quite rigid, as if he had not moved at all. Tully ran screaming with rage at him and managed to hit him once in the face but only succeeded in leaving himself open for two heavy blows back that once again sent him reeling. He spat blood onto the floor and tried to shake away the blurred vision. He turned back round to McArthur and saw the crowd was no longer cheering or baying for either man's blood.

Tully felt his right cheek and winced in pain. He realised he must look in some state. Knowing he had lost already he stumbled over to McArthur and swung one last desperate punch. McArthur ducked the fist easily and hit Tully squarely in the chin, knocking him backwards onto the ground, where he lay unmoving.

The crowd once again cheered and several men went over to congratulate McArthur. The elder examined Tully briefly, pronouncing him unconscious before walking over to McArthur.

'McArthur is now King,' he said. 'It is decided.'

McArthur went over to Ernest and Jon and grabbed them by the collars.

'Thank you,' Ernest said. 'We're very grateful. It was all a misunderstanding, you see.'

'We won't kill them here, like ruffians,' McArthur said, addressing the crowd. 'This square has seen enough violence for one day and, after all, it is supposed to be a place of business. Take these men out to that field over there and gather wood for a bonfire,' McArthur instructed. 'If they are to be killed for killing our king, then their deaths should fit the crime. Burning at the stake.'

'What?' Ernest said. 'You can't be serious. We're innocent.'

A huge cheer went up amongst the travellers.

'Hail the king,' the crowd began shouting.

Ernest and Jon were swept up by the crowd and brought to the field. In no time at all, enough wood was gathered for a huge bonfire, and Ernest and Jon were tied to the very top of the mass of branches.

There was a freezing cold wind blowing at their high altitude and Ernest and Jon began to shiver. The crowd gathered round them in fevered excitement.

'We shall make this quick,' McArthur said. 'Because we have horses to sell. Do you have any last words?'

'Yes,' Jon said, through chattering teeth. 'Yes, I would like to say something. I would like to apologise and . . . and to say that, though it is true my friend and I were unkind to one amongst you, we did steal from the young boy, we did not mean to kill anyone. We were just protecting ourselves, from pain or death, as any reasonable person would.'

There were cries of derision from below.

'Silence,' McArthur called. 'While I am king we shall have respect for all the living. This man seems an honest sort. Having met and talked with him, I believe him to be corrupted by the other. By all accounts, it was the other who stole from Jackie, and who probably killed our king. I recommend amnesty for him. Does anyone object?'

There was a respectful silence.

'Cut him down,' McArthur yelled.

Two young boys scurried up the bonfire and cut Jon's ropes. Ernest turned to him.

'Don't go,' he said. 'I have a terrible fear of being burned alive.'

Jon turned away and shimmied down the bonfire. McArthur nodded to him briefly before turning his attention back to Ernest.

'Having saved your life once today,' he said. 'I don't feel as bad taking it away. You are, by all accounts, a morally devious and questionable character. You steal, and shirk, and cheat your way through life and, had I leave you drown in mud, it would have been a more fitting death.'

McArthur lit a clutch of tightly wound sticks in his right hand and prepared to light the bonfire.

'Wait,' Jon said. 'He didn't do anything but protect himself. It's not his fault he's the way he is. He has awful parents. Nothing has gone right for him.'

'You had better stay out of things that don't concern you,' McArthur said. 'This is strictly a traveller matter. We have been abused by men like this for centuries. Discriminated against.

Hunted like animals. Beaten and murdered. We've had our food stolen and our homes wrecked. We are welcome nowhere. All we have is our tradition, a tradition mocked and ridiculed by the city folk and the country farmers alike. This man interfered with tradition. He showed a blatant lack of respect. He killed our king. His death will be a marker. A marker that we will not take our treatment lying down. Not while I'm king.'

The sticks had gone out while McArthur was talking and he lit them again.

'However,' McArthur said. 'he is a human being and I will afford him the right of a condemned man. Do you have any brief last words?'

Ernest thought a moment.

'I should like to read a poem,' he said. 'From my manuscript.'

McArthur nodded.

'Very well,' he said.

'I'll need my hands freed,' Ernest said.

McArthur nodded and the two boys scurried up the bonfire to free Ernest's hands. Ernest reached into his bag and took out his battered muddy manuscript as the two boys scurried back down the bonfire.

'It is a poem about death,' Ernest said.

McArthur nodded.

'Hurry it up,' he said as his torch went out again. 'We have horses and money to be exchanged.'

Ernest cleared his throat. He looked up into the grey expanse of sky and read:

'funeral

>It was cold in the graveyard
>I bowed my head but did not pray
>The priest wore a grey anorak
>My father had never seen his father's grave before
>Or at least, he could not remember.

I saw my grandmother lying in a box
From the inside
Cold fingers on dark wood.

We were all together once again
As a family
But she could not ask her questions
And we could not patiently repeat them when she
        didn't hear
And we could not smile at her bad jokes
And she could not laugh out loud at ours.

I thought about the priest
As I watched him meekly pray
Of how hard he must try to look serious
And how inside he must long to scream or laugh
Or dance about the grave.

There was a long silence
After the priest stopped praying
Is that it? My father finally asked
And he was told it was.
Is that it? I asked my brother
And he answered me it was.
Is that it?
Came a voice from the coffin
But we were already gone.'

Ernest stared down at the group below him. Wails of sorrow
came from various members of the crowd. Almost every one of
them was crying. Even McArthur had his own handkerchief out
and was blowing his nose loudly.

'I had a granny recently passed away,' he said, through the tears.
'It all came back in a flood.'

He blew his nose again loudly and wiped away the tears. He
cleared his throat and tried to compose himself.

'We cannot kill this man,' he called to the gathering. 'This man is a poet, a poet of great depth and originality. The travellers appreciate this great art more than most. We have a great tradition of poetry and storytelling. I have heard some of the finest poets in Ireland and this man ranks highly amongst them. If we were to kill him it would go against all moral obligations we have, and rid the world of a great artist, something I myself could not live with. We must let him go.'

A great cheer went up. Ernest was cut down from the bonfire and held aloft on the shoulders of the crowd as they travelled back to the square in celebration.

6. The Dead Are Laughing

'You must stay for the meal tonight,' McArthur said to Ernest and Jon, when the others had resumed the horse-fair trading.

'We would love to,' Ernest said, 'but we have no time. We must get to Galway. We have very important business.'

'I am sorry,' McArthur said, 'about those things I said. If I had known you were an artist I might have been more understanding.'

'Tosh,' Ernest said.

'How are you travelling to Galway?' McArthur asked.

'We had hoped to buy a horse,' Ernest said.

'Buy?' McArthur said. 'We couldn't allow that. We must give you a horse for your pains. We cannot have you leave the travellers' fair, having nearly met your deaths at our own hands, without some kind of recompense.'

'What about the king?' Ernest said. 'Aren't you angry?'

'Ah, he wasn't too popular in any case,' McArthur said. 'Secretly a lot of people would have liked to shake your hand. But tradition is tradition.'

McArthur brought a giant grey horse, the colour of stone walls, over to Ernest and Jon.

'This is one of the finest horses here,' he said. 'I had chosen this one for my caravan, but I think it is the least we could do.'

'Thank you,' Ernest said. 'We are very grateful.'

Ernest and Jon stared at the giant horse for a long time.

'No saddle,' Jon observed.

Ernest nodded.

'What's the problem?' McArthur said. 'You don't need saddles now. That's just a bunch of pollycock. Just grab hold of the mane.'

'Of course,' Ernest said.

Ernest and Jon continued to stare at the horse.

'How do we eh . . . how do we get up there?' Ernest asked.

Jon shrugged. McArthur sighed.

'I will give you a boot up,' he said, cupping his hands together.

'Good,' Ernest said, nodding his head but not moving.

'Hurry up,' McArthur said.

'You don't have a car?' Ernest asked.

'Your foot,' McArthur instructed. 'In here.'

Ernest put his foot on McArthur's hands and was lifted up onto the horse. Jon did the same and sat behind Ernest. The horse exhaled loudly as they sat into him and shifted backwards and forwards.

'Geeyup,' Ernest said.

The horse remained still.

'It doesn't appear to understand,' Jon observed.

'Go!' Ernest shouted.

'You have to kick him,' McArthur said.

'Kick him?' Ernest said. 'Won't he be angry?'

'Kick him.'

Ernest tapped the horse with his foot.

'Kick, man. You must tell him who is boss.'

Ernest looked down at the powerful beast below him.

'He is,' he said.

McArthur sighed.

'I will give you a hand,' he said and slapped the horse hard on its rump.

The horse screamed, reared up on its hind legs and went galloping off through the streets of Clonmeg. Ernest grabbed hold of the horse's mane tightly and Jon grabbed hold of Ernest's jumper.

'Good luck!'McArthur called out. 'If ever you need a favour from the travellers you only have to mention my name!'

The horse sped through the main street of Clonmeg and directly into a minor traffic jam ahead.

'Whoah,' Ernest called out.

But the horse did not slow down. Instead it cleared the first car by jumping directly over it and the second by climbing onto its hood. After jumping two more cars they were clear of the traffic jam and, in a few moments, the town.

'How do you steer this thing?' Ernest asked, as they galloped furiously along the road out of the town.

'I have no idea,' Jon said. 'Try pulling its mane.'

Ernest pulled tightly on its mane and the horse screamed again, galloped off the road and jumped over a wall into a field. It reached the end of this field and jumped the next gate. Ernest and Jon buried their heads as low as they could and held on tight as the horse galloped on and on. The countryside blurred around them with the horse's monumental speed.

In very little time their backs ached from the pain of the constant jumping. Ernest moaned and groaned with every stride of the horse. Finally, after hours that seemed like years, the horse slowed down in a quiet country field. It stopped, rose up on its hind legs again and began pacing round and round the edge of the field.

'Nice horsey,' Ernest cried wearily.

The horse muttered and spluttered and continued to pace the field until finally it stopped by a clump of deep green grass, bent its head, and began eating.

'Ow,' Jon said, beginning to feel the full extent of his pain for the first time. While they had been travelling he had been concentrating so hard on holding on that he had barely noticed the agony he was in.

'What should we do?' Ernest said, as the horse continued to eat.

'Off,' Jon said. 'While we have the chance.'

Ernest nodded. He stared down at the considerable distance to the ground.

'It's a long way,' he said. 'There are no stairs.'

Ernest lifted a stiff and painful leg over the horse, so that both his legs hung over one side. He stared down at the ground. It seemed a very large distance away. Ernest closed his eyes and jumped. He hit the ground and rolled over so that he ended up right beside the patch on which the horse was feeding, staring into its passive eyes.

'Are you alive?' Jon asked.

'I don't know,' Ernest replied.

Jon lifted his leg over the animal and prepared to jump. He closed his eyes and pushed off. He landed with a thump on the ground and rolled over next to Ernest. Both men lay on their backs staring at the dull afternoon sky, contemplating the various points of pain throughout their bodies.

'People do that for sport?' Ernest said.

'Not without a saddle,' Jon said.

'Men were not meant to travel on animals,' Ernest reflected. 'Especially not me.'

Jon nodded. Eventually their spluttering circulation managed to reach back into their legs and bring back feeling. Jon stood slowly up and moaned. Ernest held up a hand and Jon dragged him up off the grass.

'Where are we?' Ernest asked, in between the groans.

'I don't know,' Jon said. 'We could be anywhere. How long were we travelling?'

Ernest shook his head.

'I think I lost consciousness,' he said.

They were once again in an area full of green fields. But this time there were no cattle, no animals of any kind in fact. The borders of the fields were not marked out by gates or bushes or fences but by stone walls. They stretched out for as far as the eye could see. Miles and miles of hilly fields with grey stone borders. The fields were also littered with pieces of grey jutting out from the middle of the green.

Upon closer inspection Ernest and Jon realised the grey objects were stones. Huge boulders and rocks of every size littered the land in front of them every few feet. Ernest and Jon walked slowly over to one of the stone walls.

'To think,' Jon said, 'somebody actually made these by hand.'

Ernest had trouble with this notion.

'By hand?' he said.

He examined the walls, the hundreds of impossibly heavy rocks, placed one on top of the other.

'It would take years,' he said. 'How could they?'

'It did take years,' Jon said. 'They could because they had time.'

'Why don't they fall over?' Ernest said. 'Surely, the first gale and they would topple?'

Jon shook his head.

'The wind passes through the gaps.'

Ernest nodded and stared at the wall with a new-found admiration for the people who had built them. Such work. Such tiresome endless work.

'How did they do it?' he said again. 'Where did they get the energy?'

'They're not like us,' Jon said. 'They're not used to couches and TV.'

Ernest nodded solemnly and the two men began walking.

'Goodbye horse,' Ernest said, as they left the field. 'You're free forever from the backsides of idle men.'

The horse exhaled and chewed contemplatively on the grass.

'We're no longer in the Midlands,' Jon noted as they walked.

'How can you tell?'

'The land,' Jon explained. 'It's no longer flat.'

They continued to walk slow weary steps. Suddenly, they heard a low grumbling sound.

'Hungry?' Jon asked.

'No,' Ernest said.

There was another low grumbling followed by a high pitched scream. The two men stopped dead in their tracks and listened.

There was a low moaning sound coming from directly ahead of them, over the crest of a hill. The sound was falling and rising in pitch intermittently, from the low rumbling to the high-pitched scream. Jon and Ernest cautiously climbed the hill and looked over.

Beneath them there was a large rocky field which was full of hundreds of small gravestones packed in between great rocks that jutted out of the earth haphazardly. The moaning and screaming appeared to be coming from the graveyard.

'Let's turn around,' Ernest said.

But Jon was not listening. He had already begun to descend the hill. Ernest, not wanting to be alone, ran down with him, cowering behind his back from whatever was making that sound.

Jon approached the first grave and a terrible shrieking cry rushed out at him. Ernest almost had a heart attack and fell down on his knees behind Jon.

'It's the wind,' Jon said. 'Just the wind, passing through the headstones and these rocks.'

Ernest stood up. He felt a breeze as the moaning sound continued, and felt a gush of wind every time it changed into a high pitched squeal.

'Oh, yes,' he said. 'I thought it might be.'

Each headstone was no more than a few feet away from one of the giant rocks.

'It must be a children's graveyard,' Jon said. 'They're all so small.'

The wind picked up again and grumbled as it passed through the maze of headstones and rocks.

'It's creepy,' Ernest said. 'Who in God's name would have a graveyard out here in the middle of nowhere?'

'I would,' an old man who appeared from out of nowhere said.

He was standing at the head of one of the graves, with a spade in his hand.

'And you are not in the middle of nowhere,' he said. 'You are in Almore, County Galway.'

'Galway,' Ernest said. 'We're in Galway?'

The man nodded once.

'You are near enough to the coast,' he said.

Ernest nodded. He noticed for the first time that the old man was standing next to an open grave. The curious thing was that the grave was only a few feet wide and long, yet it was at least eight feet deep.

'I see you are staring at this open grave,' the old man said. 'and wondering why I have dug so deep, yet it is only a few feet wide. I'll tell you.'

For a second the wind picked up and slowed down in quick succession, making a kind of echoed high-pitched noise as it zig zagged and cut between the rocks.

'It sounds almost like laughing,' Jon said.

'Some say that,' the old man said. 'Some say it is the dead laughing. If it is, I can tell you, they are harmless enough. Some say that life is nothing but a play for the dead, to amuse them in their eternal boredom. Of course, I'm no great expert on the subject, although I've known a few that's died in my time and I've spent enough days here amongst the graves to know a thing or two.

'But I was dealing with the depth of these graves, and now I will tell you exactly why it is.

'This land once belonged to my grandfather and, when he died, he passed it down to my father. My grandfather was a foolish man with more money than he had sense and he was tricked into buying this useless rocky land by a conman from the Aran Islands. But he was rich enough and, although he soon learned the land was useless, he did not stop long to ponder his mistake. He had all new mistakes to make and, somehow, despite his own naivety, he managed to hit upon a few good deals and keep himself in the life of luxury he enjoyed and was accustomed to.

'In his later years, however, my grandfather came under the spell of the drink and of course it ruined him, like it does all good men, for it is only the bad men can survive in its clutches.

'So, when my own father, his son, was of age, there was not much left for him to inherit because it had all been gambled and drunk away. My father had been severely traumatised as a child by the sight of his own father's drunken foolishness and had, as a consequence, become fierce anti the drink and most other vices. He was determined to make an honest living from hard graft, but the only beginning he had was this old stretch of stony land. He was determined to do something with it, though, symbol as it had become for him of his own father's stupidity and the clear difference there was between them.

'So every day, for weeks on end, he would come out to this field and set about breaking up the rocks, so that he could till the land. But there are some things that, no matter what the strength of will of the individual, no man is capable of doing and, despite his tiresome work, making this field into agricultural land was one of those things. Mother Nature had that battle won all over. When my father broke up rocks, there would be more rocks underneath, when he cut away boulders, he would find they reached further into this earth than even he could dig. In short, it was hopeless and, because he was not a foolish man, he gave up trying.

'Following this, my father worked as a labourer for many years, till he could build up the savings he needed to buy real land and, because he was a shrewd man, he bought the best land at the cheapest price. From there on he became very rich, and married, and a short time afterwards I was born. So rich, in fact, had he become, that he had taken on staff to do most of the work on his farm so that, as I was growing into a young man, my father found he had less and less to do.

'He had labourers working the fields and feeding the cattle. He had accountants to do his accounts. Salesman to sell his cattle and crops. Investors looking after his money.

'But my father was not a man who enjoyed sitting still and, of course, the thing he turned to to keep himself occupied was this old stretch of green and grey. He was as determined as ever, in his old age, that he would find a use for the land. It had become forever in his mind the symbol that he was not his father, and until he could find a way of profiting from the land he would never be truly happy.

'So every weekend, without fail, he would take the long journey from his farm, to this land, and he would simply stand and stare out over these fields and think. He knew there was no point in breaking up the rocks. He had learnt that lesson well enough. But he was sure, he felt positive, that there was something, some way in which he could use the land.

'He had a small cabin built on the far edge of the land and gradually, as time went on, he began spending more and more time here, just standing, watching, staring out over the land, and trying to think of a use for it.

'Of course, in the end it killed him, as sure as the drink had killed my grandfather. It ate him up inside, you see. He could not think of anything. It was useless. The most useless land. He knew it but could not accept it and spent every waking hour here, just staring and thinking. He got pneumonia one particularly cold January day and died, right out here in these fields.

'We buried him here, thinking, well, at least it will come to some use. The only problem we had was that we could not find one small stretch of land that would fit his coffin in lengthwise. We were constantly coming across giant rocks and boulders that we could not shift. So I hit upon the idea of burying him standing up, and although my mother was slightly disturbed by the idea, nobody had any real objection, and that was what we did.

'Around this time I was finishing school, and, because I had no desire to go to college, began to look for something to do with myself. My mother had taken over the management of our large farm and there was nothing much to do there but help the labourers, something which, as I felt inclined to work which would occupy my mind as well as my body, I was not particularly interested in.

'I was looking for excitement, a challenge, and I chose this piece of land. I knew I was taking a terrible risk. I knew that it might be the death of me as it had been the death of my own father but I could not resist. It had a strange allure for me. It was this, and the fact that I wanted to solve the riddle my father could not solve, that brought me here. I wanted to give this land a purpose, to honour his memory.

'My mother thought I was mad. Everyone did. I came to live in the small cabin my father built and stayed here for weeks, months, staring out over the land, as my father had done, and thinking. Thinking what can I do with this mess of grass and rock?

'There were times, I don't mind telling you, when I came close to giving up. There were numerous occasions when my bag was packed and on my back. But I couldn't leave. I could never get much further than a few feet, before I would look out over the land, and at my father's grave in the distance, and know that I could not leave.

'It was while I was on a trip to the city for supplies that the answer came. Funny, how things happen, all that time my father and I spent staring out over the land, searching for an answer that was not there. It was in a local newspaper. A small article. Hardly of great notice or concern.

'In fact, I read over it without thinking very much. I read on for several pages before suddenly, I realised the enormity of what I had read, a few pages previously. With a trembling hand I moved the pages back. I knew how close I was. I stared at the headline in the article for a long time without daring to read on. I was afraid something would change. That it had not said what I thought it said. Finally, I gained the courage and reread the article and my first excitement was confirmed.

'The article, you see, was about the price of land in the West. How it had skyrocketed in value over the last few years. The reason being that so many emigrants, and there were no greater amount of emigrants than in the West, were returning home rich. Or, if not returning home, wanting to buy a second home in the West.

'If they were not the emigrants themselves, it was the sons or daughters or grandchildren of the emigrants, wanting a home in the place they had heard so many stories about as children. Property, needless to say, was of the highest value but I knew that there was no hope of selling the land for that purpose. The cabin that my father built was on the only bit of rockless ground, but even then, it was no more than a few feet long and wide and the possibility of building a house was out of the question.

'The article's particular focus was not, however, based on the price of property, it was focused on the price of graves. You see, not only were these rich emigrants and their relatives wishing to buy property in Galway, but they wanted to be buried here as well. There was something of the comfort of being laid to rest where your ancestors were laid to rest. But there simply was not the land for these graves. Any available land was, of course, being used for property, and therefore nobody, not the emigrants, nor the people of the small villages, could really afford the prices for these plots of land to expand the existing grave sites.

'It was after reading the article, and not paying much attention, that I suddenly thought of my father and his own grave in these rocky fields. I knew immediately that I had found the answer. I would sell each plot of land, to the highest bidder, so that they could be buried in Galway, amongst their ancestors. Furthermore the plots would still be cheaper than they could get anywhere else, the only condition being that they allow themselves to be buried standing up, because there is only so much room between these rocks that will not budge.

'And so, here I am, three years later, and I have one field full of graves and I have two more already reserved and I have found not only a purpose for this rocky land, but a profitable one.'

The wind began chattering its high-pitched laugh as the old man finished his story and stared off into the distance.

'It is only since I have put these graves in here,' the old man said after a long while, 'that the wind makes that laughing sound. And some say it is just the wind going through the headstones and the rocks. A freak occurrence. And some say it is the dead laughing. Perhaps they are laughing at all the living, and the comical play that we are acting out for them. Perhaps they are just laughing at the fact that their coffins are vertical. Perhaps it is the sound of my grandfather and my father, laughing at what has become of the field, after all their efforts. I am no great expert, and know only that, whatever the reason for the sound, it is harmless enough.'

The old man resumed his silence for a short while before stepping back into the open grave.

'And now if you'll excuse me,' he said. 'I have still a few feet to dig and it will be getting dark soon.'

'Which way is it to Skriel?' Ernest asked.

The old man began digging.

'If you climb that hill over there,' he said, pausing to point with his spade. 'And keep going straight, you will eventually come to a road that will take you along the coast to Skriel.'

Ernest and Jon thanked the old man and walked out of the graveyard as he resumed his digging.

When Ernest and Jon climbed over the hill they were amazed by the contrast between the landscape they had just come from and the one before them. The fields in front of them were of the smoothest green short cut grass. There was a small wood on the left and a small picturesque lake to the right. There was not a stone in sight.

Jon and Ernest climbed down the hill, and onto the smooth green grass.

'You know,' Ernest said. 'I'm beginning to see what they mean about all this countryside lark. I mean, it is beautiful. Look at this place. And it's completely free. Nobody to tell you what to do. You know? No traffic. Nobody telling you where you can and where you can't stand.'

'You can't stand there!' came a voice from out of nowhere.

'Goddammit, Jefferson, get these people out of my way!'

Jon and Ernest stared around the seemingly empty field. Suddenly two men appeared from just underneath a small incline in the grass. Jon and Ernest approached them and saw that they were standing in a sand bunker below the incline.

'Just what in the sam hill do you think you're doing?' an old man with an American accent dressed in red and green plaid trousers with a bright yellow jumper said. 'Don't just stand there, Jefferson, take out my nine iron and beat the hell out of these people!'

The other man, Jefferson, who was tall and skinny, grabbed a nine iron and began wielding it at Jon and Ernest in a comical fashion.

Ernest and Jon stood and watched him dance for a while but get no closer to approaching them with the golf club.

'Jefferson,' the American man said, 'you are a waste of good oxygen, you hear me? Put that club back in there and stop dancing, you little shrimp. I told you to beat the hell out of them not to try and make 'em laugh to death!'

'Yes sir,' Jefferson said forlornly.

The American man stared at Jon and Ernest furiously through his thick-rimmed glasses.

'Am I going to have to come up there myself?' he said. 'Just what in the hell do you think you're doing, blocking my shot? Don't you know you're on private property? Just what kind of a backwater shit hill town is this anyway?'

Jon and Ernest found themselves frozen to the spot, so enraptured were they with the American man's fluid speech.

'Hey! Speak English, bozos?' the American man said. 'Jefferson, get these people out of my way. No, don't. Don't move. I don't want you making a fool out of yourself. Cause when you do that, you make me look bad, you hear me? And I don't like looking bad. I don't pay you to make me look bad. Don't these people have any respect? Do you know who I am? Ask them if they know who I am, Jefferson!'

Jefferson cleared his throat.

'Do you know who I am?' he asked.

'Not *you*, you apathetic moron,' the American man said. 'Me, me. Do I have to draw you a picture?'

'No, sorry,' Jefferson said, turning to Jon and Ernest. 'Don't you know who this is?'

Ernest and Jon shrugged their shoulders and shook their heads.

'Just what sort of tin can shit factory is this place?' the American man bemoaned. 'Don't you get TV over here? Don't you have movies? Jefferson, are you trying to tell me that these people don't even have goddamn movies in this piss-soaked peasant shack?'

Jefferson shook his head.

'No, sir,' he said. 'They get the movies. I'm sure they know who you are, sir. I'm sure it's just the golf outfit, sir.'

'Well, don't just stand there, you mealy-mouthed mother,' the American man said. 'Tell them who I am here and maybe I can get the bit of respect that I am accustomed to so's I can take this lousy shot and finish the goddamn hole.'

'This is is Frank J. Carvery,' Jefferson explained.

Ernest and Jon blinked blankly back.

'You know?' Jefferson said. 'You must have seen the disaster movies, right? Of the Seventies? Like, Inferno, Tornado and Hailstorm?'

'Hailstorm was the Eighties, you pea-brained pissant!' Frank J. Carvery said.

'I think I saw Inferno,' Ernest said. 'I thought that was Steve McQueen.'

'You don't know what the hell you're talking about!' Frank J. Carvery shouted. 'I ought to punch you in the mouth for just saying that. Forget about it, Jefferson, it was a ridiculous idea to begin with. These people don't know culture. I don't even know what the hell I'm doing here anyway. I can play courses ten times better than this in Florida and get a suntan while I'm at it.'

He turned back to Ernest and Jon.

'Just what in the hell are you doing here? You're not one of those goddamned environmentalist groups are you? Crying cause you want to convert this into some kinda playground for a load of dope-smoking faggot-kissing no-hope hippies and their no-hope children? Well, I tell you what, do it. Do it for all I care! Come along Jefferson, pick up the damn ball. We're getting the hell out of here.'

The American began walking out of the bunker and off down the field as Jefferson desperately gathered up the ball and the golf clubs.

'We're going to go back to that shit bucket they call a hotel and we're going to call my travel agent,' the American man said as he walked, 'and we're going to give him hell. Best golf course in Europe! I never heard such bullshit in all my life. Hurry up will you Jefferson you lame-brained weakling. What's the matter with you? If you exercised now and again you might be able to lift the occasional club without having a breakdown. Get a move on, for God's sakes man! Have some respect.'

The American man disappeared into the distance with Jefferson stumbling behind him under the weight of the mass of clubs, leaving Ernest and Jon to stand staring after them bemusedly.

'What was that all about?' Ernest asked.

Jon looked around and noticed for the first time, the various flags and bunkers scattered throughout the landscaped field.

'Apparently we are on a golf course,' he said.

Ernest nodded.

'I see,' he said.

'The playgrounds of the rich and overweight,' Jon said, shaking his head. 'How sad. How sad that, in this place, where people had to work their fingers to the bone just to survive for centuries, men now come from all over the world to hit a little white ball around artificially beautiful patterned fields and hills, and the same people now survive by feeding off their excess cash.'

'That's reality,' Ernest said, walking off. 'Which is exactly why we must rob to become rich, because people like us don't survive unless we are entirely broken men like that guy carrying the clubs.'

Ernest and Jon walked through several holes of the lush golf course until they came eventually to a small stone wall, just over which was a long, narrow, tarmacadamed road. Jon and Ernest stepped over the wall and stood by the roadside, waiting for a car to come by so they could hitch a ride.

It was getting darker, and a cold wind was picking up, but Ernest felt in good spirits.

'Look at this,' he said happily. 'A main road. A real main road. With tarmacadam and everything.'

'Very nice,' Jon agreed unenthusiastically.

'I'm feeling very confident about things,' Ernest said. 'Everything is going swimmingly. Okay, there have been minor setbacks and death threats but still, we're here, in Galway, with only a few miles left to go, and we have all night in which to find Copper's house.'

'We don't even know which house he lives in,' Jon said. 'Skriel might be huge for all we know. There might be hundreds of houses.'

'Everything is okay,' Ernest said, ignoring him. 'Did you see the way I milked that crowd? The travellers. It has given me a new sense of purpose. A belief in myself. Clearly I am a poet after all, despite two hundred rejection letters. When I get the money I am going to buy all the buildings in which the publishers are situated, and I am going to tear them down with them still inside.'

'Don't you think your own success would be enough?' Jon said. 'And that any petty recrimination would only be admitting that they affected you?'

'No,' Ernest said. 'Well, maybe. But it's only a bit of fun.'

Ernest spotted a car come careening down the road in the distance. He held out his hand and the driver, who was travelling at a considerable speed, slammed on the brakes.

For several seconds the car skidded before stopping a few feet away from Ernest and Jon.

'Look at that,' Ernest said. 'The very first car stopped. Things are looking up.'

They got into the car. The driver was an immensely fat man whose gut was so large that it pressed against the steering wheel.

'Hello,' the man said, giggling. 'I though I'd pick you up.'

'Thank you,' Ernest said, 'we're going to Skriel.'

The man nodded and started the car.

'I'll drop you off in Bannon then so,' the man said, pressing down hard on the accelerator. 'That'll get you well on your way.'

Ernest reached desperately for the seatbelt as the car picked up an immense speed. He grabbed one end of the belt but found that the other end was not attached to anything.

Outside, the sun had almost set over a grey cloud sky. Jon stared out the window. He found something quite sinister about the darkening narrow road, lit up by the strong headlights of the car as the scenery blurred away to their sides. The driver continued to increase his speed.

'In a hurry?' Ernest asked, trying to appear unconcerned.

The man giggled.

'No, no,' he said. 'No, I always drive this way. Oh yes, I do get in some terrible trouble for it I can tell you. I get in some awful fierce trouble with the police. But I love speeding. I am addicted. There is something primal in it I have found.'

He slammed on the brakes suddenly as another car appeared ahead. He dimmed his lights and pulled over to let the other car drive by, before slamming down on the accelerator again.

'They're terrible dangerous, these roads,' the driver said. 'They're not wide enough you see. Not nearly. And they have an awful lot of trucks come through here on their deliveries. If you ask me now, a road is no place for a truck. No, that's not quite what I meant.'

The driver giggled and paused as he tried to clear his thoughts. One of the aspects Ernest found most distressing about his driving was the fact that he continually turned around while talking to them, and never once altered his tremendous speed.

'Ah yes,' the driver said. 'I have it now. It's not good for the brain, all these high speeds. The body is not meant to travel like this. It does terrible things to your insides I can tell you. But it is an addiction, and I suppose there are worse ones a man could have.

'But I was telling you, in any case, about the trucks. What I meant to say was that I don't think the roads should be used for those heavy deliveries. Especially not the country roads. It is terrible dangerous, and not good for the roads. And they are far too wide, those vehicles, in any case. God bless the days when goods and such were all delivered on trains and canals, like they ought to be. One of these dark nights I'm going to go straight into one of those big trucks, probably a truck full of petroleum, and the whole thing will blow sky high.'

The man giggled for several seconds and turned a sharp corner in the road. His gut was so enormous that he had to take a great breath so that he could turn the wheel enough, not exhaling until the road had straightened out again.

'It's not my fault at all,' the driver said. 'I only have two pleasures in this life and one of them is driving. The other, as you may have noticed, is eating. It's a product of low self-esteem you see. My father did not speak to me from the age of three because I urinated accidentally on his favourite suit. He never forgave me for that and did not speak to me for my entire childhood. He was a tough man. It was a great comfort to me, however, when, years later at my sister's wedding, after I had gained four stone in three years, he said these words: "That son of mine, you could feed off him for a year." He said it with great affection, though, and died soon after that.'

The driver wiped a tear from his eye with one of his huge arms.

'A great man, truly,' he said, nodding. 'He chose his words very carefully. Unfortunately however, I was a highly sensitive child and did not understand. I chose food as my only comfort, and was mocked and ridiculed as a consequence by every child in school and in the village. I do not blame them, of course. They were just having a bit of a laugh. They were nice children really and even when they tried to drown me in the village swimming pool I did not blame them. Of course it was impossible, because of the buoyancy of my round body.

'As soon as I was old enough I began driving, and as soon as I began driving I began speeding. One of the terrible things you see, about being so immensely fat is that each movement you make, no matter how small, takes an enormous amount of energy. When each of your arms weighs several stone alone, just picking up a cup of tea becomes a tremendous tiresome effort. And as a consequence, whenever you do anything of a physical nature, it is always painfully slow.

'But in a car, especially the automatic cars they have nowadays, all you need do is press down on the accelerator and you will move. I can't tell you how freeing that is to me. How alive I feel. Unfortunately, I became addicted to it. I became addicted to the speed I have in this car and nowhere else. The police have stopped me hundreds of times. I have paid thousands of pounds in fines. I have sworn blindly to judges that I will reduce my speed. I have no desire to kill anyone after all. But it is no use. I have not got the strength of will. The temptation is too much. The speed too glorious. And now I must let you out.'

The driver slammed on the brakes of the car, and after skidding for several seconds, the car stopped by an old country pub.

'Are we here?' Ernest asked.

'You are here,' the driver said. 'This is Bannon.'

There was nothing around but a couple of old pubs and a sleepy road full of bed-and-breakfasts. Ernest and Jon got out of the car, and waved at the driver, who waved very briefly and sped off down the road at upwards of one hundred miles per hour.

A cold wind blew as Ernest and Jon stood by the roadside. It had grown almost completely black in the time it had taken them to get there. Ernest shivered.

'It's cold,' he said.

Jon nodded. They stood outside shivering for some moments before deciding to go into one of the pubs to warm themselves and to ask for directions to Skriel.

7. Father Barnaby

When Ernest and Jon walked into the pub they could not see a thing. There was a fire burning at one end of the room and the smoke was such that Ernest and Jon could barely make out where they were walking. They spluttered and coughed their way to the bar. When they got there they could not make out, with all the smoke, whether or not there was someone serving behind it.

'Hello?' Ernest said.

'*Dia dhaoibh*,' came a voice from the smoke.

'Hello?' Ernest said.

'*Dia dhaoibh*,' the voice repeated.

'What is that?' Ernest asked, turning to Jon.

'*Céatá anseo?*' the voice said.

Suddenly, a hand appeared in front of them and began fanning the smoke away from the bar. The smoke cleared enough for Ernest and Jon to make out a small, bald man with a moustache, standing behind the bar.

'*Dia dhaoibh*,' the man said. '*Ceard atá uaibh?*'

'He seems to be talking in some strange foreign tongue,' Ernest said.

'Irish,' Jon said. 'I think he's speaking Irish. They do that round here.'

'What do you want?' the man said suddenly in English. 'Don't the pair of you have any Irish?'

'I'm afraid not,' Jon said.

'And why not?' the man demanded. 'Isn't it the language of your country?'

'We're not from the country,' Ernest explained.

'Not *the* country,' the man said, '*your* country. Where are you from at all?'

'Dublin,' Ernest said.

'Dublin,' the man said, nodding. 'That's no excuse. A cousin o' mine is from Dublin and she's fluent altogether.'

'I used to be fluent,' Ernest said. 'But I got hit in the head and experienced selective amnesia. It was quite tragic. I lost all my French as well.'

'You lost your sense too,' the barman said, laughing wildly. 'You lost your sense too!'

'We were looking for directions,' Jon said, when the barman's laughing died down.

'There's no directions without drink,' the barman said gruffly.

The smoke began thickening again and the barman once again disappeared behind the white cloud.

'We'll have two Guinness then, please,' Ernest said licking his lips.

A hand appeared and fanned the smoke away. A middle-aged woman with dyed blonde hair stood in the exact spot the bar man had been in, holding two Guinness in her hands.

'*Ceathair phunt, le bhur d'thoil*,' she said.

'What?' Ernest said.

'*Ceathair phunt, le bhur d'thoil*,' the woman repeated.

'What is she talking about?' Ernest asked.

'I think she wants money,' Jon said.

The woman sighed.

'Don't you have Irish?' she said.

'We've been through this,' Ernest explained. 'With the other guy.'

'I was asking for four pounds,' the woman said. 'Don't you have numbers even?'

Ernest shook his head.

'Everything went,' Ernest said. 'In the accident. Tragic. The only thing left was the conditional future tense.'

Jon handed the woman a five pound note as the smoke thickened again. A hand came out to fan the smoke away, and when it cleared the small bald-headed man handed Jon the change.

'That is very impressive,' Ernest said admiringly.

'I think the fire's a bit out of control,' Jon said to the barman.

'What's wrong with it?' the barman asked.

'Well,' Jon said. 'It's just a little smoky.'

'Oh yes,' the barman said. 'The chimney's blocked.'

'I see,' Jon said.

He considered, for a short while, asking why then the fire was lit, but decided eventually that there was no point in having the conversation.

Ernest and Jon struggled through the smoke to the far end of the pub and, after a lot of bumping and feeling out, found a pair of seats.

'We have to be very careful,' Jon said, as they sipped on their pints. 'We are in the Gaeltacht now.'

'Where?' Ernest said.

'Don't you know anything about Ireland?' Jon said.

'I know about where I live,' Ernest said. 'I know my bus route. Why should I know about the country? They're all quite obviously insane.'

'It is just that attitude that will get us in trouble,' Jon warned. 'We have to be respectful. Irish is a first language to a lot of the people around here. They don't like outsiders. They especially don't like people from Dublin.'

'Why not?' Ernest said.

'How should I know?' Jon said. 'Maybe it's because generally people from Dublin are arrogant. Maybe they resent that it's the capital. I don't know. Maybe it's the difference in culture.'

Ernest nodded.

'They really speak Irish?'

'They really do,' Jon said. 'It's sad to think it's dying out even here. I've always been sorry I couldn't speak it.'

'You're joking?' Ernest said.

'No,' Jon said, defensively. 'I'd love to be able to speak the language. It's our language after all.'

'It's not my language,' Ernest said. 'I mean, I've nothing against it but it's certainly not mine. I was taught it at school, like I was taught French and German at school. The good thing about your own language, I've always thought, is that you don't have to be taught it, apart from when you're a baby obviously. It comes naturally to you.'

'Don't you think it's sad, though?' Jon asked. 'Don't you think we'll lose something culturally when it goes?'

Ernest thought a moment.

'I have no idea, to tell you the truth,' he said. 'It must be sad for these people. The people who speak Irish as a first language. It must be sad seeing less and less people speak it with every generation. But how can it be sad for us? When we never have spoken it. When our parents have never spoken it. Their parents. It was lost generations ago, and if we tried to take it back now it would just be contrived.'

'Bloody Dubliner,' a voice said, from the smoke.

Several pairs of hands began fanning away the smoke and when it cleared Jon and Ernest saw that they were sitting at a table surrounded by three tough-looking young men. They stared menacingly at Ernest and Jon. They had red faces, thick woollen jumpers and brown protruding teeth.

'What are you saying?' the same voice said. 'You think you're all so fucking great. You think Dublin is the be-all and end-all of the world. You've forgotten your own heritage, your own beginnings, your own language. You're nothing but West Brits.'

Jon stood up.

'Let's go,' he said.

'I haven't finished my drink,' Ernest said.

'Come on,' Jon said.

'Go on you West Brit,' one of the men, whose red curly hair was protruding from his woollen hat, said.

'That's a lovely perm you've got,' Ernest said. 'It suits you.'

The man looked confused for a few seconds then stood up. All in all, he was at least six foot seven.

'Holy Jesus Christ,' Ernest said.

Jon grabbed Ernest's arm and they ran out of the pub. They heard laughing from behind them as the door shut but nobody followed.

'Jesus,' Jon said. 'I warned you. I warned you they don't like Dubs.'

'How was I supposed to know?' Ernest said. 'I've never been outside Dublin before. How was I supposed to know the countryside was full of madmen?'

It was pitch black outside.

'Why is it so dark?' Ernest asked. 'I can't see a thing.'

'I told you, this is the country,' Jon said. 'It gets dark in the country. They don't have streetlights.'

'Why not?'

'They just don't,' Jon said, sighing. 'They don't have the money. These are tiny streets.'

'I've never seen it so dark,' Ernest said.

'This is what night looks like,' Jon said. 'You don't get to see in the city.'

'We must get on,' Ernest said. 'In the morning, Copper will be heading back to Dublin and it will be too late.'

Jon shook his head.

'When are you going to get over this?' he said. 'Are you seriously intending robbing and murdering this man?'

'Not murdering, necessarily,' Ernest said. 'That was just me getting overexcited. But the money, yes. Hell yes. Why not? We deserve it. We've come this far. What else is there?'

Ernest began walking down the street, the wind blowing directly into his face. Jon sighed and followed him. They began to hear a strange noise as they walked. They stopped dead in their tracks.

'What is that?' Ernest asked.

The strange swelling, shaking sound came again. At that precise moment the moon came out from behind the clouds and lit up Galway Bay, right in front of them.

'The sea,' Jon said. 'It's the sea.'

'The Atlantic,' Ernest said. 'I've never seen it before.'

They heard the waves crashing against the shore and recognised it as the sound they had been hearing. They walked onto Bannon pier and stared out at the black still ocean, like a massive oil spill.

'What are those mountains in the distance?' Ernest asked.

'They aren't mountains,' Jon answered. 'They're islands. Those are the Aran Islands.'

Ernest stared back at the mountains sceptically. He had felt sure they were joined to the coast by a thin stretch of land. He looked closer and saw the stretch of land ended long before it ever reached the islands.

They walked back off the pier and onto the stony beach, full of stones of all different shapes and sizes, hundreds of shades of grey spread out among small pools of water, so that Ernest and Jon had to carefully choose the path they walked on to avoid getting wet.

Ernest continued to stare at the Aran Islands. He could make out a distant set of lights on their coast.

'People live on those?' he said.

Jon nodded.

Ernest shook his head. He felt himself drawn to the islands. The tide was out and Ernest decided to walk out as far as he could to the edge of the beach to get the best possible look at them. There was a huge rock sitting at the point where the beach met the waves and Ernest decided the best vantage point would be on top of this giant boulder. He began heading towards it with Jon following.

'I like walking on the rocks,' Jon said. 'I always have done. Ever since I was a child and my parents brought us to Dún Laoghaire. They would walk the pier and we would run about on the rocks, sometimes hunting for crabs, sometimes just jumping about. There's something soothing about it, I find. You can't think about anything else but which rock you are going to next, which is the steadiest, what your next path of rocks is going to be.'

'I never went to the sea,' Ernest said, as they stepped closer to the boulder. 'We might as well have been living in the middle of the desert for all it mattered to us. Mostly I forgot the coast was there at all. We didn't go for trips or picnics in my family. We watched TV in uncomfortable silence and waited for each other to leave the room so we could put on what we really wanted.'

They arrived at the large boulder. Ernest chose his last path to it, involving one treacherous jump across a large puddle, and after successfully completing the jump, he climbed up onto the boulder. Jon did not chose as wisely. He picked a safer-looking route, but one which involved a seaweed-covered rock, and sure enough his foot slipped and was drenched in the cold water.

He climbed up onto the boulder after Ernest with his foot still wringing. Ernest stared out at the distant set of lights on the islands.

'Why would anybody choose to live there?' he said. 'The cold wind from the Atlantic constantly blowing at them.'

'It is amazing,' Jon said. 'To think that people fished in these waters. That that is how they survived. By jumping in their tiny boats and pushing off through the cold sea.'

'They were insane,' Ernest said.

Jon nodded.

'Human beings,' he said. 'They're funny things. They get just everywhere. You can't keep them out.'

Both men stared for a long time at the distant set of lights before finally deciding to head back.

'Let's go and steal from our landlord,' Ernest said. 'It's the very least he and we deserve.'

Ernest turned and was alarmed to see that the tide was already rushing in towards the beach. He screamed and began scrambling down the boulder. Jon followed quickly after and the pair of them began jumping from rock to rock in a desperate attempt to make it back to shore before the sea closed them off. They got about halfway when it became obvious that they were not going to make it.

There was no safe path to the shore. Not even a risky jump to attempt, and the water kept on rising.

'Back,' Ernest screamed and they began scrambling back to seek the relative safety of the large rock. They made it just as the sea swept over the route they had taken and covered it completely.

Jon and Ernest climbed to the top of the rock and watched the sea rush in around them.

'This is wonderful,' Ernest said. 'Just wonderful.'

Jon watched helplessly as the water rose. He felt almost like laughing.

'It's so silly,' he said. 'There is nothing we can do. We have absolutely no control. We're actually going to have to sit here till we eventually drown.'

'We're safe on this rock,' Ernest said.

'You can't be serious,' Jon said. 'We're not safe. The water level will rise far above this rock.'

'We're fine,' Ernest said. 'We'll just wait here till the tide goes out. Everything is okay.'

Jon realised Ernest was not going to listen to reason. They waited in silence and as they did so the water level slowly crept up the rock towards them.

'I'm going to swim for it,' Ernest said, getting up and staring at the black stretch of water to the coast.

'Don't be ridiculous,' Jon said. 'You won't make it.'

'Of course I'll make it,' Ernest said. 'It's not so far.'

'It's not the distance that will get you,' Jon said. 'It's the cold. You can't survive in that kind of cold, let alone swim anyplace. Our best chance is to try and attract someone's attention on the shore.'

For the next ten minutes they yelled and screamed and clapped towards the shore but there was no response.

'It's useless,' Ernest said eventually. 'We're going to die here.'

Jon could not help but agree. It was deathly silent apart from the slow swelling sound of water moving,

'So close,' Ernest said. 'We came so close. What a ridiculous way to die.'

Jon said nothing. He turned and stared out at the Aran Islands.

'I hate the sea,' Ernest said, as his feet, hanging over the side of the rock, dipped in and out of the cold waters. 'I don't see why so many people feel comforted to live on its shores. Doesn't anybody find it disconcerting? The constant erosion. Every day a little more land gone, the sea a little closer. I don't see anything tranquil in that. It does nothing for me but make me think of death and destruction. It reminds us, with each wave, that one day all of us will end up in the water. That the sea will eventually get all of us.'

The water was almost at their level now. Drops of spray sprang up from the waves and cooled their faces.

'What do you suppose we should do?' Ernest asked, quietly.

'Slip in ourselves, of our own free will, or wait for a wave to overpower us?'

Jon shrugged.

'Doesn't really matter, does it? One gives the illusion of control when we don't have any.'

He took out his inhaler without thinking and took a deep breath. He stared at his inhaler and smiled.

'I don't know why I bothered,' he said. 'Habit I suppose.'

Ernest began shaking. He could not take his eyes from the water. He was staring into it, trying in vain to penetrate its murky depths. It was almost like a moving solid. A liquid stone.

'It should be easy enough,' Jon said. 'We won't feel much pain. The cold will see to that. The important thing they say is not to panic, although I don't see how you would go about remaining calm. They say, if you can survive those first few minutes in the water, the initial shock to the body, that you have a fair chance. The tide is moving towards the shore, we might get washed up. Somebody might see us.'

'Can we talk about something else?' Ernest asked.

Jon looked at him. Ernest smiled.

'Sorry,' he said, knowing he was being ridiculous. 'I know it's kind of relevant but I'm having difficulty coming to terms with the fact this is real.'

Jon nodded silently. Another wave crashed against the rock, and the tip of it covered the entire rock and wet Ernest's feet. Ernest stood up. He stood alongside Jon on the highest part of the stone.

'Not long now,' he said, trying to remain jovial.

Jon nodded. Another wave crashed, a little higher. The wind picked up and as it did so the waves came in a little quicker.

'I used to like watching the waves,' Jon said. 'Not for any soothing effect. I used to like watching them far out in the sea and trying to guess which would be the biggest when it came into shore. I don't enjoy it so much now.'

As if to emphasise his words, a huge wave crashed against the rock. Jon almost lost his footing but Ernest grabbed his arm at the last second.

'Thanks,' Jon said.

'Not that it makes much difference,' Ernest said.

'Look at that,' Jon said, pointing out into the sea.

It was a wave. A giant wave. Still far out in the sea, but getting bigger all the time as it headed towards the rock. Jon and Ernest braced themselves for it's impact.

'Are you there?' came a voice from the sea.

Jon and Ernest looked out into the darkness. The wave was getting closer. They could not find the source of the voice. Suddenly a boat appeared from out of nowhere, moving towards them.

'Yes,' Jon yelled. 'We're over here.'

It was a small motorboat, an old man with a long beard at its helm. He moved the boat to within a few feet and cut the engine as the wave was about to hit.

'Jump,' he shouted.

Jon jumped towards the boat and landed in the stern with a crash. Ernest paused a fraction of a second and looked towards the sea. The wave was rising as it hurtled towards the rock. It was enormous. Like the frothing open mouth of a whale. Ernest was momentarily transfixed by the sight of the massive closing wave, until the screaming voice of Jon snapped him out of it. At the last second he jumped into the boat as the rock was engulfed by the wave.

'I thought you might have been one of the others,' the old man said, after the small boat itself had settled from the impact of the wave.

'Haven't we met you before?' Jon asked.

'You might,' the old man said. 'I don't remember myself, I have to say.'

'Thank you,' Ernest said. 'We're very grateful. We were stuck.'

'I heard you calling,' the old man said, nodding. 'But I wasn't sure, now, if it was a trick. Because the wind does funny things and you have to watch out for the others of course.'

'Thank you,' Ernest said again. 'If you could just take us back to shore, we'd be very grateful.'

'It's shore we're going to all right,' the old man said as a fog enveloped the boat. 'The shore of Inis Ochair.'

'Inis Ochair?' Ernest said.

'That's right,' the old man said, pointing into the mist. 'The fourth Aran Island.'

'There's only three Aran Islands,' Jon said.

'I'm glad you've told me that now,' the old man said sarcastically. 'Because that means I've been living a lie. There's a fourth and plenty know. That's where we're going now.'

'But we have to get back to shore,' Ernest said. 'We have an appointment. It's urgent.'

'It's a lucky thing, you know, that I heard you as I was going for my usual walk,' the old man said. 'Because I wouldn't usually come out in the boat on a night like it is.'

'Excuse me,' Ernest said. 'Please, we need to get back to the shore.'

'I can't help you with that,' the old man said. 'I don't ferry people to the mainland. I haven't gone there in fifteen years and I don't plan on doing so to please you.'

'Why not?' Ernest said, desperately, taking out the money from his pocket. 'I'll give you a hundred pounds.'

'You could give me all the money in the world,' the old man said. 'But it won't change the truth.'

'How do you know where you're going?' Jon asked, as the boat chugged through the thick mist.

'When you've travelled these waters as long as I have, you get to know a thing or two.'

Jon nodded. The old man cut the engine again and the boat suddenly struck ground. He then jumped out of the boat and, though he looked old and weak, dragged the boat onto the beach with Jon and Ernest still in it.

'Please,' Ernest said, as they stepped out. 'We have to get across that bay. It's a matter of life or death.'

The old man shook his head sadly.

'What about if I were to rent your boat?'

'You wouldn't make it,' he said. 'There's rocks as big as houses in that bay and you'd never make it through. You'd better wait until the morning. There's few on this island who'd even go out on a night like it is.'

The old man began walking away into the mist. He turned around, just before disappearing.

'You're welcome to stop in my home if you like,' he said. 'It's the first house you come to up the hill. I'll leave you to decide.'

Jon and Ernest stood on the beach in silence, with the sound of the waves crashing against the shore behind them.

'Forget it,' Jon said. 'We're not going to make it.'

'We have to,' Ernest said.

'Look, Ernest,' Jon said. 'We're lucky we're alive, we've escaped death on this trip more times than I can remember.'

'Which is why we must go on,' Ernest said. 'That's exactly the reason. Don't you understand? There's a purpose to it all. Can't you see it? We were thrown out of the flat so we could finally get up off our arses and do something. That was what we needed. Otherwise we would've drifted in and out of the dole queues for the rest of our miserable lives.'

'So we're destined to rob Copper?'

'Why not?' Ernest asked. 'Look, things have been going well because we have kept focused on our task. If we stop now and fail, something terrible is going to happen.'

'You're delusional,' Jon said.

'Maybe,' Ernest said. 'But I am going to get back to the mainland, before morning.'

Jon shook his head.

'How?'

Ernest began walking in the direction the old man had gone.

'I'm going to find the old man and ask him where there's somebody with another boat,' he said. 'There's got to be someone round here who appreciates money.'

Jon slowly followed him. They climbed a large hill and as they got higher they eventually broke through the mist and, for the first time, could see the island.

They were standing on what appeared to be a large circular hill. Below them, was the mist and then the sea. Scattered over the hill were a variety of tiny cottages, each with a puff of smoke coming from its chimney and a dull yellow light in its window.

Ernest knocked on the door of the first cottage they came to.

'Come in,' said the familiar voice.

The old man was sitting in front of a raging fire, with a cat in his lap and a dog lying contentedly by his feet.

'Have a chair,' the old man said. 'The kettle is hot if you would like coffee.'

'No, thank you,' Ernest said. 'We're not staying. We were just wondering whereabouts we could find somebody else with a boat.'

The old man nodded.

'You're going back then,' he said. 'I thought you would.'

'Yes,' Ernest said. 'Well, we have an appointment. We need to get across tonight you see.'

'I haven't been back in fifteen years,' the old man said, staring into the fire. 'That's when I came to this island. The locals don't talk to you: the islanders. They don't talk to outsiders. Which suited me just fine. I was sick of people. Sick of conversation. You know, there is a story, and I don't know whether it is true or not but I shall recount it to you all the same.'

'We are pressed for time,' Ernest said. 'If you could just tell us where to get the boat.'

But the old man did not hear him, or did not choose to hear him. He just stared into the fire and in a soft, hypnotic voice, began to recount the story.

'Apparently, not so long ago, there was a foreigner who came to these parts on holiday and fell in love with the place. He found this island particularly enchanting. He was an intelligent man, somewhat weary, who was looking for somewhere he could call home, after years of wandering.

'He was one of those displaced children, born in some country or other, during one of the many short stops his wandering parents took, as they searched in vain for something that they could not and would not find. So he was born in one country and raised in countless others and he never had a fixed home or friends or even a fixed language to speak.

'As a consequence, this young boy learned to speak dozens of languages and to remain quite distant so that he would not involve and hurt himself in the short-term world he lived in. He was extremely bright, however, and lived for his books which, upon leaving, were one of the few things he could take with him. He read hundreds of books. Thousands. He never went to school but was more schooled than any child his age or older. He was terribly alone.

'When he grew old enough and responsible enough, and this, for him, was a far younger age than any normal child, he separated from his parents, whom he loved dearly but could not help resenting a little for his confused upbringing.

'He decided, upon separation, that he was not going to be like his parents, constantly shifting and searching for who knows what. He was going to find a nice quiet friendly place and he was going to buy a house, and live in the one spot for the rest of his life.

'So he began looking for the perfect place and moved from city to city, town to town, looking for a somewhere that would fit his simple criteria. But he could not find anywhere. This city was too noisy, that city too small. Another was too unfriendly, another too interfering.

'Finally one day, to his horror, he realised he had become just like his parents. Constantly moving from place to place in short stinted spurts, searching for something he would not and could not find.

'He had, with this realisation, lost almost all hope of ever settling down and it was then that he came to Ireland. He started off in Dublin first, then moved to Thurles, then to Cork and on to Galway, and to the many small villages along the coast.

'One of the things he enjoyed most about a new country was being able to learn its language. This man had an extraordinary gift for language. He could learn in a few weeks what it would take most of us years to grasp.

'Some scientists say, and this is an aside, that there is a unique part of the brain which deals with language and that, once you start learning, this place in your brain becomes more active so that the more languages you have the more active your brain is. In effect what these scientists are saying is that each language not only has its own verbs, nouns and tenses, it has its own way of working in the brain. That each language is a whole different thought process. Therefore, nothing can ever be truly translated into a different language, no phrase, no single word.

'That is why it is a true tragedy when a language dies, because it is not just the words that die, but the real meaning behind them.

'This man, in any case, was somewhat disappointed, upon arriving in Ireland, at the level at which Irish was spoken. He had become fluent in English long ago and was disappointed he could not find anyone in Dublin, Thurles, or Cork, with whom he could try out some of the preliminary things he had learnt to speak in Irish.

'He had learnt most of the other Celtic languages and he could not understand why the country had given up on a language that he had heard was so rich and diverse and strangely poetic.

'In Galway though, Connemara, specifically the Gaeltacht area, he found there were people who did speak the language. Indeed, who spoke it as their first language. Not only that, but they were very friendly to him in these small villages. There were so many native people, you see, who hardly spoke Irish at all. A lot of the younger people, particularly, refused to learn. They watched TV, and went to the cinema and read books that were in English. It was dying out, and the older people were pleasantly surprised to see an outsider who was not only willing to try and speak a few words to them, but wanted to learn more. It gave them hope and, in hardly any time at all, the man was as fluent as the most fluent local, in the local dialect.

'But then the time came for him to move on and it was with a heavy heart that he contemplated leaving, because he had almost found the perfect place amongst these small villages. Almost. Something was still not right and he began to wonder would he ever find a place that would fit his standards. He felt sure that he would not. He felt sure that he would be wandering forever, like his parents, only worse because at least they had each other.

'The day came for him to leave. On the bus journey back into Galway to get the train, the driver stopped for a short tea break, at the ferry point to the Aran Islands. He decided, on a whim, that he should at least see one of the Aran Islands before he left, and, abandoning his bus, he crossed that very day to this island.

'As soon as he arrived he fell in love and I can give you no real reason except to say that he saw something here, that he did not see anywhere else. The people were friendly, the local pub warm. The scenery was beautiful. It was small, but not too small. Connected to the world but cut off. He knew he had found the place.

'He set about buying a small house immediately and within a matter of days had found a place and moved in. On his first morning in the house, the man felt happier than he had felt in years. He looked out at the view from his bedroom window, of the whole of Galway Bay and smiled.

'He walked out into the clean fresh air, stared around at the small village of which he was now a member and he felt, for the first time, as if he truly belonged somewhere.

'And on that same morning he decided he would call in on his new neighbours, whom he had met as a tourist, and tell them the news of his settlement. The first woman he called on, with whom he had talked for several hours in a local pub, and whose company he had enjoyed very much, was slightly bemused when she saw the tourist back on her doorstep.

'"Did you miss the ferry?" she asked him.

'He told her his news. That he had bought the house and that he was planning to live on the island till his dying day. He gave her a gift and invited her around for dinner that very night. The woman thanked him, with a small polite smile, but said that she could not go that evening and that she could not talk right now because she was in the middle of making breakfast. With that she stood up, led the man to the door, and wished him a good day.

'The man was a little confused by her reaction but, he thought, he had probably come on a little too strong. He might have been contravening some sort of tradition or etiquette by asking her to dinner so soon. He would have to learn to be more tactful, he decided, as he walked to the next house.

'When he called in, to a middle-aged man he had met on the ferry on his way over, he was surprised, once again, by the cold reaction he got from him when he told him his news about the house. The man had simply nodded wordlessly and told him that he could not stay to talk because he had an appointment.

'Although slightly disappointed with his first two encounters, he was not put off. He had caught them on a bad day, he thought, or perhaps he was doing something wrong that he did not know about. So with the third person he visited, he was extremely cautious, only telling them about buying the house at the very end of the conversation. This person, an older man, had been very friendly upon the man calling in. He had made him tea, and offered him something to eat and while they chit-chatted about nothing much the conversation continued to be very friendly, but when the man mentioned, finally, that he had moved in to a house on the island, the old man's reaction was quite sudden and stark.

'"You'll have to leave now," he said. "I'm very sorry. I'm after remembering I need to get some work done on the roof immediately. I'm sorry now, but it can't wait."

'The man nodded vaguely and walked out of the old man's house. He called in on three more houses that day, but everywhere he went, no matter how cautiously he approached the subject of his house, he was immediately treated coldly and some excuse was made to make him leave. He simply could not understand it. What could he possibly have done wrong?

'Perhaps, he thought finally, it was some sort of religious day that he did not know about. Perhaps a day which called for silence, or where talk of anything other than God is not allowed. It could be anything, he thought. He knew so little about these people.

'He caught the ferry that same day into Galway and bought all the books he could find on the people and the customs of the Aran Islands. When he got back to the island he spent the the next few days and nights reading them and learning about even the smallest customs that the people of the islands had or were still practising.

'After spending this time studying he once again felt confident to go out and engage the locals in conversation. He had found no reason why anyone, on that previous date, should have treated him the way they did, but he had learned, in his studies, that the locals were a very conservative and in some ways inhibited people. He decided to be much more subtle in his approach to them.

'He felt, in reality, he had been a bit of a fool, inviting everyone round to his place on the first night. Of course it wasn't done. He felt like a bumbling tourist and was determined never again to make the islanders feel as uncomfortable as they had clearly felt on that first day.

'He went walking round the island that morning, and saw many of the islanders about. He greeted every single one of them and they greeted him back, although he was disappointed to see that there was something of an air of discomfort about them as they greeted him. He decided not to try and pressure them and did not even try to engage them in small talk on that morning.

'The next few days passed like this, the man going for the occasional walk, greeting anyone he saw and them greeting back but always with a certain degree of reticence.

'Finally after two weeks of this, the man grew weary of his solitary company and, while on one of his walks, approached one of the men he knew, who had returned his greetings.

'"Fine day," he said to him.

'The old man looked out over the sea, avoiding his gaze and nodded silently.

'"Are you off to the boat?" the man asked, seeing the old man had fishing tackle in one hand.

'The old man looked at the fishing tackle in his hand as if it had just appeared there and then, for one second, looked the man in the eye before, without another word, wandering straight off towards the sea.

'The man stood quite still, in shock, and watched for a long time as the old man walked away. He had been completely shunned. As if he were some unsavoury character the old man did not want to be associated with.

'The foreign man could not understand it. This old man had been very friendly towards him when he had arrived on the island as a tourist. He could not understand what he had done to offend him so. Still, shaking off the incident as a once-off (after all this man might have been known for such strange behaviour), the man greeted the next islander he saw warmly, and when he was greeted back, approached the woman.

'"Lovely day," he said to her. "The rain has cleared up nicely."

'The old woman nodded sadly.

'"I can't stop," she said. "I'm in a hurry."

'With that, she took off down the road. The man had countless other encounters on that day and each time he was either completely ignored or some excuse was given, and the person would hurry away as if he had some contagious disease.

'That night the man went back to his home, alone and weary and feeling quite hollow inside from the way he had been treated. What could he possibly have done to deserve such treatment? he asked himself. He scoured his memory but could find no incident which could have justified their behaviour.

'Perhaps they just don't like me, he thought in the end. But they had seemed to before. They had seemed to enjoy his company. To laugh at his jokes. What had he done wrong?

'Over the next few weeks he tried, on countless occasions, to engage the islanders in conversation, always without success. He invited them to dinner, he bought gifts, he did everything he could think of but nothing worked. When he entered the local pub, it would go extremely quiet and whatever table he sat at, people always moved away.

'At night, sometimes he would cry a little. He felt so alone. It had taken him so long to find this place and now it was like a living hell. But he found he could not leave. That would have been the obvious thing to do, after all. He had moved here, it had not worked out, all he had to do was start moving again. But he couldn't do that. He had found the place. The place he was looking for. He knew that if he started moving again he would never stop and he could not face that.

'Besides, this was where he had chosen. He had known from the minute he got here that this was where he was to live and die and he could not give up simply because he was an outcast. The island had chosen him as much as he had chosen it. He could not leave.

'So he stayed, and for as long as he lived here he continued to be ignored almost totally by the locals. They would always greet him, if he greeted them, but never anything beyond a simple hello. The man lived a long and very lonely life here and eventually, one night in his house, died in his sleep.

'The curious thing was that, when news of the man's death spread round the village, the villagers were genuinely saddened to hear of his passing. Indeed, the man's funeral, a few days later, was one of the biggest these islands have ever seen. Practically every single villager on the island came to pay their respects to the foreign man. There were genuine outbreaks of grief amongst the villagers present. Many of the women, and some of the men, cried openly. If you did not know the circumstances and came upon the scene, you would think this man had been the island's most cherished and popular member.

'You see, the simple truth was that the villagers had liked the man a great deal. As a tourist, they were able to joke and laugh and talk for many hours with him. But when he became a villager, you see, the rules changed. These islanders have come to rely on the tourists. They need them to survive. So they are quite willing to ignore certain failings on the part of tourists, because, after all, the better time they have, the more money they are likely to spend and the more likely they are to come back or tell their friends to visit.

'But this is not to say they didn't genuinely like the man, when he was a tourist. They did. They were pleasantly surprised, as the people in mainland Galway had been, to find an Irish-speaking tourist, one who was friendly and kind, and had a similar sense of humour to their own.

'But when he became an islander, when he bought the house and committed to staying, the rules changed. He was no longer a tourist and therefore the differences he had were no longer acceptable to the islanders. And it was really only one difference which had caused this man to be so ostracised. It was really only the one thing.

'It was not, as you might imagine, that he was an outsider, or that he was a foreigner. It was not that he spoke Irish with a strange accent. It was not even that he was too friendly or over-bearing or patronising to the villagers, or any aspect of his personality or indeed his behaviour.

'It was one thing. One thing which separated them from him and one thing that was, to them, unforgivable.

'It was the fact that he had learnt his Irish on the mainland of Galway county. The fact he had learnt to speak Irish in those small villages on the coast and that it was this dialect which he was fluent in.

'You see, there are dialects of Irish all over the different parts of the country, as is the case with many languages, and the changes in the dialect are sometimes so minute as to make them hardly recognisable to any one but the people who speak it themselves.

'As a tourist, the islanders recognised that this man's regional dialect was from the mainland, but as a tourist, it did not matter to them particularly. And the man, not being familiar with the island's dialect, did not realise he was speaking any differently from the way he was being spoken to. But there was a difference. The tiniest of differences.

'When the man bought the house and began calling on the islanders, they knew immediately that they could have nothing to do with him. As a tourist, they could accept the wrong dialect. But if he was to be an islander, a true islander, he would have to learn to speak in their dialect or they could not speak to him at all.

'This was something that went unsaid amongst the islanders. There was no town meeting called or leaflets distributed on the subject. There was no active campaign against him. It was just something each and every one of them knew immediately to be the case, without having to discuss it or even vocalise.

'So when, every day, or every few weeks, the man would greet them, they would always greet him back and would wait to hear which dialect he spoke to them in. And as soon as he put one foot wrong, as soon as he uttered one word in the wrong way or context, they would have to make excuses and walk away. They could not hear the mainland dialect, not from another islander. It was an insult to their ears.

'But the real tragedy is that this man, for whom language came so naturally, who could learn hundreds of different dialects if he put his mind to it, never knew what he was doing wrong, and so could never set about correcting it. More than that, because the islanders would not speak to him, he could never learn his mistake.

'If they had spoken to him, even for just a few weeks, his keen ears and mind would have begun to notice the differences in their dialect and his own and he would have corrected them, but he was not given that chance.

'To learn he had to hear them speak and to hear them speak he had to know the dialect. So he was destined to be alone.

'And when he did die, almost all the villagers paid their respects and some wept openly because they admired this man immensely and felt tremendously sad that he would no longer be around. They felt no guilt about the way they had treated him, though. They simply had no choice.'

The fire had almost died out and the old man stood up and threw three lumps of peat onto the shrinking flame, sending a cloud of smoke pummelling around the room. He sat back down in his chair with a deep sigh. The dog looked up at him for a second before settling back down beside his leg. The cat began purring again as soon as it jumped into his lap.

'I don't get it,' Ernest said. 'What's the point?'

'Point?' the old man said.

'I mean . . . I don't get it. What's the point of the story?'

'I don't know,' the old man said.

'Well,' Ernest said. 'What does it prove? Where's the . . . It's just depressing.'

'Do you think so?' the old man said. 'Yes, I suppose you're right.'

Ernest stood up in frustration and began to pace the room.

'Well, was it really necessary?' he asked. 'I mean, why even relate something like that? There are no redeeming features to it. It's just . . . purely depressing.'

'Yes,' the old man said.

'What's it got to do with me?' Ernest asked.

'I don't know,' the old man confessed.

·

'Well, is it supposed to help me?' Ernest asked. 'Is it supposed to make me think twice about going to the shore?'

The old man thought a minute.

'I don't know,' he said. 'It's just a story that's told and that I thought I'd tell to you.'

Ernest shook his head in frustration.

'Right,' he said. 'Do you or don't you know where we can get a boat?'

The old man nodded

'Walk down the path,' he said. 'The third house on the left. Liam Clahavan. He might take you. If anyone will. It's a bad night for it.'

'Thank you,' Ernest said.

He turned to Jon, who was still sitting in a chair next to the fire, staring into its flames as they wrapped around the new pieces of peat.

'Are you coming?' he asked.

'Why do you stay here?' Jon asked the old man. 'I mean, if the islanders are like that. If they shun you. What made you want to live here?'

'Well,' the old man said, 'if you'll recall, I never said anything as to whether the man was happy or not. Lonely, yes, but some men are happiest when they are alone, even if they wish, with all their heart, that things could be different.'

Jon nodded.

'Thank you,' he said, standing up.

The old man nodded once and returned his focus to the fire, raging once again.

Jon and Ernest left the warmth of the old man's house and stepped out into the blustery darkened night.

'Ridiculous,' Ernest said, as they walked. 'I ask him for a boat, and he tells me someone's life story. I wouldn't mind if it had a point.'

Jon did not say anything.

Ernest knocked on the door of the third house on their left. Both men shivered as they stood on the doorstep. Jon looked up at the black clouds against the dark blue sky and wondered to himself whether or not it would rain.

The door of the house swung open. A man with huge sideburns dressed in bright red pyjamas stood in the doorway of the house and stared at them for several seconds without speaking.

'We're tourists,' Ernest said finally. 'We want to hire a boat.'

The man continued to stare at Ernest. He scratched his belly under his pyjama top.

'Want to hire a boat?' he said in a thick western accent. 'For the morning is it?'

'No,' Ernest said. 'No, for now.'

'For now?' the man said. 'Sure it's the middle of the night.'

'Yes, but we have an appointment. It's very important. Look, Liam isn't it? Liam, we're willing pay you one hundred pounds.'

Liam scratched his stomach again and sighed.

'Rough night,' he said. 'I don't know what appointment'd get me across those waters on a night like it is.'

'I'm offering you a hundred pounds,' Ernest said. 'Surely that's an incentive? It'll only take twenty minutes there and back.'

Liam nodded. He stepped out onto the cold muck in his bare feet and looked out over the bay. It began to rain lightly as he stood watching the sea.

'There's a storm on its way,' he said.

'One hundred and twenty five pounds,' Ernest said. 'To get us over there right now. Before the storm hits.'

'I don't know now,' Liam said. 'You never can tell how fast they're going to hit.'

'Look, it's just a little rain,' Ernest said. 'I don't see how that means there's a storm coming. One hundred and fifty pounds. We can't say any fairer than that.'

Liam nodded.

'Look out there,' he said, motioning. 'I've seen four men from this island die in that bay. Two of them on nights when there wasn't a cloud in the sky. The sea as still as a lake. I've seen storms rush in here in less time than it takes for a man to spit. I think I know a thing or two.'

'One hundred and seventy five,' Ernest said. 'That's all we have.'

Liam shook his head.

'It's not about the money so much,' he said. 'Although I can see from what you're saying that you need to get over there in a bad way. I am examining the waters and wondering to myself if this is the night they will take me. It's not a matter of money. All the money in the world wouldn't do me much good at the bottom of Galway Bay. So, I am staring out at the waters and wondering is it tonight they'll try and grab me.'

Liam continued to stare for a long time. Finally he nodded.

'I'll take you,' he said. 'For one hundred and seventy five pounds.'

'Fine,' Ernest said. 'Great.'

Liam went into his house and shut the door. Jon and Ernest stood in the rain and waited till he came back out, fully clothed, and led them back down to the small beach, through the fog. When they got to a small dark wooden boat with a pair of woodwormed oars, Liam began pushing it out off the sand.

'Wait,' Ernest said. 'We're going to cross the bay in that?'

Liam nodded.

'What else?'

'It hasn't got an engine,' Ernest protested. 'It hasn't even got sails.'

'You don't want sails in this bay,' Liam said. 'You'll be half way to America before you know where you are. Jump in,' he instructed, as he began pushing the boat through the waves.

Jon and Ernest ran alongside the boat and jumped inside. Liam grabbed hold of the two oars and, with two powerful arms, began pushing the boat out into the sea against the waves.

When they were a little way from the island the fog cleared entirely leaving them in still and total darkness. The only sound was that of the oars gently dipping in and out of the water.

'Are you a fisherman?' Jon asked Liam as he rowed.

'A fisherman?' Liam said, shaking his head. 'There's not many of them left these days. Most of us have a relative, you see, who died in the waters fishing. Every year there'd be one. There's easier ways of making a bit of cash these days. No, I am a tour guide operator.'

'Why have you got all this fishing equipment in the boat?' Jon asked.

'This is where I do my tour,' Liam said. 'That's my job. I bring all them Scandinavians and Germans and Americans out here and I show them what the locals used to have to do to eat. I dress up as a peasant and I talk like a peasant, and for twenty pound a head I give them the experience of life as a fisherman of the Aran Islands.'

'Don't you find it demeaning?' Jon asked.

Liam shrugged.

'I can't say I do,' he said. 'One of my brothers is over there in London working as a brickie. The other fella went to University College Galway and is now a clerk in a bank in Galway city. I have visited them both on numerous occasions and, I have to say, neither of them like what I do. Most of the villagers these days are separated between them that work for the tourists and them that don't. And in the beginning there was a fierce amount of dislike between the two groups.

'A lot of people thought we were pandering to outsiders and that it was undignified but the group who opposed have grown less and less in number as time has gone on. There's not many of them left now. A few old folk. Some of the young fellas though, fellas like me two brothers, have grown up with the tourism, and grown to resent it. I suppose I can understand it. Having them fellas gawping at you and taking photos day in and day out. But I deal with the reality, and the reality is there's far worse things than codding a few tourists out of their money. And as far as me two brothers go . . . well, the one has this big foreman fella shouting at him all day and calling him a thick Paddy, and the other has a manager who, although he never raises his voice, treats him far worse.

'I'll take a few gawping tourists any day. At least you can put one over on them with no real damage. They're impressed by what they see even if it's not the truth. All they want is a bit of a show anyway. I don't have many dissatisfied customers.'

The waves began picking up as they reached the halfway point between the island and the mainland. Liam looked up into the sky.

'I don't like the look of it,' he said.

'We're halfway there,' Ernest said.

Liam nodded.

'I suppose you're right,' he said and began rowing again.

The rain suddenly started again. They were surrounded by the smashing sound of it hitting the sea. A wave crashed against the side of the boat and knocked one of the oars out of Liam's hands. It slipped into the black ocean before he could grab it back with his grasping hand. Liam stared at his one remaining oar.

'That was not good,' he said. 'Of course, they should, by right, have been tied on someplace. I always forget that part of it.'

He stared at the oar a while longer as the rising waves continued to batter against the boat.

'What are we going to do?' Ernest asked.

'Have any of you an idea which way the tide is going?' Liam asked.

'You're the one who spends his life in a boat,' Ernest said. 'I thought you knew what you were doing.'

'No,' Liam said. 'No, not really. It's all an act you see, for the tourists. I never really learned much about it. To be perfectly honest, I don't really like boats too much. It was purely a financial consideration.'

A huge wave crashed into the boat and knocked all three men down. When Liam sat up again he noticed that he was no longer holding the second oar.

'That's a bit of bad luck,' he said, nodding. 'Ah well, there's not much you can do in these waters but go round in a circle with the one oar.'

'What are we going to do?' Ernest asked.

'Well,' Liam said, 'as near as I can figure, we'll have to sit inside this boat, hold on very tight and hope the waves don't turn us over. If we're lucky we might drift back towards the island or even towards Galway. If we're unlucky we'll drift out into the Atlantic where we will probably die of starvation and dehydration.'

Ernest stared into the black night as the boat slowly rose and quickly fell on the huge waves. He thought he could make out the lights of Galway mainland only a few hundred feet away. Another giant wave crashed against the boat, knocking them to the floor again. Ernest spat the salt water from his mouth and stood up in the boat, desperately trying to find the lights again.

'Sit down,' Liam instructed.

Jon saw his friend standing and tried to speak but found he couldn't. He was holding on with whitened knuckles to the side of the boat, trying desperately to stop the sickly swelling feeling in his stomach as the boat rose and fell.

'Get down, dammit!' Liam instructed Ernest, who was continuing to stare out into the night.

'The lights,' Ernest said. 'I have to find them.'

Ernest stood staring for one more fraction of a second before being swept over the side of the boat by a giant wave. Liam tried to grab him as he slipped over but only managed to tear a bit of wet material from his jacket.

He showed the scrap of material to Jon forlornly. Jon stared in disbelief over the side of the boat. Another wave crashed into the boat and sent him reeling back. When he sat up again he saw Liam was no longer in the boat.

'Oh Jesus,' he said.

He did not believe in God. That was what went through his mind in those few seconds. It had been his natural instinct as a child to say a prayer whenever in trouble. His mind had been browbeaten by all those priests and their adoring talcum-powder-smelling lady teachers.

'Bow your heads, children, and pray for the souls in PURGATORY.'

'Bow your heads, children, and pray for those poor unfortunate BLACK BABIES in AFRICA.'

'Bow your heads, children, and pray for poor JOHNATHEN OWEN, who is in HOSPITAL this week with MENINGITIS.'

But the priests in the school were wholly unlikable, and everybody kept trying to tell him that God was so full of love and kindness and forgiveness, so he could not understand it.

There was Father Mint, who beat children as young as six with a thick leather strap. There was Father Hay, who would stand in the middle of the schoolyard during break time, and hit on the head with his open hand any boy whom he caught running. There was no school policy against running. It was just that Father Hay took exception to it. He couldn't stand watching kids running around. He really used to belt them if they came close enough.

Then there was Father Iris who, during Confession, would scream at you if you confessed to the merest of crimes, such as forgetting to say your bedroom prayers, or arguing with your sister, and give you two hundred Hail Mary's to pray and tell you where you were going if you didn't say them.

Then there were the old fools who, while not cruel, did not exactly inspire Jon or persuade him, as a young boy, that they fitted the image of those portrayed as God's representatives on earth.

There was Father Barnaby, a plump man from the country, who was headmaster of the junior school for a little while during Jon's time there. Father Barnaby used to come into class each day when he was headmaster and always began by staring at the floor for several seconds as if he could not remember why he was there. He would hum, and haw, and smile shyly at the teacher, and smile shyly at the class, and then, as if as a last resort, ask the boys had any of them seen the game of hurling that was on yesterday, and the teacher would sigh.

One of the other things Father Barnaby would frequently ask was whether anybody could name the three colours of the hurling team of his beloved home county, Offaly, and everybody always knew the answer because he asked it nearly every day. The teacher would sigh and occasionally somebody would be bored enough to answer him just to get him out of the room or onto his next question.

If the kids were feeling bored enough or they were in the middle of some exam or other when Father Barnaby called in, they would try and keep him in the room as long as possible. They would do this by trying to get him to tell them one of his famous jokes. Father Barnaby told the worst, the most obvious, and most unfunny jokes in the world.

He must have had a book some place called *One Million and One Awful Jokes*, because he was always telling them and no two of them were ever the same. The thing was, though, if you got him in the right mood, Father Barnaby could while away as much as a whole afternoon telling his dreadful jokes, and some-times, such as when they were in the middle of a test, this is what Jon's class tried desperately to get him to do.

The teacher would go completely red in frustration and sigh every couple of seconds and look at her watch but she would never say anything, because he was the headmaster after all, even if he was some bumbling old fool who didn't know what was expected of him and so wandered from class to class humming and hawing and telling bad jokes.

So when Father Barnaby told the punchline of his terrible jokes —and his jokes always had punchlines; he didn't go in much for situational humour—the whole class would erupt in an explo-sion of pure fake laughter, to try and convince old Barnaby that he was just about the funniest man in the world and that if he would only stay and tell a few more jokes they would all be tick-led pink.

People would go way overboard in their attempts to convince Father Barnaby they found him funny. They would roll on the ground squirming and shaking and holding their sides as if they'd split. They would jump off their desks as if the humour was just too much for them and they could not take it. They would laugh and scream for five full minutes, and the teacher, meanwhile, would look just about ready to have a nervous breakdown.

And sometimes Father Barnaby was so pleased to see he had made all the kids happy, and that he might just have a reason for being headmaster after all, that he would tell more jokes, and sometimes he would get so carried away on the tide of laughter that he would spend the whole of the afternoon telling jokes.

Jon had always felt kind of sorry for Father Barnaby, although mostly he carried on and faked laughter with the others. But sometimes he would stop pretending and look Father Barnaby in the eye and see how genuinely pleased with himself he was and feel terribly guilty and want everybody to stop faking. And some-

times when Father Barnaby was staring at the floor and not saying anything and the teacher was looking so impatient, Jon would
get very agitated, because he could see Father Barnaby was making a fool of himself and that everyone knew it but himself and
even though he didn't notice, Jon noticed for him, and felt em-
barrassed for him too.

The school was mostly split up into those two broad groups of
mean and sadistic or harmless and bumbling old priests, and even
though there were a few in the middle, it was the priests at either
end of the spectrum who most affected Jon.

As a young boy entering the school, he had been so wide-eyed
and in awe of these men, dressed in black, the pure white collar
round their necks. He believed what he was told about them and
when they spoke he listened attentively, thinking that, whatever they were saying, it must be important. But having seen
them be cruel, cruel to himself and to friends of his, cruel in a
way his parents had never been cruel, he began to wonder. After
all, all those books, everything he learned in Catholicism, spoke
about forgiveness, of a kind God.

One day, in class, one of the brainier of the kids, Anthony
Davids, was sitting, as usual, beside Jon in the classroom and, as
usual, he was being attentive and listening to the teacher. There
were two boys behind them, however, who were talking while
the teacher read, giggling with each other in secretive conspira-
torial whispers.

The teacher was already impatient with the class at this point,
having warned them twice already to be silent as she read, and
on this third occasion she looked up, with furious eyes magnified
by her thick glasses, and stared down at Jon and Anthony.

'Is that you two talking?' she said. 'How dare you! How dare
you talk while I'm reading after I've asked twice already for silence. I want one hundred lines from both of you tomorrow
morning: I must not talk in class. To be signed by your parents.'

Jon nodded forlornly but Anthony was horrified. He had never
even been given lines before. The worst part of it all was having
to get his parents to sign it. He really never had been in trouble
before.

'It wasn't me,' Anthony said to the teacher. 'Please, miss, I wasn't talking.'

'Are you answering me back?' the teacher said, in a quietly outraged voice.

'It wasn't me,' Anthony said, as if he knew he shouldn't be saying it, but could not help himself.

'Right,' the teacher said. 'Get up to the top of the class. Immediately.'

Anthony shook his head, but began moving.

'It wasn't me,' he said again, staring at the floor as he walked.

'You'd better shut your mouth right now young man,' the teacher said. 'We'll see what Father Mint has to say about your insolence.'

The thing about being sent up to the top of the class was, that sometimes, it could work out fine. You never knew when Father Mint, who was headmaster at the time, was going to arrive. If you were sent up to the top of the class with five minutes to go before lunch, you had a good chance the teacher would forget about you after the break and you would not be punished, but if you were unlucky enough, as Anthony was, to be at the top of the class during one of Father Mint's daily visits, then you were destined for the strap.

'What have we got here?' he asked as soon as he arrived, a tall thin man with pure white teeth that he regularly flashed at the boys just as he was about to strike down with that leather strap.

'It wasn't just the fact that he was talking,' the teacher explained to Father Mint. 'It was the insolence of him. The bare-faced insolence. I saw him talking myself.'

Of course, Jon knew that to be a lie, and for one second, he contemplated putting his hand up and telling her as much, but he did not. He kept his hand down and watched as Anthony shook his head vigorously.

'It wasn't me,' he said, a tear beginning to come down his cheek.

'Are you standing there calling Mrs Brown a liar?' Father Mint said, in a booming furious voice.

Anthony shook his head and wiped the tears from his cheek.

'It wasn't me,' he repeated, and he looked as if he knew what his words would mean.

'Right,' Father Mint said, his mouth tight and furious.

He took out the small thick piece of leather from the pocket of his long, draping, black clerical skirt.

'Hold out your hands,' he instructed.

Anthony wiped another tear away. He was sobbing uncontrollably now.

'Hold out your hands!' Father Mint yelled.

Anthony held out his two hands, face up. Father Mint struck them hard and fast with the strap. He struck them four times more and each time Anthony let out a terrible short whimper of pain. As Jon watched he felt as if it were his own hands being struck. He could almost feel the stinging pain with each strike.

'Now sit down,' Father Mint instructed, when he had finished. 'and don't be telling lies.'

But he had not been telling lies. He had been telling the truth . . . and this was one of the first chinks in Jon's belief in the priests. The longer time went on, the more often he saw that priests could be as wrong as anyone. They could be as mean, or they could be as foolish. He saw they were not any wiser or closer to any spirituality than anyone.

Of course, this didn't mean there wasn't a God. The fact that the Church was full of men like that did not really reflect on a God, if there was one. But in his growing up, the two had always gone hand in hand and Jon found that when his faith in the Catholic Church collapsed, so did his faith in God.

All of these thoughts went through Jon's head in the few seconds that he was alone in the boat. He realised that a belief in God might have helped him at such a time. He wondered to himself if his thoughts on the subject had been allowed to grow independently of the influence of the priests and their loyal teachers, he would perhaps still have had a sense of God, or at least something that would give him hope that his life might continue, once his body had breathed for the last time.

He had thought he would die from the asthma. He smiled to himself as he thought about that, then he laughed out loud, because he was smiling as he sat in a small wooden boat, in the middle of Galway Bay, while a storm raged all around him.

At least he wouldn't die in a hospital, he thought. His worst time in life had been those few weeks, after that terrible initial attack of breathlessness. The boredom. The helplessness. What was perhaps worst was the realisation, sitting in that hospital bed, that one day he would probably die from the same disease he was there for now. Knowing the instrument of his death. He even knew what it would feel like. The sudden realisation that you weren't getting enough air. The desperation of it. The lungs, being able to take in less and less, as if a new weight was being added to your chest every few seconds. As if your ribs were closing in on your spine, and squeezing your body flat.

There was an old man sitting opposite Jon in the hospital. An asthma sufferer, like himself. He was there when Jon arrived and there when he left. A wheezing old man, with clouded eyes and a lost expression. The nurses all knew him by his first name and he smiled weakly at them and cracked bad jokes as they fixed his pillow and helped him with the many machines he needed to help him breathe, huge bulky things with long snake-like pipes and springs and balloons that inflated and deflated as he slowly breathed.

Jon hated looking at the old man. Hated his weak smile and his bad jokes and his good nature. He looked at this old man and knew he was looking at himself. He was destined to sit where the old man sat, and to breathe through the many machines, and to wheeze with every single painful breath, and to be utterly helpless. He looked at the old man and hated him intensely because he was his future.

Jon laughed now, at his thoughts then, as he sat in the boat shivering. He had been so sure. He wondered now at his certainty that he would even live to be so old. That man was well into his eighties. He realised, as another wave crashed inside the boat, if a man lives that long he is lucky. He is lucky just to be able to walk, to be able to go the toilet on his own. He had seemed happy enough. Maybe it wouldn't have been so bad after all.

Just before Jon was swept into the water as the boat was overturned by a huge wave, he thought to himself that even if the old man had been happy, he didn't think he could be happy that way. He'd rather live his life on his own terms than go into hospital and spend those final few months helpless. Not to say that he didn't want to live long. He did. He just didn't want to have to rely on others. Not when everybody was so mean; people in hospitals. It wasn't that they meant to be, necessarily. They tried to be nice. But they weren't. They were short. They were rude. They were patronising. Even the nicest nurse or doctor was more patronising to you than you would take from anybody on the outside.

Human beings just aren't all that caring, Jon thought. To ask them to be caring as a profession is a joke. I think I'd rather be hit by a piano from above, he thought, or by a bullet or anything quick, before I got to the point where I had to rely on nurses and doctors and sucking and spewing machines. And with that thought a huge wave crashed against the boat and knocked it over, sending Jon into the icy waters.

8. Copper Downey

As Ernest hit the water all he felt was a tremendous burning pain. A pain like nothing he had ever experienced. A pain that cut through every part of him. It screwed and twisted every molecule, every cell. Like a hundred million different Chinese burns all over him. He tried to scream but could not. Somewhere in the back of his mind someone was trying to tell him to remain calm but he was ignoring them. He thrashed in the water, not really aware where he was at all, just trying to rid himself of the shattering burning he felt all over.

Ernest awoke, and stared at the sun, peering at him from just above the horizon. He smiled to himself and sighed. He stared from the sun to the moon, which still hung, slightly faded, in the pale blue sky. He wondered to himself what the word was for such a morning, when the moon and the sun are both visible. He frowned and tried to think. He was sure there was a word for it. He was no good at calling up such things. His memory did not store or recall such information very well.

It was while musing in this way that Ernest remembered once again who he was. He had not been aware of anything but trying to remember the word for the sun and moon morning. It had not particularly mattered to him at the time what his name was, or why he was there. But now he remembered, and with the memory came a shock that made him sit up.

I am alive, he thought.

He was lying on a patch of brown seaweed on a sandy beach. To his left was a figure completely covered in seaweed from head to toe.

'Jon,' Ernest tried to say, but he found his mouth was almost completely numb. He moved his jaw up and down. His tongue felt as if it was six times its normal size in his mouth. He could not remember how to manipulate it for speech.

'Jaaa!' was all he could say.

The seaweed figure began moving. It sat up, looking like some sort of strange genetic experiment. A hand rose up from its side, and tore the seaweed from its face. It was Jon. He stared at Ernest for a long time with a blank expression, before leaning over and spewing out several litres of water onto the sand. Ernest smiled, glad to see his friend was alive.

After a little while both men stood up and, after balancing on their feet for several minutes while the earth rose and fell towards them, they began to walk in slow unsteady steps. A little way down the beach they found the small wooden boat they had been travelling in. It lay, entirely intact, upside-down in the sand.

'The boath,' Ernest, whose tongue was slowly beginning to defrost, said.

Jon, who did not seem as badly affected, nodded.

'Do you think he's dead?' he asked.

'Not dead,' came a voice from underneath the boat.

Ernest and Jon scrambled to lift the boat up and, sure enough, Liam lay on his back underneath. He smiled up at them.

'Well,' he said, 'that was a close thing.'

The three men stood on the beach and took deep breaths and stared out at the sea which had almost killed them and had then placed them, quite gently, on the sandy shore.

'Well,' Liam said. 'She must have had her reasons.'

Ernest nodded.

'Where are we?' he asked.

Liam slapped his stomach and stared around the beach.

'Skriel,' he pronounced.

Ernest looked around them, at the sandy beach, and the small, old-looking pier. He nodded appreciatively as he stared.

'Skriel,' he said. 'We've arrived. We must go, immediately.'

Jon shook his head.

'Forget it,' he said. 'Count me out.'

'You heard him,' Ernest said. 'We're here for a reason. We should, by rights, have died out there last night. We've got to hurry. Look at the sun. He'll be leaving soon.'

'I should go and get some oars,' Liam said as he stared at the boat, scratching his stomach.

Ernest took the soggy twenty pound notes from his pocket.

'Here,' he said. 'I'm only sorry we can't give you more.'

Liam shook his head.

'Ah, I can't take that. Not with the boat capsizing and all that,' he said. 'Besides, it wasn't about the money. Still, I think you must have a purpose on these shores all right. I've never known the sea to be so kind. Usually, now, it is as ruthless as any predator.'

Ernest turned to Jon, as Liam walked off down the beach.

'You see,' he said. 'We've got a purpose.'

Jon shook his head.

'Thank you,' he said. 'Maybe that's true, but in my case it is certainly not to rob and murder a landlord.'

'We don't have to murder him,' Ernest said. 'I don't want to kill anyone any more than you do. I'm just saying rob. He deserves it. Look, don't you see? There's got to be a reason for all this. There's got to be a reason we started on this journey and why we're here now. Do you honestly think it could have happened by accident? We took side roads, we never knew where we were going, we survived numerous attempts on our lives, we nearly died in that boat and yet, here we are, washed up on the shore right off Skriel, with only a little time to spare. You're going to tell me that's just coincidence?'

Jon shook his head.

'No,' he said. 'I don't know. You really want to do it? You really want to rob Copper?'

'I don't know,' Ernest said. 'Mostly, I admit, it was just talk. I was trying to get Paul to come on some kind of adventure. Mostly it was just something to do. But, after all this, I'm starting to wonder. I'm starting to wonder if maybe things don't happen for a reason.

'Look, what is there back there for us? I can't face having to find another shitty flat and live below the poverty line on what those bastards are willing to give me. I can't face six more months of sending out pre-rejected copies of this manuscript to people whose opinion I don't even want. And if we go back there that's all there is ahead, either that, or starting in some lowly menial job I'll hate and that will eat at me from the inside until I'm a walking corpse.

'I'm going to do it, with or without you. I have to. After all this, I have to.'

Jon nodded. Ernest began walking towards the road at one end of the beach. Jon sighed and followed a few seconds later and the pair walked together onto the road and into Skriel village.

'Right,' Ernest said, as they stood in the centre of Skriel village, staring around them at the small, quaint houses, the old grey church, and the tourist pubs and restaurants. 'We've got to find Copper's house.'

'How do you propose we do that?' Jon asked.

'Simple,' Ernest said. 'We'll just ask somebody. We'll tell them we're relatives or something, that we're here to visit him and that we lost his address.'

'I see,' Jon said.

They came to the first house. Ernest turned to Jon as they walked up the pathway.

'Remember, don't let on we're from Dublin,' he said. 'Obviously these people have some sort of bizarre prejudice against us just because of some kind of petty jealousy and unfair resentment. I mean, it's not my fault they live in a backwater, is it?'

'That's just the attitude that gets you on top of bonfires,' Jon said.

'Shut up. I'll do the talking.'

Ernest knocked on the door. A second later an old woman with long flowing white hair and very few teeth opened it to them.

'*Dia dhuit*,' she said.

Ernest was momentarily put off by how strange the woman looked.

'Duggit,' Ernest said finally, trying to mimic her sound. 'My friend and I are from Roscommon. We're here to visit a relative of ours, Copper Downey, but we've lost the address, you see. We were just wondering if you could tell us where he lives?'

The woman nodded, and bade them come into the house with a long white wrinkled arm.

'I've been waiting for you,' she said as she led them into the hallway.

'This is it?' Ernest asked, looking around the musty old house. He turned to Jon.

'She must be Copper's mother,' he said.

The old woman turned around to see why they weren't behind her and began waving them forward again, into the back of the house.

'It's gone so cold,' the woman said, as she led them through the house.

'Yes,' Ernest said. 'It has, hasn't it? I expect you're wondering why we're so wet. Well, it was the ferry you see, it crashed and we all got soaking wet and, of course, I lost the address of the house. Is Copper in by any chance?'

The old woman nodded and motioned them to keep following her. She led them finally to a small dark back room which contained nothing but old boxes full of clothes and a boiler.

'Here we are,' the woman said, pointing to the boiler.

Ernest and Jon stood staring at the boiler for a long while and then looked back at the woman. She was nodding serenely as she watched them.

'I'm glad you came so soon,' she said. 'It's gone so cold. It's gone so cold I can barely feel my hands.'

Ernest nodded.

'I'm sorry,' he said. 'There appears to have been some sort of mistake. We're looking for the house of Copper Downey.'

'What?' the old woman said, before sighing. 'What, now? You'll have to speak up. I haven't had them cleaned this week. Are you going to get the things out from your van?'

'No,' Ernest said. 'No, you don't understand, we're just looking for Copper Downey's house.'

'She must think we're here to fix her boiler,' Jon said. 'It is freezing in this house.'

'That's all very well,' Ernest said. 'But we don't have time for this.'

He turned back to the old lady.

'We're not here for the boiler,' he yelled. 'We're looking for someone.'

'What?' the old lady said. 'You don't think you can get it done? You haven't even looked at it yet. The other fella always has a good look at it first. You haven't got your tools.'

'No,' Ernest said. 'No, we're not repair men.'

'What's wrong with it?' the old woman said, a look of great shock on her face. 'I've had it thirty years and it's been fine. It heats up the place something great, so it does. I never have any trouble with it. My son sometimes has a look at it for me but he's away. It's so cold in the house, I can barely feel my feet. Would you like a cup of tea, while you're working?'

Ernest sighed. It was no use.

'Maybe we should have a look at it,' Jon said.

'Are you insane?' Ernest said. 'We don't have time.'

'She's freezing, for God's sake,' Jon said, before turning to the old lady. 'Haven't you got anyone in the house? No other relatives?'

The woman shook her head.

'My daughter is away,' the old woman said.

'We have to do something,' Jon said. 'It's awful. A woman her age alone in a big house like this.'

'What the fuck do you want us to do?' Ernest whispered. 'I agree with you. It is awful. It's terrible. But we don't know anything about boilers. How are we supposed to fix it when we don't know anything about it?'

'We could have a look,' Jon said defensively. 'We can't just leave her here on her own.'

All the while the old woman was staring at them with a small serene smile on her face. She was happy, satisfied that the men whom she had phoned had come so quickly to fix the boiler. She was enjoying the attention. Meanwhile, Ernest and Jon continued to argue.

'We've got to go,' Ernest was saying. 'We don't have time for this. Copper will be leaving for Dublin soon and it'll be too late. I don't like it any more than you do, but that's the reality. We can check in on her on our way back, when we have all of Copper's cash. We can leave her enough money for a new boiler.'

'I'm not leaving her here on her own,' Jon said. 'She could die in this cold.'

'Fine,' Ernest said. 'Stay here. I am going to rob Copper Downey.'

Ernest stormed out of the back room and proceeded to get lost in the maze of corridors and rooms that wound through the large house. Finally he ended up in a darkened dead end. He fumbled for a light switch and clicked it on.

Ernest let out a sigh. He was in a room full of countless numbers of photos framed and hung on all four walls. He recognised the old woman in a large number of the photographs. There were pictures of her with small children, pictures of her at weddings, several pictures of her with a smiling bald man. In each of the photos the old woman was smiling the same small smile.

Staring around the room Ernest began to pick out black and white photos of her when she was a young woman. She was quite beautiful. There were several of her sitting with a bunch of friends, a cigarette balanced elegantly in one hand.

It made Ernest think. It reminded him of his grandmother. Of when she had died. He had only ever known her as an old woman. In a way that had made her death easier, because to him she had always been old, and old age is equated with death.

But not long after she died, his mother brought back some old black and white photographs, stored away in her attic for who knows how long, and amongst them were some of his grandmother as a young woman. These photos of her had had a profound effect on Ernest. There was one in particular, in which she was standing in the doorstep of a house, with the sun hitting her face, the coyest of smiles on her as she looked away from the camera, down the street, not really looking at anything but just laughing at the fact she was being photographed, and thinking about that as she stared away.

She was twenty-one years old, the same age Ernest was as he looked at it, those few days after she died. It shocked him. She had always been so old. Always been coughing and groaning when she sat down and sighing when she got up. It had shocked him to see his grandmother looking so young and beautiful. To think of her as a young girl with the same hopes and ambitions that he had, the same dreams of what was to come. Looking at that photo, he realised for the first time that his grandmother had lived for almost ninety years. She wasn't just a kindly old woman who spoiled them with sweets.

Staring around him, at the old woman's whole life set out in photos around one small room, and thinking about his grandmother, Ernest felt depressed. He turned off the light, feeling more than a little ashamed, and found his way, after several wrong turns, back to the boiler room.

Jon was standing on a box altering several levers and checking nuts and bolts on the boiler. The old woman was watching, with that same small smile on her face and Ernest stared at her for a long time, thinking of that young girl on the doorstep. Thinking how strange life was.

'Have you got the tools?' the old woman asked when she noticed him.

Jon turned too. Ernest stared at the floor.

'You were right,' he said. 'I'm sorry. I got carried away. Of course we should stay and help.'

Jon nodded.

'I don't know if we can,' he said, turning his attention back to the boiler. 'I just don't see anything wrong. Not that I know anything about these things. But I can't see anything obvious.'

Ernest nodded gravely and examined the boiler.

'Neither can I,' he pronounced finally.

After a little while they gave up and went back into the living room whereupon the old lady made them all tea. She didn't seem too bothered that they couldn't fix the boiler.

'My Frank's very good with it,' the old lady said. 'He just gives it a tap with an old spanner and it starts up again.'

The old lady laughed, a long unabashed laugh that Ernest and Jon could not help but join in with.

Ernest stared at the clock above the old lady's head. It ticked and tocked loudly as they sipped their tea. He could not help but feel agitated. They had come so far and here they were, sitting, drinking tea, while probably just a few houses away, Copper was preparing to leave for Dublin and take the secret of where he kept his money with him.

'What kind of boiler is it?' Ernest asked, standing up suddenly.

'I don't know,' Jon said. 'Gas?'

'What kind of fuel does your boiler take?' Ernest asked the lady.

'Oh, it doesn't take fuel,' the old lady said. 'Would you like some more tea?'

'It must take something,' Ernest said loudly. 'Gas, oil?'

'Oil,' the old lady said. 'That's right, the man comes with the oil. A young fella. Oh, he's a lovely man. He always stays for his tea. He likes the chocolate biscuits. I'm not allowed have them any more but I sometimes keep them for the guests. And Maggie, Maggie likes the chocolate biscuits.'

'Is that your daughter?' Jon asked.

'My daughter?' the old lady said. 'No, my daughter is away. She's working. No, Maggie keeps me company. Frank wanted me to get a dog, you see, for the burglars, but I don't think I'd be able for one. And we've always had cats in our family.'

Jon and Ernest nodded silently.

'There must be some kind of outside container then,' Ernest said. 'For the oil. My house used to have oil heating. She might have run out, or something might have clogged it up, she could have had a leak, any number of things. We should go check.'

'Where's your container?' Jon asked the old woman.

'Oh, I don't have one,' the old woman said. 'No, I don't have trouble with that. I know a good few now that needs them, but my lungs have always been good. My Paddy used to have one though, I think I might have one upstairs.'

'No,' Jon said. 'Not an inhaler, a container. Where do you keep the oil?'

'Oh,' the old woman laughed for a full minute. 'I thought you meant . . . Oh yes, it's out the back.'

Ernest began racing down the many corridors till eventually he came to a door that led into the back garden. He pulled the bolt on the door and rushed outside into the overgrown garden full of weeds. He stared around the garden and for those first few seconds could see little sign of any oil container. Then he spotted a particularly large bush and, sure enough, when he pushed back the weeds and ivy there was a large solid rectangular container underneath. Jon had joined him at this point and the pair of them stared at the huge tank for a few seconds wordlessly.

Ernest banged on the side of it. It thudded low and deep.

'There's something in there,' Ernest said. 'Whether it's rain or oil, who knows? We'll have to open it up and check. Give me a boot up.'

Ernest stood up on top of the oil drum and looked around for the opening. He stepped on several branches as he walked around and began kicking them off the side, trying to uncover the lid so that he could at least get a look inside.

'Found it,' he said, staring at the rectangular door that opened outwards. He fashioned a long dipping stick from a branch and, lying down on his stomach, pressed the stick as far into the oil drum as it would go.

When he removed the stick he saw that it was covered in a brown slime, almost halfway up the bark.

'There's oil in there all right,' Ernest said. 'I can't say anything about the quality of it, but there's enough of it in there to keep that boiler going.'

Jon nodded and felt quite ineffectual standing staring up at Ernest.

'What can I do?' he asked.

'Do?' Ernest said. 'Oh, nothing. I'll just have to go in there, that's all.'

'Go in there?' Jon said. 'Are you mad?'

'It's perfectly safe,' Ernest said. 'I think I can squeeze through the lid. I have to see if something's blocking it. It's probably just a bunch of leaves.'

But Jon, who had been claustrophobic since he was a young child, could not understand how anybody would go into that small, dark enclosure.

'It's not safe,' he said.

'The sooner I get in there,' Ernest said. 'The sooner we can get out of here.'

The old woman peered out at them from the kitchen window, smiled to herself, and turned away to put on another pot of tea.

Ernest stretched a foot into the tank, until it finally hit the bottom and he could feel the oily goo creeping up all the way to above his knee.

'It's definitely full enough,' he said, and his voice reverberated inside the drum, as he lowered his body down.

Jon climbed up onto the top of the drum but could not look inside the lid. Just thinking about Ernest being in there was making him feel claustrophobic. He pulled out his inhaler and was going to take a deep breath when he realised that it had been completely drenched and that he should probably wait, just in case the sea water or some chemical in it had some bizarre effect on the inhaler that he did not know about.

Thinking about this made him think about the stuff he had to inhale into his lungs, the chemical, and how he didn't really know what it was. He knew its name, the scientific term. But he didn't really know anything about it, except that when his lungs tightened up, or his cough got bad, he would inhale it in short held puffs, and it would make him feel better.

He started to wonder to himself whether the stuff itself was actually doing him any good, and whether the whole thing wasn't just psychological. Perhaps, he mused, some great psychologist had teamed up with the doctors one day and said:

'Look here, fellas, we can't really beat this thing asthma with any of your fancy drugs, and the new tests and trials aren't going too well either. Nothing's working out, nothing that really works one hundred per cent, and the things that come close have awful crippling side effects.

'Now, I've been doing a few tests of my own and I've discovered a remarkable thing. If you just give all these people a little inhaler gizmo, like this one here, and scent it with something that tastes a bit like medicine but is, in fact, just a harmless oxygen spray, these people actually convince themselves they feel better. What's more, you tell them there's a couple of minor side effects, (because everybody expects side effects and if you don't give people them they feel cheated because they know there's no such thing as a free ride) not only will they cure themselves, but they'll make sure they feel the side effects you told them about as well.

'What say we all pool together and sell these things and, that way, we can all make a fast buck and cure people at the same time?'

Jon was still pondering these thoughts when Ernest called out to him. He was fumbling around in the pitch dark of the oil drum and Jon could hear every tiny sound he made ten times amplified as it hit against the walls.

'I've found something,' Ernest said, in his strange reverberating voice.

Jon was snapped from his thoughts and peered down the opening of the drum, but he couldn't see anything through the black.

'There's something stuck,' Ernest said. 'I think it's an old rag or something. It's blocking the oil pipe leading to the house.'

There were loud sloshing sounds coming from the drum as Ernest attempted to remove the rag. Jon could here his thudding steps as he pushed and pulled and struggled to get it out of the pipe. Finally he heard one last slosh and Ernest's voice.

'I have it,' Ernest pronounced.

A moment later he emerged from the opening with a black soggy rag. Ernest was feeling a little strange from being inside the tank and breathing nothing but oil fumes so he just concerned himself with inhaling the fresh air for a while and did not pay any attention to the rag he was holding.

But Jon was watching it. He was watching more and more of the oil drip off the rag and, for some reason, he kept watching, because he thought there was something a little funny about it. He watched it for a long time, and finally one big blob of oil dripped off it, and he could see, for the first time, a pair of small unblinking eyes.

'Eh . . . Ernest.'

But Ernest was too busy breathing the fresh air and he held his hand up to show Jon he would talk to him in a minute.

More of the oil was dripping off and Jon could now make out a pair of small crumpled ears, and the red gums of an open mouth.

'Eh . . . Ernest.'

'What?' Ernest said, in between breaths.

'I don't think it's a rag.'

Ernest didn't seem to hear him for a long time, then he looked up at Jon, his face scrunched in confusion. He must have deciphered Jon's words by then because next he looked at the rag. He screamed immediately and dropped it back into the oil.

He climbed out of the drum and began wiping his hands on everything available while trying to hold down the sick that was creeping up his throat.

'Jesus Christ!' he said, as he wiped his hands on leaves and creepers. 'What was that thing?'

Jon shrugged.

'It looked like some kind of animal.'

'Jesus Christ!'

When Ernest had finished pacing up and down on the oil drum and cursing he stopped quite suddenly for several seconds and began a low mumbling curse sound.

'What is it?' Jon asked him.

Ernest just shook his head, and continued to curse.

'I don't believe it,' he said finally aloud. 'I don't believe I was so fucking stupid.'

'What?' Jon said. 'What?'

Ernest stared into the opening of the oil drum.

'I'm going to have to get it out,' he said, shaking his head with bitterness. 'I'm going to have to get back in there and fish that thing out with my bare hands. I'm so fucking stupid! Why didn't I just throw it away some place? Anywhere but right back into the tank where it's going to clog up that damn pipe.'

Jon nodded sympathetically. By rights, he knew, he should have been volunteering for the job. But he couldn't. He simply couldn't.

'I'd go but . . . ' he said.

'No,' Ernest said. 'No, I know. It's my fault anyway. I'm the one who dropped that thing in there. It was dead wasn't it? It looked dead.'

'No,' Jon said. 'No, it was definitely dead.'

Ernest nodded and tried to hold on to that thought as he jumped back into the oil drum. Jon sat on the side of the drum and for the next five minutes, listened to the low moans of Ernest as his hand passed through the oil looking for the dead thing that had been blocking the pipe.

Finally, the long continuous moan ended and Ernest's head popped back up out of the drum. There was a squelch as the animal was plopped onto the lid of the drum. Both men stood over it and watched as the oil slipped away again.

'What do you think it is?' Ernest asked, as his head lolled about the place from feeling so lightheaded.

'I don't know,' Jon said. 'A big rat?'

Ernest didn't like that thought at all. He didn't like the thought that he had just fished out the world's largest rat from the oil drum.

'It's too big,' he said, shaking his head. 'It's far too big.'

Jon noticed something at that point. A small silver thing, shining in the sun for the first time as the oil slipped away. He lent down and examined it closer, holding his nose to keep the awful stench away.

'It's got a collar on it,' he said.

Ernest bent down.

'Well,' he said, moving his hand towards the collar. 'I suppose I've touched it already.'

He grabbed hold of the collar and moved it around so that they could both clearly read the name that was written on it.

'Oh shit,' Ernest said. 'Maggie.'

Jon nodded sadly.

'Poor thing,' he said.

Ernest wiped the oil away from his hands again and the pair of them climbed slowly down from the oil drum.

'Do you think we should tell her?' Jon asked a few moments later, as they walked back towards the house.

'I don't know,' Ernest said. 'Who knows what it would do to

her? She might have a heart condition.'

Jon nodded. The old lady spotted them from the kitchen and was there to meet them as they came into the house, with a large pot of tea.

'Tea,' she said simply, not too interested in what they had been doing.

They stayed for one more cup of tea, and as Jon sat chatting with the old woman, Ernest tried the boiler. In the time they took to finish the tea the heating was back on.

'What do I owe you?' the old lady asked them as they told her they had to go. 'You've done a marvellous job. I must ring you now always. I hadn't rung the place more than ten minutes before you arrived. Wonderful service. The place is heating up lovely.'

'It's on the house,' Ernest said, as they backed away towards the door. 'Really, there's a special offer on this month.'

The old woman nodded.

'Marvellous,' she said. 'I'll ring you two always now.'

'No problem,' Ernest said. 'It was our pleasure.'

'And I can go and call for Maggie again,' the old woman said. 'Because she loves to sit in front of the radiator.'

Ernest nodded and felt terrible.

They left the old woman's house as she continued to thank them profusely and promise she'd stick with their company.

'Maybe we should have told her,' Jon said, as they walked back onto Skriel's main street.

'Look,' Ernest said, 'we did what we could for her. Her house is warm. It's a lot more than most people will do these days.'

Jon nodded.

'She can get another cat,' Ernest went on.

'But still,' Jon said. 'Throwing it into the neighbours' garden.'

'Look,' Ernest said, 'they'll break it to her gently. They know her. It was the right thing.'

'What are we going to do now?'

'Carry on,' Ernest said, going down the garden path of the next house, 'till we find Copper Downey's house.'

'He might have left already.'

'Well we'll find that out,' Ernest said, as he rang the doorbell of the house.

A middle-aged woman came to the door and looked Ernest up and down suspiciously. Ernest remembered, for the first time, how ridiculous he looked.

'Hello,' he said to the woman. 'Sorry to bother you. My friend and I are relatives of a man in this town, Copper Downey. We were involved in a crash, that's how I got all this oil over me, but em . . . we lost Copper's address. He's our uncle you see.'

'Never heard of him,' the woman said, and slammed the door in Ernest's face.

Ernest sighed.

'How could she have not have heard of him?' he said. 'Everybody knows everybody in these places.'

'Weren't you listening to that guy's story on the island?' Jon said. 'The people round here aren't much different. They're suspicious. They don't give out people's addresses to strangers.'

Ernest nodded but he wasn't listening. He had spotted a young man walking down the street towards them. The man had a huge hairy belly that was sticking out from a check shirt which he had open save for a couple of bottom buttons. The man's hair was whipped up into a huge quiff and his teeth were a yellowy brown.

'What are you doing?' Jon asked, as Ernest approached the man.

But Ernest was not listening. The one thing he had on his mind was finding Copper's address and he didn't care who he had to ask.

'Excuse me sir,' he asked the man. 'My friend and I are looking for the address of Copper Downey. We were supposed to meet him in town about a car he's selling but we got a bit delayed and . . . he's expecting us. Do you know which of these houses he lives in?'

The man looked Ernest up and down very slowly and spat, an inch from his shoe.

'Are you from Dublin?' he asked.

'No,' Ernest said. 'No, not Dublin. I'm from Kerry. In fact, we both are. I realise I have a Dublin sounding accent but I sent away for one of those tapes, you see, how to speak Dublin 4 in less than three weeks. Actually, bit of a con really, took me six months before I had the whole thing down.'

The man nodded.

'A tape?' he said, spitting again.

'Yes,' Ernest said. 'Anyway, do you know Copper Downey?'

'I know him,' the man said, nodding once.

Ernest nodded

'Could you, by any chance, let us know which is his house? I assure you, he's expecting us.'

The man spat again and put one hand up to his quiff, as if to make sure it was still there.

'Fucking Dubs,' he said. 'I can't stand fucking Dubs.'

'Me neither,' Ernest said, giggling. 'Fucking Dubs. Coming over here, stealing our cattle.'

The man looked very curiously at Ernest.

'Is that right?' he said. 'Do they come over here for the cattle?'

'Oh yes,' Ernest said. 'Yes, they have no scruples whatsoever. They keep them for fertilisers, you see, for their gardens. And for free milk of course. Oh it's all the rage in the Dublin middle classes. If you haven't got a cow, now, you're not with it.'

'Bastards,' the man said, shaking his head.

'Bastards,' Ernest agreed. 'So, could you tell us where Copper lives?'

The man with the quiff sniffed loudly. He turned around and pointed down the street.

'You go down about two miles out of town,' he said. 'You'll see a big house with red bricks. It's not that one. It's the next one. It's got a big balcony, like, and it's next to the sea. You can't miss it.'

'Thank you,' Ernest said. 'We're very grateful.'

The man with the quiff nodded once and walked off down the street in slow ambling steps.

'You see,' Ernest said. 'You just have to know how to approach them.'

He fumbled with the musket as they walked on the road out of town.

'I don't think it's going to work,' he said.

'No,' Jon said. 'I think you'll find when gunpowder gets damp it becomes quite unreliable.'

'Oh yeah,' Ernest said. 'Well, never mind, he won't know the difference.'

'We're really going to do it then,' Jon said. 'We're really going to rob our landlord.'

'What else?' Ernest said.

'Well perhaps we shouldn't have wandered around town asking people for directions to his house then,' Jon said.

'It couldn't be avoided,' Ernest said dismissively. 'Besides, we'll be out of the country long before the investigation starts. Do you know what the police are like round here? They deal with poachers and the occasional gun-toting farmer. They're about as sophisticated as a pair of curtains. We'll be fine.'

'So, where is it exactly you want to go?' Jon asked.

'What?'

'Where is it you want to go, after we've done this? The reason I ask is just that I'm not sure I want to leave.'

'Why not?'

'I don't know,' Jon said. 'I just . . . I'm kind of used to the place. I don't like travelling. I like to know where I am. Miserable as it is, I kind of like Dublin.'

'Well, you could have mentioned this,' Ernest said. 'Before we traipsed across the country to rob this man.'

'It didn't occur to me. To be honest I thought you were joking. I mean, up until the last few days you have never done anything really all that crazy. Not in the criminal sense anyhow. I was trying to determine whether or not you had finally lost all reason.'

'Well, I have,' Ernest said. 'I have lost all reason and I'm going to rob this man.'

They came to a large house with bright red bricks. Far in the distance, down a road that led to the sea, they could see a large grey house with a balcony.

'Right,' Ernest said. 'We're here. I'll quite understand it if you want to stay behind or go home or do whatever it is you think you have to do. Personally, I can't see any alternative for us. We need money. We don't have a home. We don't have jobs. We can't even draw the dole unless we have a fixed abode. Personally, I don't plan to starve on the streets just because this evil bastard landlord wanted to squeeze a bit more money out of his cramped little flat. Think about it, will you? Think about what sort of a man would give someone 48 hours' notice to leave their flat. Think about a man who owns five huge houses across Dublin and collects whole truck loads of cash from them. And finally, think about wearing these balaclavas over your head because, I, for one, don't plan to be identified.'

Jon stared at the balaclavas in Ernest's hands.

'Balaclavas?' he said.

'Yes,' Ernest said. 'Balaclavas. That way, we can conceal our faces and stay in this God-forsaken country without fear of being arrested. I was only talking about going on a little holiday in any case, while they were doing the investigation. Some place hot. I haven't been on a holiday in donkey's years.'

'What if we're identified?' Jon said. 'What if we're identified by the old woman, or that guy we just got directions off.'

'Please,' Ernest said. 'That woman's going to turn in the people who fixed her boiler? She doesn't know who we are. She thinks we're from Boilers 'R Us. She's probably half blind anyway. And as for that guy, I don't think he looked one of us in the eye the whole time. In any case, look at us, we're covered in seaweed, muck and oil. There's a layer of grime over us that has set and been growing the past three days. My own mother wouldn't recognise me. Bad example. Your own mother wouldn't recognise you.'

Jon nodded.

'That's true,' he said.

'Well then?' Ernest said, holding out the balaclava. 'It's up to you.'

'Where did you get them?' Jon asked finally.

'Paul's,' Ernest said. 'You'll have to tear strips for your eyes and mouth.'

Jon nodded and took one of the balaclavas. Ernest and Jon ripped the balaclavas in the appropriate places and pulled them down over their faces.

'Right,' Ernest said. 'Let's go.'

'How does this work?' Ernest asked. 'I mean, do you think we should burst in there with guns ablazing or just politely knock.'

'I don't know,' Jon confessed. 'This is my first time.'

They were standing in the driveway of the huge grey house with its large balcony that looked out over several acres of land. The back of the house was on the edge of a tall cliff and Jon and Ernest could hear the sea crashing against the rocks below. They had observed Copper's car sitting in the drive and both men knew, when they saw it, that this was finally very real.

It was hot under the balaclavas, and talking was not easy.

'Maybe we should just knock,' Jon suggested.

'You can't knock when you're about to rob somebody,' Ernest said. 'It's just not done.'

'It's some house,' Jon said, walking backwards and taking in the whole of the pristine three-storey building.

'Somebody will see you,' Ernest said, motioning Jon back.

They stood for several seconds staring at the various bits of brass on the door.

'Well?' Jon said, finally.

'I'm thinking,' Ernest said. 'Maybe we should split up. You go round the back and I'll stay here.'

'What for?'

'I don't know,' Ernest said. 'It sounded good in my head.'

They were still talking when Copper Downey opened the front door of his house to collect the milk. He leant down and picked up the usual three pints of milk, without noticing Ernest and Jon standing there, stood up and shut the door again.

Ernest and Jon stood blinking for several seconds.

'Shit,' Ernest said eventually.

Copper Downey opened the front door once again and was about to place a note for the milkman in the milk tray when he noticed two pairs of muddy feet in the doorway. He looked from the muddy feet slowly up to the balaclava-covered faces and began to scream. This in turn made Ernest and Jon scream. Ernest pointed the gun at Copper's face which made him scream louder still and they all stood there screaming for several minutes before anything else happened.

Eventually the screaming died down leaving Ernest somewhat at a loss what to do next.

'I'm a supporter,' Copper yelled, finally, holding a pair of shaking hands above him.

He was a very thin man with a thick moustache that did not suit him. His wiry frame was cowering as he held his hands high above him and muttered desperate prayers in between assuring the two men, whom he felt sure were members of the local I.R.A unit, that he was a supporter.

'A supporter of who?' Jon asked curiously.

'Youse,' Copper said. 'I always give when Tom Kenny comes round collecting. You can ask him yourself. I always give my fair share.'

Ernest finally decided what they should do next.

'Into the house,' he instructed.

Copper and the two of them moved into the living room of the large house.

'Down on the floor,' Ernest screamed and Copper lay flat down on the rug next to the fireplace.

'What's going on?' came a voice from behind them.

Ernest and Jon turned with a start. A young girl with curly blonde hair, dressed in a school uniform, was standing at the bottom of the stairs and staring, with a very confused look on her face, at her father on the floor and the two men standing over him.

'Ahhh!' screamed Ernest.

'Oh God,' Jon said.

'Ahhh!' screamed Copper.

The girl was the only one who wasn't screaming. A few seconds later she was joined by a young boy a little older than her. He put his hand on her shoulder and stared quizzically at Ernest and Jon.

'What's going on?' he asked.

Ernest stopped screaming.

'Kids,' he said, shaking his head. 'I don't believe it.'

Jon shook his head.

'Oh God,' he repeated.

A third child, the oldest thus far, joined the two children at the bottom of the stairs. She put her hand on the boy's shoulder.

'Who are you?' she asked.

'Look,' Ernest said. 'We're friends of your father's. You go on back upstairs and keep very quiet till we've gone.'

'Why are you pointing a gun at him if you're friends?' the boy asked.

'A game,' Ernest said. 'It's all a game. If you just go back upstairs we can finish playing.'

'I want to play,' the little girl said, walking forward and lying down by her dad on the floor.

'It's not a game,' the young boy said. 'You're robbers aren't you?'

Another boy, younger still, came ambling down the stairs. He was dressed in pyjamas and was rubbing the sleep out of his eyes.

'What's going on?' he asked. 'Why isn't everyone at the table?'

The eldest girl hushed him up but he wouldn't be quiet.

'All I ask,' he said, in a mock serious voice, 'is that you all sit down at the table in an orderly fashion while I make the breakfast. Now, is that too much to ask?'

The young girl lying next to her dad giggled at the boy's impression.

'Is that too much to ask?' she giggled, poking her dad in the ribs.

'Please,' Ernest said to Copper. 'Please tell your kids to go upstairs for a little while. I promise you, we have no desire to hurt anyone.'

Copper nodded.

'Kids,' he said. 'I want you to go upstairs. These men and me are playing a game. I want you to go upstairs and wait for me to come up, okay? I'll be up in a few minutes.'

The kids nodded reluctantly and began moving back upstairs. The young boy in the pyjamas and the young girl lying next to her father were the only ones to stay behind. The young boy began running round the kitchen table, singing at the top of his lungs 'Is that too much to ask! Is that too much to aaaasskk!'

The young girl giggled and joined her brother running round the table and singing.

'Is that too much to ask! Is thaat tooo much to aaaask!'

Ernest watched in horror as the two kids went round and round the table.

'Please,' he said to Copper. 'Please make them go away.'

'Lorna, Michael!' Copper said sternly. 'Have you made your beds this morning?'

Lorna and Michael stopped running round the table. They stared over at their father.

'No,' they both said in unison.

'Well go and do it,' Copper said.

The little boy sighed grumpily and the little girl mimicked him.

'Go and do your bed! Is that too much to ask!'

The boy began singing as he ran up the stairs.

'Go and do your be-ed. Go and go and go and go and doooooo your beddddd.'

The little girl giggled in delight and followed her brother up the stairs, singing along with him.

Once they had gone Ernest turned the gun back on Copper, making sure not to look Jon in the face as he did so.

'Right,' Ernest said. 'We want your money. All of it. Every bit of cash you have.'

'I don't have any,' Copper said. 'I swear to you.'

'Bullshit. We know you have cash. If not in the house, then somewhere else. You'd better tell us where it is.'

'I don't have any money,' Copper said. 'I swear to you. All I have is what I have on me. About thirty pounds. It's upstairs . . . '

'I'm not talking about thirty pounds!' Ernest yelled. 'I'm talking about the cash, the cash you collect from your houses in Dublin every week. We know you have it, we know you keep it somewhere here.'

'Cash?' Copper said. 'I don't have any cash.'

'You'd better tell us or, so help me, I'm going to use this,' Ernest said. 'We know you're a landlord so there's no use pretending. We know you only collect the rent in cash. You'd better tell us where it is.'

'I'm not pretending,' Copper said. 'I'm not pretending I'm not a landlord. I do pick up the rent in cash. But I don't keep any of it. I don't have it in the house. I swear to you.'

'Bullshit. We know you don't trust banks. I'm getting very impatient, Copper. I want to hear you start talking.'

'I'm telling you,' Copper said desperately. 'I'm only telling you the truth. I don't keep any of that cash. It all goes . . . it all goes to the bank. It all goes in the bank on Friday.'

'I said, we know you don't trust banks!' Ernest screamed.

'Yes . . . yes. That's true but . . . for a reason . . . that's why . . . I'm sorry, if you'll just let me explain. I can't seem to get the words out.'

'Calm down,' Jon said. 'Let him talk, for God's sake.'

'Okay,' Ernest said. 'Okay, calm. Fine, we're all calm. There's no problem. Tell me, what the hell are you talking about?'

'My wife,' Copper said. 'My wife died . . . she died two years ago. I took out several loans . . . on the strength of the life insurance you see. I bought two more houses in Dublin. So's I could make sure and look after the kids. Some security.

'But . . . it hasn't come through, the life insurance. She died in a car, you see, and they're trying to claim it was reckless driving. It wasn't. It wasn't reckless driving. We have witnesses, medical reports, the whole lot. But they're not satisfied and they say they won't pay. I had to take out another loan just to pay for the legal fees. I don't . . . I don't trust banks any more. You're right about that, but it's not that I don't save with them. It's that I have no money to save with them. All the money, you see, nearly every penny I earn, goes right back into the banks. It's been so long now, I have overdraft upon overdraft.

'And every year they put more penalties on me because I'm not keeping up the repayments, so that every year I owe more and more no matter how quick I pay them back. And now, because of the amount of interest and penalties and legal fees I'm paying, even if the insurance does come through it still won't be enough. It still won't be nearly enough.

'I tell you, I have no money. Only last week I had to throw

most of my tenants out of their flats, because if I didn't charge more for the places, I would've had to sell the houses. I had to throw them all out with only 48 hours' notice, and it broke my heart doing it, but I'm so desperate now that I have no choice.

'They have me, they have me under their thumb, and they're making sure they squeeze every penny I have, and me with four young kids. I've gone in there I don't know how many times. I've begged with them. I've pleaded with them and every time they tell me, *Of course, Mr Downey, of course. We're not animals, of course we won't repossess your house, of course we'll come to some arrangement over penalties, an agreement on your repayments.*

'But the minute I'm gone they start writing letters, the minute I'm out the door they sit at their computers typing. They write them so quick that by the time I'm home there's already a big pile of them waiting for me. Polite, formal letters, telling me that, *it would be wise*, if I were to pay such and such an amount immediately, otherwise they will have to, *regrettably enforce penalties as stipulated in the terms of your loan*. They're oh-so-polite and understanding in person, but in those letters they tell you what they really mean.

'So I swear to you, I promise, I have no money in the house, and every bit I ever do have goes on those kids upstairs.'

Ernest slumped down onto the couch.

'I'm so sorry,' he said, shaking his head.

Copper looked up hesitantly from the ground.

'That's awful,' Ernest said. 'That's just . . . just awful.'

'How could they do that to you?' Jon said, shaking his head. 'With four young kids.'

Copper nodded and wondered to himself just what sort of burglars these two men were.

Ernest stood slowly up.

'We'll be off then,' he said. 'Sorry to have bothered you.'

Ernest looked at Jon and the pair turned around and began walking towards the door. Ernest paused a moment before leaving. He reached into his pocket and took out the remaining twenty pound notes and change, approximately one hundred and seventy-five pounds, and placed the money on the table next to where Copper Downey was still lying.

When Ernest and Jon stepped forlornly out of the garden of Copper Downey's house, Ernest turned right and began walking towards the sea.

'Where are you going?' Jon said, calling after him.

Ernest did not answer. He simply stared straight forward and continued walking towards the cliffs. Jon began walking a few paces behind him.

'You know, we probably shouldn't hang around here,' he said to Ernest. 'We should probably get out of this area.'

But Ernest wasn't listening. He walked straight on until they came to the edge of the cliff, then walked along its side, staring down at the choppy sea below. They walked for fifteen minutes along the cliff face, till it jutted out into a triangular point, high above a clutch of large rocks.

Ernest walked out onto the very edge of the cliff and stared at the rocks below. Jon, still a few paces back, began to feel alarmed.

'Ernest?' he said. 'Ernest what are you doing?'

Ernest turned around, as if noticing Jon for the first time.

He turned back out towards the sea. A cold mean wind picked up and shook his jacket as he stood staring. Ernest took off his balaclava and threw it down the cliff, watching it bang against the wall of the cliff a couple of times before finally hitting the sea. He watched the waves toss it from rock to rock for a while.

Jon took off his balaclava and put it in his pocket.

'Ernest?' he said.

Ernest did not turn around. When he spoke it was in a low monotone devoid of feeling.

'It's useless,' he said. 'No-hope fucking useless. I had thought for one minute, for one fragment of a second that maybe there might be some kind of sense or purpose for me in this stupid world.

'I thought, maybe my delusional drunk plan isn't so delusional after all. Maybe that's the answer. Maybe it's all been building up to this point. Maybe I was meant to have joyless parents and to wander in confusion throughout childhood knocking into all the objects that were put in front of me. And then, as a teenager, doing everything so spectacularly wrong and being beaten down all the while. Not growing taller but gradually shrinking till they have me so small I can't do anything for myself. Till I can't face anything except shuffling along in an endless ordered queue marked damaged product of no-hopers gathering their dole and giving it right back to the bastards who gave it to them in the first place, just for the privilege of being able to eat with the others, and pay rent with them and fit in on their terms, and every once in a while having to grovel in front of them so they don't cut me off at the knees. So I know exactly where I stand and that I better remember that I couldn't cut it in the real world and I should feel very grateful indeed that they don't take me out someplace and shoot me for being so useless.

'Maybe, I started to think, there is a way out. Maybe the way out is simply to do the unexpected. To follow through on one of those crazy no-chance schemes that run around my mind and constantly evaporate when I come to reason, like I'm supposed to, like maybe they want me to.

'And then we started it, the drunken stupid plan, and I hold onto this plan with all my strength instead of letting it evaporate because, even though I know it's crazy, what else is there left to try? My last chance saloon and suddenly, things start to work out.

'Okay, we come across obstacles but instead of being beaten down by them, for the first time in my miserable existence I start to overcome them, and gradually, we get nearer and nearer so that, finally, I let myself wonder if this isn't it after all. The answer to all our worries. And that my problem has not been lack of talent or lack of ability or being some kind of runt who doesn't fit in but simply lack of focus, and now that I've finally focused, something is beginning to work out.

'And after all that, after getting closer and closer and letting it all build up till, finally, we're standing on Copper's doorstep and I'm sure we're doing the right thing. Till, finally, we go in there and, of course, it's not only *not* the right thing, it's not even close. Nowhere near, in fact. It's about the furthest thing possible.'

Ernest turned to Jon

'Didn't you ever wonder,' he said, 'while you were in there, how different Copper was behaving? How polite he was, how humble?'

'You were holding a gun to his head,' Jon pointed out.

'No,' Ernest said. 'No, that's not it. That wasn't it at all. It was the way he looked, even. He didn't even look like himself. Like that same evil bastard who used to collect from us every week and who used to let himself in unannounced and used to shout at us if we were late, and never used to do any repairs.

'See, the Copper Downey we knew didn't have any kids. He lived alone, in a big house, with nothing but bundles of cash for company. And it was that Copper Downey that we were after. Not that guy in there. But we'll never get to the real Copper Downey, because people like you and me aren't supposed to succeed.'

'What are you talking about?' Jon said, shaking his head.

'It's simple,' Ernest said. 'It's really so perfectly simple. Men like the real Copper Downey, they succeed. And men like you and me never do. Whatever happened, when we called in on him, he would have had some excuse. If it wasn't those kids and his wife and all those overdrafts then it would have been something else. Something, anything, to keep us from success.'

Ernest took his manuscript out from his bag and threw it out over the cliff. For a few seconds the wind caught it and it flew through the air on its own, the pages flapping like a hundred different wings, before it crashed down into the sea.

'Why did you do that?' Jon asked quietly.

'They were right not to publish it,' Ernest said. 'Not for their reasons, because it was still better than most of the crap they do publish. But because nothing's the same now, and I needed to go on this journey to find out where I really stood, and start again. And everything will be a little bit different now.'

He sighed.

'It doesn't matter anyway,' he said. 'Maybe Emily Dickinson

had the right idea. Storing away her poems in the attic and never being bothered whether or not people saw them, or she got the approval of some publisher or the wider world. She knew. She'd learned the lesson.'

'Look,' Jon said. 'You're just depressed. Why don't you step away from the edge and we'll talk about things for a little while. You don't really want to jump.'

'Jump?' Ernest said. 'Who said anything about jumping?'

'Oh,' Jon said. 'I don't know. I just presumed . . . '

Ernest looked over the edge.

'Are you crazy?' he said. 'I could really hurt myself.'

Jon nodded.

'Of course.'

Ernest looked at his Mickey Mouse watch.

'Shit,' he said. 'We have to go. We've got to be in Dublin in two hours to sign on.'

He began rushing back towards the road.

'But Dublin is at least three hours away,' Jon called after him.

'Exactly,' Ernest said. 'Which is why we must hurry.'

And both men ran off as fast as their short legs would carry them.